MEN AT I
MONSTERS
AT MIDNIGHT

Erotic Stories of Shapeshifters, Demon Lovers and Creatures of the Night

Edited by

CHRISTOPHER PIERCE

STAR *books*

P R E S S

Herndon, VA

Herndon, VA

Acknowledgments

Special thanks to STARbooks Press, Mickey Erlach and John Nail.

Dedication

For Master Matt, as is everything.

CONTENTS

INTRODUCTION
I LOVE MONSTERS

Mankind has always been both repulsed and fascinated by monsters. Since I was a kid, monsters of all varieties and dispositions have haunted not only my nightmares, but also my good dreams and waking hours, too.

Some monsters are pure terror, with no redeeming qualities of any kind. The shark from *Jaws* is a good example of this kind of monster. Other monsters not only frighten, but also intrigue us, like the grotesquely beautiful xenomorphs from the Alien Quadrilogy. There are monsters that we pity, like Frankenstein's creature or the hapless King Kong, who never stood a chance against the savagery of humans.

Then we have the monsters that are sexy. Those are the ones this book is about. The vampire is the most prominent example, of course, as their endless popularity can attest to, but for me werewolves, demons, devils, incubi and (male) spirits are just as hot. These are monsters that enthrall, arouse and fascinate as well as frighten.

Some of us long to be their victims, others wish to cross over to the dark side and become monsters themselves. Whichever kind of monster lover you are, I know you'll find plenty to sink your teeth into in this collection.

Enjoy the stories.

Christopher Pierce

NOCTURNAL NOLAN
R. W. Clinger

Nolan Volmere III never sleeps at night. He never eats. He never seems to have ugly days with bad hair. And never is he tired, instead always filled with a sense of dark energy. It's as if he doesn't age at all, always twenty years old, a junior at Rothmore College, my roommate, my obsession.

In truth, I could die just looking at him: blond mussed hair that semi-conceals his eyes, a hulking six-three frame, chiseled pecs with saucer-size nipples, taut abs like a ladder, thighs of molten steel, charcoal-colored eyes with crescent-shaped slivers of blood red, and colorless skin that forbids the consumption of a late summer tan.

At night, he leaves our shared dorm and parties. Where does he go? Who does he party with? Why is he always back before dawn? I'm afraid to follow him because … he might hurt me for crossing a privacy line between roommates. No, he wouldn't hurt me, claiming me a friend, someone he trusts, and yet …

I can't keep my gaze off him, studying his sculpted body when he changes into a pair of blackberry-colored jeans and an onyx silk shirt at dusk, preparing to attend yet another Rothmore drinking party without me. Helplessly, I see him as a god in my addicted mind. The guy is absolutely perfect in every conceivable way. Rhapsody of the untouched. The subject of my affected desire.

It's laughable to think he wants anything to do with nineteen-year-old me. Nolan is perfect compared to me, Rand Falls. I'm sure I'm not his type. There is no way he can be into a biology major with brown hair and blue eyes, a five-ten structure and a hairless chest. I'm out of Nolan's league. Statistically speaking, I'm beneath him in so many ways. Honestly. This evening he chooses no underwear as he pulls up his skin-tight black denim. And to no avail, as if he is performing for my needy interest, my growing hunger, I take in his soft seven inches of drooping cock and bushy blond hair of triangular pubes. My face is half-concealed by a vintage paperback copy of Stephen King's *Salem's Lot*, and I relentlessly bite at my lower lip, seduced by his changing time.

3

With flaps hanging open on the denim, he says, "You're watching me again, Rand."

I say nothing, gulping saliva down the back of my tight throat.

"It's okay …" he says. "I know you like me. I don't mind if you watch me."

He doesn't know what I want to do with his skin. He can't possibly know. Shirtless, his steel-plated chest shimmering in the blue-purple light that shifts inside the dorm room's open window, he quickly slides up to my side, holds my hips with his strong palms, draws his lips to my neck, and …

I'm shivering, terrified, but trusting that he won't hurt me. His touch is a deathly cold, but enlightening at the same time, exactly what I want from him. Afraid for my life, knowing I have crossed a line by watching him dress, I nervously mutter, "Don't … don't hurt me, Nolan …. please don't hurt me."

He sniffs at my flesh and draws his tongue against the twitching veins on my stiff and goose-pimpled neck. One smooth and soft lick turns into two, and he whispers, "Never, Rand … I would never hurt you. I like you too much."

I can't move, frozen under his touch. I awkwardly shudder at his licks, but find the moment completely enjoyable, a thrill for personal reasons, since he is so adorably strong and hot.

"Hungry," he whispers against my neck, "so hungry for you."

What comes over me is … unthinkable. I move one of my palms to the now-firm stake between his legs, and begin to massage all of its nine inches up and down. In doing so, I turn my head down to his cold lips, kissing him for the very first time, crossing yet another scathing line in our roommate relationship.

As if frightened by mortal touch, he quickly backs away from my lips and right hand, and murmurs, "Not yet … not until I hunt."

"Hunt?" I ask, totally confused.

He doesn't answer me. Nolan stands in the middle of the room, pushes his still-hard goods into his tight denim, zips up, grabs his silk shirt, and vanishes from our room, unseen again until well after midnight.

September-hot entombs Room 242 inside Shelton Hall. Exhausted from studying for a biology exam on metamorphosis, I decide to sleep in the raw, passing out in a matter of seconds after my head hits a goose-feather pillow. I dream of nothing as a thick blackness finds me, cradling me within its chilly and hulking arms.

Three o'clock in the morning? Four o'clock? I wake to Nolan's icy lips against my navel, kissing my skin. Groggily, I inquiry, "Nolan? … You're back."

"Hush," he whispers, rolling fingers along my sides. He finds my nipples and gently pinches them. His mouth connects with my navel a few times as he inhales my corporeal scent. His lips drag down and over the line of curly hair between my navel and pubic triangle. Sharp eyeeteeth gently nip at my skin, but they are careful not to break it. A long and drawn-out inhalation of my pores is heard. Nolan gasps with satisfaction by my sleepy smell, and whispers in the moonlit room, "My God, Rand … if you only knew what you do to me."

"What?" I question, once again confused, but fully awake for the time being.

"Your scent … your mortality. I crave it. I crave you."

I realize he's naked as his body slips up and along my own. Our nipples kiss as our chests meet. Our firm cocks tango in the post-summer's early morning heat. There is nothing warm about him though, besides his emotions for me. His body is frigid and bloodless against my own. His lips touching mine feel like ice. I truly believe he has no soul.

In truth, his body temperature is not a concern. I'm turned on by his closeness, fully consumed by his erotic spell and passion-driven attention. I cannot push him away and decline his arms gripping my sides, his firm cock aligned with my solid cock, and his lips indulging in our furtive kiss. Windblown and mesmerized by our embrace, I feel bubbles of pre-ooze leak out of my rod and squeeze against our connected skins. Again, I tremble beneath his touch, uncontrollably shivering with selfish delight.

His heart – what heart? – is unfelt. There is no rhythmic beating above me. There is no ticking or blood pumping inside his icy-stern torso. There is no …

Overtop me, in our compromised positions, Nolan slowly pulls away from my lips and whispers, "So thirsty for you … can't have you … won't have you." Again, I'm baffled by his words. I don't understand what he is saying. But my attempt at translating his puzzling comments fall short as his face, mouth, and lips caress the center of my chest and drop to the patch of curly V-triangle hair between my legs. Down there, Nolan inhales me sharply, and exhales with self-satisfaction. Again, he confuses me by saying, "If I can't have you in full, I shall have you in part."

Nolan covets the extension of meat between my legs. Slowly, he slips my center into his icy mouth while holding the base of my stem with his right hand. Like no other man in my life before him, I have never felt this way about oral sex: sated, on a higher plane of sorts, and completely intoxicated. My eyes roll into the back of my head, and I lose my breath. For a second or two, I feel as if I pass out, becoming lethargic and unconscious. This is not the case, though. It is a strong feeling of wanted and needed passion between my mysterious roommate and me, a pivotal entanglement of college guys who just happen to have an indulgent attraction for each other's skin and the unexplored avenues of combined male-sex.

Honestly, I am embarrassed to confess that it only takes him three consecutive licks and sucks on my seven-inch rod before I cream inside his cool mouth. With my fingers buried in his blond mussed hair, my load fills his throat and core. To my surprise, Nolan is not disappointed at my quick explosion. In fact, he craves my seed to the fullest, filling his insides, sucking my cock dry, and draining every ounce of sap out of my system.

Finished with his task, coming off and up from my sweaty skin, he accomplishes the craziest thing. Nolan kisses my forehead, lips, and neck. He whispers, "Sleep for now," and brushes both of my eyelids with his right palm.

The motion is so immediate and soothing. I know it is a spell of sorts, sending me into thick dreams, returning me to my night's rest, spent from our secret connection and his mouthy pleasure, abandoning his unshared secret with me that he is not human, of another world and time and …

The next night, I decide to cross yet another line between us. At dusk, when the sky is nothing but a brilliant purple mixed with sleepy orange and fiery pink, I follow him to one of his parties on the other side of the campus. Nolan enters a Victorian frat house with luscious jocks that drink too much. He stays for approximately three hours, chatting with the jocks, enjoying their festive party.

Peeping in the frat house's windows, I observe his fondness and attraction for a redheaded rower with bulging muscles and emerald-colored eyes. I hear Nolan call the jock-male by his last name,

Utley. I witness his seduction of the man. It's as if Nolan hypnotizes the rower, convincing him to leave the party with him. It's as if Utley is under Nolan's mind-spell and ...

Side-by-side, shoulder locked to shoulder, the two students make their way out of the frat house and into the night. Nolan leads the rower astray, walking with him into the nearby woods, traveling a good half-mile through the dark without a flashlight, and without being cautious of scratching and biting tree limbs or heaping brush. In truth, I have to use my cell phone to follow them, keeping its blue-green light low to see the narrow pathway that divides the woods.

Once at a moonlit clearing that is inhabited by truck-size rocks, the two men undress, dropping their party clothes to the ground. Upright, naked in the glare of white-gray light, they hold and kiss each other. Shadowy mouths, tongues, chests, and firm cocks meet, just like the scene from the night before between Nolan and me in Room 242. Hungry for Nolan, Utley falls to his knees, pivots palms on Nolan's hips, and spins my roommate around, forcing him to lean against one of the massive rocks. Nolan balances himself on the rock by using his palms. Inviting Utley's body to collide with his own, he cocks his legs apart, and whispers, "I'm yours tonight ... do whatever you want with me."

Approximately fifteen feet away, hidden among a collection of brush, wide-eyed and granite-hard in my jeans, I observe Utley using his palms on Nolan's tight rump, spreading his cheeks apart. The rower soon dives his face into my roommate's bottom, dipping his tongue inside Nolan's center. Two consecutive dips are just a prelude to the dozen that follow. Having an upright nine inches of dreamy shaft-shadow between his legs, Nolan begins to moan and groan. He arches his neck in the sinister light, and takes in the almost-full moon with an insidious desire. He murmurs with helpless satisfaction, captivated by the rower's tongue-and-mouth visit.

This act within the deep woods continues for the next ten minutes. Lapping and licking. Moaning and groaning. And Nolan's back arching with pure bliss. I watch in awe, pleased with their man-connected-to-man act, caught in their lair of sexual excitement and bliss. I'm bone-hard between my legs, but I refuse to become a trio in their hideaway embrace, allotting them their one-on-one privacy. Nor do I pull out my own meat and begin to bang it behind the brush.

Instead, I choose to watch the dining rower and nocturnal Nolan without self-pleasuring.

It is Nolan who abruptly stops Utley's post-midnight snack. My roommate spins around with his waving night's flag, and seriously chants, "Suck me off ... Take my cum into your system."

Still under Nolan's uplifting spell, Utley stays on his knees and holds the base of Nolan's cock with both hands. The rower lifts the shaft up and begins to cordially and swiftly suck Nolan's sack with fine pleasure. Utley flawlessly travels in a northward direction with his mouth, licking Nolan's entire pole from base to cut cap. His obnoxious and animal-like slurping is heard even from my cozy distance.

Moved with elation by the rower's mouth-massage, Nolan murmurs chaotically within the night. And once Utley places Nolan's rod inside his throat, working its mass in a north and south motion, Nolan arches his neck, stridently inhales and exhales, stares into the bright moonlight, and begins to grow the longest eyeteeth I have ever seen in my life.

It can't be. I'm seeing things. There is no way Nolan's eyeteeth turn into dagger-like weapons. I'm imagining this. I'm ...

The fratboy on his knees continues to blow my roommate, faster and faster, performing a rhythmic motion that leaves me fascinated, and causes pre-sap to leak between my legs. His head bobs up and down on Nolan's meat, forcing the ageless junior to whimper in orgasm, and cling to the rock with his strong hands. As if on cue, Utley pulls away from Nolan and begins to stroke my roommate's joint up and down. After five speedy man-handling jolts, I hear Nolan wildly grunt and see three arcs of his shimmering, almost-silver goo exit his thumper and decorate the clearing.

Once his cream-fest is over, he pulls Utley up by his arms, and informs, "We have to finish you off now."

Nolan spins the naked rower around and pulls Utley's jock-back to his rippled chest. One hand locks against the fratboy's torso while his other hand begins to crank the rower's beef in a to-and-fro motion. Nolan's handy movement is swift and diligent, and causes Utley to fuck his palm in a steady manner. When Utley is almost ready to fire his load into the clearing, huffing and puffing, exclaiming that he is about to come, I witness the craziest and most unbelievable thing.

Nolan tilts his head back into the moonlight, and his four-inch fangs shine in the night's ambient gloom. His eyes turn into a fiery red and …

Nolan is going to bite Utley's throat with his opened mouth, sinking his fangs into the student's corded neck while he shoots his last load. My heart races within my chest with jealousy. My pulse heightens to the fullest. And I think: My God, Nolan … don't do it. Take me instead. I'm not afraid of you.

Abruptly, he stops just in the nick of time before feeding on the rower in the clearing. Nolan hears my thoughts. In fact, he turns his view to where I hide in the nearby brush, and pushes Utley away from his alert body.

You hear me, I think. You're a vampire … and you came here to feed on the rower. I know your secrets … and I have no fear of you.

What transpires next is rapid. I run away, bolting back through the woods, taunting and teasing Nolan. I stumble over a rock, scrape my knee on the ground, and rise for a continued run. I call over my shoulder, out of my mind, willing to play his game, "Catch me if you can, Nolan! Come and get me! I'm yours for the taking, if you want me!" But my game soon ends as branches scratch at my arms and hands in the deep woods. A tree limb smacks against my face and …

I forget that I am mortal and tumble backwards onto the September earth. I immediately fall into a blurred world and … all I can remember is the moonlight shining into my eyes, and Nolan standing over my frozen body, coveting me with his fully grown fangs and devil-red eyes.

Just before dawn, sunlight ready to bleed into the dorm room, I wake in Room 242 with Nolan at my side. I feel his cold breath on my face, which causes an instant erection between my naked legs. Amused to see him, I sit up and beg, "Hurt me if you want. Feed on me. I know your secret now, and I'm not afraid of you."

Fingers caress a cheek and lips, and he explains, "I can never hurt you. I will never feed on you. I'm falling for you."

I ignore his comment, having other concerns on my mind. I ask, "The rower? What happened to him?"

"He's fine. I listened to your request and … he's safe in his frat house for now."

To my surprise, Nolan climbs between my legs, sniffs my asshole like an animal, breathes cold breath against my balls and explains, "I can't control my sexual craving when I'm around you anymore. I used to be able to restrain myself, but now I've grown keen for your smell and likeness."

"Fuck me," a mere whisper escapes my stiff throat inside the room.

Again, Nolan abides by my wishes. Although he is strangely immortal, clean for eternity, he applies a condom and lube to his shaft and … What comes over me as he pushes the first three inches of his dick into my ass is tormented bliss. I grip the bed's summer-warm sheets as tightly as Nolan grips my ankles. I see things the common college guy will never have the opportunity to see: eternal lust and ageless beauty.

Nolan's next three inches of pushing shaft cause me to lose my breath, and I feel the room spin around me. A stifling coldness fills every pore on my body as drops of pre-cum leak out of my hose. I become lost with his joint inside me, dizzy but wholly bliss-filled. The last three inches of his pole ram hard into my core, and I gasp with wanted pain. Positioned on his knees between my legs, his chest gleams with a silvery beauty in the desired shadows. Nolan firmly snuggles his entire cock inside me, connects his flat torso with my drooping balls, and holds this position for a minute, teasing my charged need to the fullest.

He whispers, "I feel the cold fire between us. It's only getting stronger with my cock inside you."

I cannot respond, caught in a sex-trance by the width and length of his stake nestled inside my bottom. My pulse seizes, races, and seizes again. My body is his body for the time being, one in time and space. Slowly he pulls most his tool out of me. And slowly he pushes it back inside, one inch after the next. This continues for the next fifteen minutes: cock slipping inside me, pulling out, in and out, in and out. It is a slow and concurrent motion that drives me mad. An intoxicating movement is found between mortal and immortal friends/roommates/lovers.

I realize this sex-spell is all about me. I become Nolan's pet on the bed, and his only desire is to fulfill my every need with unending pleasure. Perhaps it is the same feeling of world-spinning elation when he draws blood from one of his terrified fratboy victims. The emotion must be similar to what I am feeling now as he smoothly and sweetly glides to and fro within my tight rear.

I can tell when Nolan is about to explode. Continuing his rhythmic bottom-beat, his eyes turn into a fiery red. Sharp, knife-like fingernails grow from his digits, careful not to shred my ankles to pieces. And fangs, four inches long, white as hell's snow, protrude from his mouth. As an orgasm sweeps through his body, he morphs into a vampire before my eyes. I swear with my body and soul, his cock becomes longer and wider within my core, driving me into my own personal state of bliss.

His eyes now burn with orange-red flame. Nolan is still cold by my touch. With exquisite passion and skill, he gently pulls out of me, loses the condom, and begins to finish himself off. One hand-stroke to his stick prompts the night-feeder to murmur, "Rand." Two strokes and a single hip-thrust forward causes him to whisper, "I want you forever." Three strokes by his working hand forces chilled ooze to leak out of his hose and dribble down and over my tight torso.

My stomach's heat and perspiration sizzles his vampiric load, dissolving it completely. For one second the cream is frozen against my flesh, but vanishes just as quickly.

With his fangs even longer and his hellbound eyes on fire, he whispers over me, "Now to please you, Rand," and he reaches between my legs with both hands, and begins to shift his palms up and down in rapid movement.

Helpless under his control, I raise my hips, fall to my bed, and raise them again. My flag is teased, stroked, and manipulated by his steady care. A state of jubilation builds within me as Nolan's palms continue to work my beef. I gasp for breath. My mouth goes dry. A stage of utter dizziness sweeps through my head, and causes me to whimper, "I'm going to shoot … I'm going to blow … I'm going …"

Coming, firing my creamy load against his stern torso, decorating his skin, I become heightened in a state of early dawn's bliss. Arc after arc of mortal sap shoots from my stake and …

Nolan slowly leans over me with his open mouth and protruding fangs. He finds the stern length of my exposed neck and sniffs its succulent flesh with pure delight. In a matter of seconds, I feel his icy lips and eyeteeth against my skin. His dark venom flushes inside my system as he begins to bite my neck. I'm injected with pain and remorse and love and kindness and need. His eternal soul flows into me, morphing me into his permanent kind, an ageless and immortal

11

lover of the night, one of him … forever … his everlasting soulmate of the bloodless damned, giving me exactly what I want.

LUNACY
Kyle Lukoff

"Cubs these days," the old wolf sighed.

The others ranged around the bar nodded their shaggy heads.

"They just don't know what it was like," said another. "Back when it was real."

A few minutes of contemplative silence passed, broken by the bartender announcing last call. Night was falling, and the full moon would rise in a few hours. The pack dispersed into twos and threes and slipped out into the gloaming, anticipating the night's hunt.

On the other side of town, a group of young almost-men lounged at the mouth of an alley. Their hair was mohawked or spiked or shaved to the skull. One had a conservative military crew cut made ironic by the face full of metal below it. Tattoos and piercings abounded. They were in constant motion, playfully shoving each other, leaping off the walls, dangling from the crosswalk lights.

One checked his watch and threw his cigarette to the ground.

"Come on, you faggots!" he yelled into the alley. "Spiky, cut the foreplay. Chester, blow your load, and let's get fucking moving!" The others howled in agreement and laughter, and a minute later a loud grunt issued from the darkness. The pack cheered. Two more young punks came strutting out, one zipping his fly as he walked, the other brushing grime from the knees of his cargo pants.

"Feeling better, Ches? We can get to work now?" Chester just grinned, showing canines just starting to lengthen.

The leader whistled and started sprinting north followed by his pack. It had been a full month since they last got to play.

Humans believed that werewolves ("lycanthropes" according to the politically correct) became thus with no rhyme or reason, that their conversion was simply a mixture of viral and chemical reactions, no romance or mystery involved. They believed the myths of random attacks, preying on children, creatures driven by lunar madness and bloodlust. This was partially true. To hear the elders tell it they were born in blood and violence, throats near ripped out, months of agonizing recovery. Baptism by teeth, as it were.

However, once turned, they found themselves part of a family, and most blended in seamlessly. They created elaborate rituals for the waxing and the waning of the moon, invented their own language for their hunts and feasts. In the few bars they deigned to congregate, they signaled their difference to others using the most subtle of signifiers – a tooth earring, a certain rip on a jacket made unmistakably by claws or fangs. You had to know what it meant to know what it meant. To the outside world, they were uniformly clean-cut, well-mannered, gainfully employed, upright men one and all. Their true nature and business they shared only with each other, in the dark and in low tones.

Wolves only fucked other wolves. Since the virus that caused lycanthropy only affected males, it meant that all wolves were what humans called gay. The older wolves fucked one another out of a sense of loyalty and obligation, relieving their baser urges without shame and without judgment. But none claimed to enjoy it, to actively seek out each other's flesh out of desire or lust.

The youth rebelled, as youth always rebel. These ones were queer, queer by birth and queer by life. Some young ones claimed they were turned by a blowjob, their dicks scored ever so gently by razor-sharp teeth, then licked clean. Others were turned by friends, who nibbled their lips or threw a particularly mean fuck, violent in their own way but done with love and what even the elders had to admit was brotherhood.

They preferred the streets to the bars, and refused to wear the symbols of wolfdom. Most chose instead to align themselves with the punks and skinheads and skaters, separate yet visible as part of a larger whole. They eschewed the rituals and practices of the elders, demarcating their lives in terms of the ebb and flow of the streets.

These changes the elders could have borne, so long as the young ones adhered to the most basic of codes.

The wolves had worked out a truce of sorts with their city. Everyone knew that wolves didn't have to kill. Their prey rarely even turned if the hunter didn't want it. A sip of blood or nibble of flesh was one means by which they survived, but it was a supplement rather than a staple. It kept their coats lustrous and their spirits up. They wouldn't die without it but would become depressed, hollow, as both wolves and men.

Still, the police and the politicians wanted to keep the wolves in check. It was terrifying, after all, to be walking alone at night, minding your own business, and having a wolf spring upon you, all hair and eyes and mouth. The therapy bills alone (covered by the city) were astronomical.

In other parts of the world, wolves were locked up in cells or camps, or banished to forests, or shot. To avoid this end, the old wolves worked out a truce. When the full moon rose, the wolves would limit their hunting grounds to the cruisiest parks, the poorest blocks, the piers most frequented by the homeless, the perverts, and other illicits. The city didn't care if those kinds of people were terrified – in fact, they preferred it. Some wolves grumbled quietly amongst themselves, predators turned into the lapdogs of the government, but none would go against the judgment of the pack leaders. None would risk being outcasts.

And yet, troublesome reports began to come in: 34, female, white, address in a fashionable block. Bitten on the leg, currently in the hospital in shock; male, 56, white, leaving his office in the financial quarter, suit jacket ruined, back mauled. After years of good behavior, some of the wolves stopped playing by the rules. In the boardrooms of the city, discussions began again of containment, of extermination.

In the bar again, on the roof deck, the moon a crescent, the older ones gathered in the corner. A few cubs stood with them, deferential, a bit apart, eager to curry favor. They were sent off to get beers for the rest, and when they came back, the discussion began.

"It must be that East Side pack," said one.

"None of us would have broken the truce. Those cubs, they don't need this the way we do," another agreed.

An elder cleared his throat. "That's right. We need to feed so we can work, earn, provide for our pack. But the young ones, they want nothing. They fuck at night and sleep at day, work odd jobs to buy beer money, sleep anywhere and everywhere. They don't even deserve to be called wolves."

One of the well-groomed cubs shifted awkwardly. He was standing just behind his mate, Franklin, an older wolf, who grabbed him and rubbed his head.

"We don't mean you, Caleb. You're one of the good ones." Caleb blushed and looked at his boots. After a moment he raised his voice.

"What are we going to do about them?" he asked. "They don't … I mean, they're not just gonna listen, right? We gotta, we gotta do something to stop them!" His voice cracked in excitement.

"Well," said a middle-aged wolf named Johann, "I know where they meet. Down in the lower district, near the waterfront. Caleb, if you're so eager, why don't you go down and join them? Hear what they have to say, what they're planning, and report back to us."

"M-me? But, I, I'm not …"

"We know," said Johann. "You are one of us, not one of them. But they don't know that. You shall be a wolf in punk's clothing. What does the pack say?"

Looking around, Caleb saw the older folk nod in agreement, and he blushed. After taking a fortifying swig of his drink he held his head high.

"This is an honor I shall accept," he said. "I will not let the pack down." The other wolves lifted their glasses to him and drank as one.

The next night, a lone wolf picked his way down the avenue then turned east towards the docks. Clad in jeans riddled with safety pins and a shredded shirt, Caleb was just the picture of a young punk, new in town and without a crew. He wandered up and down, ears perked up, listening for the sound of the pack.

He heard nothing. Caleb had expected to come across a large, roving group of angry kids, wreaking havoc and attacking anyone who came in their way. The most he saw was one lone skinhead, stomping down the street in knee-high combat boots.

Caleb decided to follow, keeping a good distance between himself and the other youth. He followed as the kid walked purposefully down the side street and slipped into an abandoned boat house. Plucking up his courage and reminding himself of his duty to the pack, Caleb followed him inside.

He was immediately lost in a crush of young bodies, spiked and pierced and inked bodies. They were milling around in the leaking, damp building, and Caleb could see them only by the illumination of a few bare bulbs hanging from the ceiling. Caleb made his way to the wall and hunched against it, trying to reformulate his face into a look of I-don't-care-I'm-waiting-for-someone. As the punks eddied around him he soon stopped being mesmerized by the outlandish dress and

16

accessories and noticed that they were slowly coalescing around the stage. This gathering had a purpose.

Just as he reached this realization, a lone lad leaped onto the stage and started yelling.

"Wooolves!" he howled, and the crowd howled back, wordless and eager. Caleb turned and moved towards the center of the crowd, hoping to escape notice.

"The old wolves say that we are all brothers with men, and that we have to live among them and with them and like them. They say that we are garou before loup, were before wolf, throp before lycan. Is that who you are?"

The motley crew howled again, one voice united in derision and pride.

"We say no to the old ways, no to the old bans! We are wolves, we are brothers, we are unlike anyone else, and we are damn proud!"

"Hey mate, you new here?" whispered one of the wolves next to Caleb. He was around Caleb's age with a bleached Mohawk, gauged ears, neck tats and typical punk garb, leather jacket and black jeans.

"Yeah," he said, "I'm just checking out the scene."

"You're hide, though, right?"

"Yeah, I'm hide. My names Cal – Cole. My name's Cole."

"Cool. I'm Joaquin."

The leader was still ranting. "They want to keep us chained! Muzzled by society and convention! Is that the life we want for ourselves?"

"NOOOO!" roared the crowd as one. Caleb shouted, too, telling himself that he was trying to remain in character, fighting against the rush of feeling in his gut. He snuck a peek at Joaquin and saw the young man grinning at him, incisors glinting in the reddish light.

"So what are we going to do?"

They assembled howled in response. Caleb joined them, eyeing Joaquin.

With that the band came on. Caleb had heard of them before, Lunacy, one of the only all-wolf punk bands in the country. The older wolves disapproved, saying it was too loud, too fast, too angry, but Caleb secretly had a collection of all the wolfpunk he could find. Lunacy was his favorite, and he found himself screaming and jumping shoulder to shoulder with Joaquin and the others. The set was long, and by the time the lead singer was done screaming into the microphone, Caleb was drenched in sweat, his voice raw and sore. On the last song, he ended up arm in arm with Joaquin, drinking beers and singing along with the band. As the music tapered off, he disengaged himself, suddenly awkward.

Joaquin leaned over and said into his ear, "You wanna go somewhere?" Pumped up on adrenaline and youthful lust, Caleb nodded before he could think about what it meant.

"Come on, I know a place." Joaquin grabbed Caleb by the arm and dragged him through the crowd, behind the stage and down below into a black, gritty room lined with pipes.

"How do you know about this?" asked Caleb breathlessly.

"I used to work here." With that Joaquin shoved Caleb against the wall and began kissing him, biting at his lips, taking just a little blood.

Caleb was fighting with a rush of feeling. This was hot, so hot, but it was fucking wrong. And what about Franklin? What about his mission? But quicker than thought Joaquin had unzipped his jeans and was down on his knees, sucking, and Caleb stopped thinking. He grabbed onto the back of the punk's mohawk and just went for it.

It was a good blowjob, too. Like all wolves Caleb liked it rough, and rough was what he was getting. Joaquin's tongue was strong and insistent, his teeth riding not too gently along Caleb's cock.

Caleb knew he was bleeding and didn't care. Both of them were hide already, right? He reveled in the feeling of Joaquin drinking him, of taking in his blood and cum and sweat, using it to keep himself strong, masculine, alive. At that thought, his cock got even fatter and harder, and he gripped Joaquin's hair tighter and started fucking his face. He heard the strangled choking sounds coming from the other guy's mouth, felt him start to drool and weep, and at the sight of Joaquin's red, straining face Caleb shot a load deep into this throat.

Joaquin swallowed greedily then pulled back, using the red hankie in his left back pocket to wipe his face. He stood up grinning. "That was fucking hot, man."

"You're telling me? Felt like I came in buckets."

"I could tell. I almost did, too."

Caleb glanced down and saw that Joaquin had unbuttoned his jeans. He wasn't wearing anything underneath, and his hard dick was bobbing like an eager pup.

"You want me to take care of that, bro?" he asked.

Joaquin slit his eyes. "Don't mind if you do." With that he kicked Caleb's feet out from under him, yanked down his pants, and flipped him onto his belly. Caleb heard him digging in his pants pocket for something, then heard him tear open a packet of lube. He spread his legs and moaned as he felt the head of Joaquin's cock push against and into his asshole. He was glad he had already come, so he could focus on the feeling of a fat piece of wolfmeat inside of him.

Joaquin pumped in and out, slowly, his dick long enough to massage Caleb's prostate, making him feel like he was being fucked from the inside out. He let out a long, deep groan.

"You like that, mate? You like the way I'm fucking you like the hot piece of ass you are?"

"Y-y-yeah, oh fuck it feels so fucking good, don't stop, don't stop!"

"Ain't gonna stop 'til I blow way up inside you, punk. Guess we both got worked up back there, didn't we?"

Caleb couldn't talk back. All he could manage was a tortured "Uh-huh," as the unbearable weight of Joaquin on his back and in his ass continued, in and out and in and out. He focused on relaxing his asshole to give Joaquin a smooth, hot ride.

Caleb had never been fucked like this before. His mate Franklin was the kind of wolf who went for cubs and other wolves because he had no other choice. Before changing, he had slept with women, and made do with his own kind out of necessity rather than interest. Their fucks were brief, and Franklin would satisfy him out of a sense of duty, but he never got Caleb off using his mouth. The cub had always wanted this kind of sex, hot and messy and full of passion, but he didn't even allow himself to believe it existed.

With each thrust Caleb felt his resolve crumbling. The older wolves talked about authenticity and truth, brotherhood and pack, and yet to even be initiated into their group took months of perseverance, to prove that you truly belonged amongst them. He had joined because he was lonely, because he didn't even know that crews like this existed. He only found out about them through the older wolves, talking about how they represented the downfall of wolfdom. When Franklin wanted to mate with him, he agreed eagerly, thinking that it finally meant acceptance into the pack. And yet, that acceptance came with a price. He had to dress like they did, talk like they did, fuck like they did.

Their world was old and staid and settled. This new one he stumbled upon was fresh and raw and alive.

Joaquin's pumping grew faster and harder, and Caleb's mind shut down. The animal in him took over and he began yipping and growling as he felt his dick grow hard again. He opened his eyes only to see his hands and forearms lengthen into hairy gray legs ending in paws with wickedly sharp black claws. Inside his asshole, he felt Joaquin's dick turn bristly as a hairbrush, and knew that the other lad must be changing, too.

The full moon, he thought, it's tonight. He had been so nervous about infiltrating the group that he had forgotten the date. He should be safe with his mate and his pack, stalking the piers and the parks, and he realized that this was why such a large gathering of young punk wolves chose tonight. They were going hunting.

With a snarl Joaquin came, and in the next instant his transformation was complete. He raced up the stairs to join his crew. Caleb, after only the slightest hesitation, followed.

Tonight, he would join his new pack.

THE WISHING WALL
G. R. Richards

"Some say they feel the walls closing in on them," the crumbling hotelier began. Her withered hands rattled as she unlocked the door. "But it's the busy season, you see. This is the only room we have left."

"It is small ..." Jesse hesitated. The galley space culminated in a twin bed crammed between two marble walls that curved up and met at a central apex. No television, no coffee-maker, no night tables, even. In one word, a hovel.

"Small, yes, but only three Euros for the first night," the hotelier went on, with a mysterious glint in her eye.

What a deal, hovel or not! "I'll take it," he said. "For that price, I might even stay the week."

"Three Euros for the first night," the ancient woman repeated. "One hundred and fifty thereafter."

Jesse's jaw dropped. The decrepit woman must be joking. In a peal of laughter he said, "Okay, you got me. Very funny." The hotelier considered him quizzically from behind thick spectacles. She made no reply. His feet ultimately made the decision. "I'll just stay the night, in that case," Jesse said. After a full day of sightseeing, he couldn't face another minute of pounding the pavement in search of a less raunchy hotel. And the bedding looked clean enough, so what the hell? Pay the three Euros and hit the sack.

When the hotelier hobbled away, three Euros in hand, Jesse shut the door. He turned out the light and collapsed fully clothed into the claustrophobic bed. As long as he kept his eyes closed, he wouldn't notice how small the space was or how close the walls felt. Long day. The drift into sleep was immediate, welcome, like a bubble bath for his exhausted mind.

The most wonderful dream overtook him as he floated in that liminal space between consciousness and the depths of slumber. As he lay in the miniscule bed, warmth crept up his body. At first, the warmth was glowing and nonspecific, but it soon transformed. The ethereal sensation heated his core until it was impossible to ignore the pulses growing outward from the core of the heat. Those pulses, like fingers, spread across Jesse's lean stomach until it became glowingly obvious what this ghostly sensation consisted of. Oh, yes, it was amply clear now. It was a hand. A male hand. Its caress was feather-soft as it traced across his T-shirt and up his chest. Jesse didn't have full-on sex dreams as often as he'd like. Hopefully this would grow into one. The hand paused when it reached a dormant nipple. It was so unusual for him to be able to feel every touch as he dreamed it. He wished hard for the hand to reach beneath his top to fondle his tits. Maybe this would be one of those lucid dreams where he retained awareness and even some form of control.

Thud, thud, thud. A knock at the door brought him bolting upright. Damn it! That was turning into such a good dream.

"May I enter?" the hotelier's weak voice asked through the door.

Could he stop her? For an elderly woman, she had fortitude. "Yeah, come in," he replied, rising from the bed.

"To turn down your bed, young sir," she went on as he opened the door.

"Oh, don't worry about that," he said. Maybe if he got back in bed right away, he'd sink into the dream again. "I was just going to sleep on top of the covers anyway. I'm dead tired tonight."

The old woman tsk'ed through her teeth as she reached across the bed to fold down the blankets. "That is no way to rest. You must fully undress. You must allow your body to breathe." Backing away from the bed, she said, "There. Now you get comfortable in the bed and have a good night's sleep."

The wide smile on her lips weirded Jesse out as she crept from the room. She didn't even wait for the tip he tried to fish from his pocket. Maybe she had a camera hidden in the ceiling or something. The old woman probably got her jollies watching young men undress in their rooms. Oh well. He stripped bare and dove into bed. The crisp sheets felt great against his back as the cool air washed over his front. Jesse closed his eyes.

A pleasant sensation of sinking into sleep overtook his mind. As his thoughts detached from the day's pleasant escapades, the touch returned. Without a layer of clothing to muffle the sensation, he could feel fingers on his skin. They seemed to be everywhere at once. Warm fingers petted his cheek and his neck. They plucked his nipples like harp strings. He smiled without opening his eyes. Last time he opened them, the sensation went away. After traveling alone for nearly a month, he'd give anything to get off without expending effort or equity.

When those mystery fingers traced a path down the hair on his belly, goose bumps rose up on his flesh. His cock was standing at attention by the time those warm, masculine hands made their way to it. They wrapped themselves around the base of his shaft, and Jesse gasped. Their grip was strong and commanding, just the way he liked it. The fingers were smooth as marble. Grasping his hard rod, they stroked it all the way to the tip. It felt so damn good; Jesse thrust his hips into the mystery palm.

"All in good time," an almost imperceptible voice whispered in his ear.

Jesse's blood ran cold. His body felt even stiffer than before. What was that?

The first voice was followed up by another that seemed to come from down by his feet. "This isn't a race, you know."

If he tried to speak, would he be able to? He felt completely mute. And what would he say? He was dreaming. It was weird. So what? Just let the hands do their thing. Still, he couldn't ease up. He couldn't shake the sense that something was in the room with him. It was more than just a dream. He needed to know for sure.

He lifted his lids until a faint glimmer of moonlight snuck in. Chickening out, he pressed them shut again. If something was there, what would he do? Who could it be? He froze. The hand grasping his rod pumped it slowly, root to tip. That sure got his blood flowing hot again. His thighs trembled when soft fingers encircled his sensitive cock head. This had to be a dream. How else could it know exactly what he wanted? He was confident. In one assured motion, he opened his eyes to find four arms reaching across his body. Two hands caressed his chest, one worked his cock, while another reached below to fondle his balls.

Jesse couldn't even scream. He couldn't move, except to roll his head to his left side. There, he came face to face with … a face! What was it? Was it a person, or … a ghost? No, it wasn't transparent the way ghosts are said to be. It was smooth and statuesque as a Roman cavalier. Its pale head gleamed in the moonlight. It smiled.

"No need to be afraid," the form chuckled. It leaned in close to lick his lips with an incredibly smooth tongue.

"Who … what …" Jesse stammered, melting just a bit at the sensation. "What are you?"

"Oh, the old lady didn't tell you about us?" another voice asked. It came from way down by the foot of the bed.

"No." If Jesse could move, he would have hurled himself out the window above his head. But he was frozen in place. "I don't think so."

The marble man to his left chuckled. "We live in the wishing wall."

The creature's strange warmth coursed inside him. It felt good. Damn good!

"I don't know what that means," Jesse said.

A second head looked up from the level of Jesse's surging cock. It was that creature – the one at his right side – whose strong hand rubbed his erection. He was upside-down, with his feet beside Jesse's head. "Tourists never hear the old legends," the one creature said to the other.

"Very true."

Their faces were beautiful. Perfect male specimens. When Jesse turned to his right, he realized just how perfect. The inverted creature's thick meat stood still, just waiting to be manhandled.

"Aren't you even going to ask about the legend?" he probed.

"Huh?" Jesse replied, drooling over the marble-smooth erection. "Sorry, what were you saying?"

The sinistral marble man chuckled in his ear. "This house was once inhabited by a pair of mystic masons by the names of Nostou and Ven. The two men loved deeply, but public sentiment of the time would not allow them to live as they wished. They worshipped each other's well-worked bodies in secret. But all secrets will out in good time, and they were soon enough caught. They were slaughtered for their love."

"Holy crap," Jesse replied. This was all so surreal. "That's harsh."

"Indeed it was," the marble man went on. "But the men were not alone in life or in death. In subsequent years, their followers constructed this wall from sacred marble."

"What for?" Jesse asked. He felt like a schoolboy between the wise creatures. He felt as if he knew nothing.

The marble man inching toward his resting cock spoke up. "Communication," he said. Jesse didn't understand. Communication with whom? Ohhh …

"You're the mystic masons, aren't you?"

Nodding his head against Jesse's thigh, the upside-down creature declared,

"I am Nostou."

"I am Ven," said the other. Tracing his smooth fingers along Jesse's chest, he whispered, "We reside here, in this blessed marble structure. Our followers named it the wishing wall because we seek to fulfill the desires of those young men who sleep between us."

"Oh," Jesse cooed.

Ven asked, "What do you desire?" but Nostou didn't wait for an answer. He lunged at Jesse's cock, taking the whole damn thing in his smooth, warm mouth. Jesse moaned. He couldn't help it. His prick grew exponentially as the mystic mason sucked it. If he didn't get something between his lips, he knew he'd let out a cry that would wake the dead.

When Nostou's fat cock beckoned, Jesse didn't resist. He turned to his right. Wrapping his hands around its base and his lips around its tip, he sucked that smooth dong. Nostou rested his heavy head on Jesse's thigh while they serviced each other.

From behind him, Ven asked, "Are you two trying to make me jealous?" He answered his own question by tweaking Jesse's nipples. It felt so damn good, he groaned around Nostou's thick meat. Jesse's hot hole twinged when Ven reached down to tickle it. He stopped sucking for just a second – long enough to say, "There's lube in my bag there. Nostou, can you reach it? The jar's in the front pocket."

"Oh very well," the excellent cocksucker agreed. He smiled in the moonlight. "If I must." Pulling the lube from his bag, Nostou tossed it over to Ven before devouring Jesse's cock. It felt so damn good he strangled the mystic man's dick with both hands as he sucked.

"There are so many potions for lovers these days," Ven said with amazement in his voice. He eased the lube against Jesse's begging asshole with his marble fingers.

"You guys really do wish-fulfillment full-out," Jesse laughed as Nostou gave his balls a smack. "Oh god," he cried, catching his breath. "God, I've never told anyone I liked that."

"We know what you like," Ven replied as he eased his marble-smooth cock head into Jesse's hungry hole. Jesse gasped. His lungs seemed to jump up and down. He couldn't catch his breath.

Nostou pumped slowly on Jesse's cock. "We know what you've wished for."

Letting Nostou's meat fall from his lips, he turned to get a glimpse of what was going on down below. His heart throbbed as Ven guided his cock into Jesse's ass, inch by inch. It burned like the devil. He thought he'd die, he felt so damn full of cock.

Nodding, Jesse said, "I've always wanted to get sucked and fucked at the same time. For as long as I can remember, this is what I've dreamed of: two hot guys coming at me from both sides. It's incredible!"

"We know," Ven replied. Forging his marble cock through Jesse's asshole, Ven reached forward to pinch his nipples. Jesse ate Nostou's meat to keep from screaming. When he urged his cock forward, Nostou deep-throated it like a pro. He thrust pretty forcefully and Nostou took it all in. He couldn't believe this was really happening.

Ven smacked Jesse's ass as he fucked him from behind. He had a sudden urge to finger Nostou's ass, but the man's entire backside was melded to the wishing wall. They couldn't fully separate from the structure, it seemed.

As Ven's generous cock rubbed like crazy inside his hole, Nostou sucked his wood. Every so often, the marble men smacked him on the ass or the thigh, or on his hypersensitive balls. The sensations were so intense he went wild on Nostou's big fat meat. When his thighs began to quake, he pressed his ass back against Ven's slick cock, and then jutted his hips fast forward so his wood reamed Nostou's throat. Jesse slid back against the marble dong, then forward into a warm and welcoming mouth. His motions were jerky, he knew, but neither man seemed to care. They gave and gave. Ven fucked while Nostou sucked. He could feel in his balls that he was going to blow. His whole body trembled. When Ven gave his nipples a mean pinch, that was all he could take. Jesse came like a geyser in Nostou's mouth. He gritted his teeth while Ven twisted his tits in tight circles.

When he was released, Jesse went spiraling into the depths of slumber. He tried his damnedest to keep his head above water, but the force pulling him down was too powerful to resist. As he fell into a dreamless sleep, he could still feel the marble men surrounding him. He could feel his happy cock cradled inside Nostou's warm mouth. His hands cradled Nostou's meat like a precious child. Ven's smooth dong rested inside his ass even as he lost grasp of consciousness.

Jesse slept more soundly than ever before. It seemed to take hours to crawl back up to life on earth from that pit of endless slumber. As sunlight filtered in from above, he realized it was time to get up. Opening his eyes seemed an impossible task.

When the door swung open, he bolted upright in bed.

The elderly hotelier stood inside the doorframe as he scrambled to cover his nakedness with the blankets that had all fallen to the floor. "I'm sorry to intrude," she said. "I've been knocking."

"Oh," Jesse replied, in a daze. "What time is it?"

"Past midday," she said. "Time to check out." As she spoke, her gaze lingered on the marble to Jesse's right side. When he followed her line of sight to a spot on the wishing wall, he felt his cheeks blush. Nostou was nowhere to be seen, but at the level of his mouth the wall was doused with cum. Speaking in a slow and deliberate tone, the old woman said, "Unless you're willing to pay one hundred and fifty Euros for a second night …"

Crazy. There was no way he could afford it. He'd have to cut his trip short if he put up that much cash for just one more night of wild sex with two gorgeous marble men …

With a heavy sigh, he told the woman, "I'll stay. I have to stay."

"Very good, young sir." Her smile seemed both gracious and self-satisfied as she backed out of the room and closed the door.

Settling back into bed, Jesse wrapped heavy blankets around his chilled body. "I must be nuts," he said to himself. "Tonight better be worth it."

As he closed his eyes and breathed in the sweet afternoon air, he could have sworn he heard chuckling to his left. At his right side, a faraway voice seemed to say, "It will be."

THE GATEKEEPER
Rob Rosen

Milton sat on his rock and scanned the syllabus for Evil 101, a required course, the only course, in fact, for the position of gatekeeper. In demon-speak, GK duty was the cushiest job in hell, though it did require some training. Torturer, now there was a tough job. There were a million-plus ways to torture a soul. A demon had to earn his Masters in Evil in order to land that job. But gatekeeper, well now, sitting on a stool and checking off names from a list didn't require all that much brainpower; hence the need for just the one course, Evil 101.

The syllabus, needless to say, was a short one: How to Recognize Evil in Five Easy Steps; How to Admit Evil through the Portals of Hell; How to Retain Evil after Admittance; and How NOT to Piss Off Satan. This last area of study, Milton was told, was key. Basically, if you perfected areas one through three, you'd sail past four. If not, well, shudder to think what Satan would do to you. A million-plus ways to torture a soul was but a drop in the proverbial bucket for him, after all.

So Milton studied. Milton passed the course. And Milton became a gatekeeper.

Cushy, he was soon to discover, however, did not necessarily equate to enjoyable; because boredom, he found out, was one of those methods of torture most frequently administered in Hell: bored out of one's mind; bored to tears; bored to death. All apt descriptions for the job of gatekeeper.

"Cushy like a pillow of needles," he whispered to himself one day after he had checked in an endless list of vile, corrupt, despicable souls. But this wasn't the worst part, no sirree. What was painfully omitted from his training was the fact that when a soul arrived at the gate, the world from whence it came, for the briefest of instances, became visible to the gatekeeper. Milton, therefore, saw snow-covered hilltops, blue sparkling oceans, valleys crammed with flowers, skies filled with stars, and soft, plush, beautiful beds. He rarely saw fire, flames, ash, and definitely no tortured souls on the other side. In other words, the land of the living was nothing at all like the land of the dead.

And so, Milton reread his notes, studied once more what had been taught to him, and discovered one very important detail: souls came in, souls stayed in, but demons, well now, there was no mention of their coming or going. Demons worked. Demons kept Hell running smoothly. Demons did the jobs Satan employed them to do. But if there was a rule as to keeping put, Milton was hard-pressed to find it.

There was, of course, one very important thing to consider, but each time he saw the other side of the gate, briefly smelled the fresh air, caught a glimmer of blue, of green, of anything but searing red or ashy black, that one thing got pushed further and further back to the recessed, cobwebbed attic of his pea-sized brain.

But of the gate, was it a two-way portal? He assumed so. After all, he had been taught in Evil 101 that souls must be retained at all costs. If a soul attempted to travel in reverse, he would douse it in molten rock, stab it with his poker, assail it with numerous devices to inflict pain and discomfort, and, if all else failed, devour it whole in his gaping, toothy maw. In other words, souls stayed where they were meant to stay.

But, he reasoned, they must be capable of leaving. And if they were capable, then so was he.

It was simple, really, what he did. One day, when no one was looking, he stopped a soul from entering, thereby locking the two worlds in place as he hopped over the threshold. A sudden burst of air hit him, cold, fresh, and damp with the first drops of moisture ever to touch his cracked, scaled, orange skin, just as a cornucopia of aromas wafted joyously up his impossibly wide nostrils, and colors of every imaginable hue shot through his orange irises, bursting forth behind his bulging eyes like a spectacular display of fireworks.

"Oh," was all he could muster. "Oh." Again and again and again.

But the last Oh wasn't out of bliss. Not by a long shot.

The gate, he quickly realized, had stayed open after his departure. And he wasn't the only thing escaping. Hell, it seemed, was seeping out, oozing forth in a thick torrent, red and viscous like a lava flow, burping up fire and brimstone in a cloud of noxious, sulfurous gas.

"Oh," he said one final time, quickly amending it with an apt "Damn."

He turned and stared dejectedly at the gate. Its hinges had melted and dissolved, its frame and door burning in a blazing instant. And then the spirits erupted outward, evil twisted soul after evil twisted soul, their eyes squinting into a light they never expected to see again. Then, all at once, the ground around Milton turned dry and brown, and the flowers wilted, and the trees dropped their leaves, and the sky turned black as night just above his head.

And then another demon popped out, red and scaly, a confused look on his deformed face.

"Satan's gonna be way mad," he moaned.

Milton trembled, and replied, "Yep, which I'm hoping we're never going to witness first-hand."

The demons were off in a flash, not wanting or daring to wait around any longer than they already had. Besides, Milton reasoned, the gate would be fixed. Had to be fixed. Somehow would get fixed?

Milton pushed the thought away as the pair followed the sun into the horizon. All around, on the periphery of it all, however, a blackness ever loomed. Like the edges of a burning sheet of paper, the flames drew nearer, enveloping, charring, turning to cinder what was once whole and unmarred. And evil, dark as pitch, wailed just beyond, rushing forward at a jarring rate. The demons felt this without having to see it; evil, after all, was their business, their very stock in trade.

"Wait," the red one, whose name was Jesup, eventually said. "Sooner or later we're going to be spotted. And, trust me, once that happens, Satan will hear about it."

"But what can we do about that?" Milton asked, leading them to a secluded cave nestled deep within a pine-lined valley.

"Transfiguration," came the reply. "Didn't you learn that in Advanced Evil?"

Milton blushed, though, of course, it was impossible to see the red through all his orange. "I, um, never made it past Evil 101."

Jesup nodded. "Which means you're a gatekeeper, right? That explains everything." And then he grinned, revealing fangs as sharp as daggers, before raising his stubby arm up in the air. "Watch, then," he instructed, his clawed hand moving up and down as he muttered some archaic language, causing the air around them to spark and eddy and spin with hurricane force.

When everything suddenly came to a silent standstill, Milton gaped in shocked surprise at what he observed, for in that small cave were now two men, naked as jaybirds, and not at all the two demons that had arrived.

"Impressive," Milton said, his eyes roaming up and down his newly-formed body, smooth along the sides, hairy down the middle, and considerably more elongated compared to his previous stature.

"Different, at any rate," Jesup amended, walking forward, his hand running down the length and across the breadth of his new-found friend. "And no scales, no vibrant colors, no horns or spikes or claws."

Milton moaned at the touch, the feeling of flesh upon flesh sending a wave of bliss coursing through his body, his eyelids fluttering as he stared down in wonderment. "This fifth limb of mine seems to be able to grow," he made note, grabbing at it with a succession of rapid strokes. "And arc up and out, and fill with the warmth of blood."

"Mmm," added Jesup, taking a hold of it. "And it throbs in my hand." He looked down, his own thick prick pointing up and out, a slick bead of translucent cum dripping up and over the wide, mushroomed head, salty to the taste, sticky to the touch.

"Oh yeah, that feels good," Milton practically purred. "What else can we do with these human forms?"

Jesup looked around the cave, his sapphire blue eyes shooting out beams of illuminating light. They landed on the far wall where a series of paintings could be seen, depictions of beasts and men crudely drawn across the stone. He walked up and placed splayed fingers atop the cool surface, a lewd smile suddenly stretching wide across his handsome face.

"These humans," he laughed, "have strange sexual customs. I can see them, up here." He pointed to his head.

"Show me," Milton pled, eagerly, his hand once again yanking at his ramrod-straight slab of meat, pleasure shooting out in all directions.

Jesup turned and walked back, his own cock swaying as he did so. He stood in front of Milton, grabbing for his narrow waist as he pulled him in with a grunt. His head leaned in, lips brushing lips, two mouths grinding, a tongue darting forth, snaking its way inside, entwining with its pair. That first kiss like magic.

Milton groaned, his hands moving out, coming to a rest on Jesup's firm, alabaster ass. "Nice," he sighed, coming up for air.

"And just the prelude," Jesup chuckled. "Lie down on the ground."

Milton pulled away and did as he was told, gathering up a pile of leaves and pine straw to cushion the stone floor with. He looked up and smiled, his demon friend quickly sinking to his knees in between outstretched legs.

Jesup craned in for a soft, perfect kiss, his mouth soon moving to the side, down a curved neck, across a rigid clavicle, bee-lining to a thick nipple, which he took in between his teeth for a suck and nibble.

Milton arched his back and moaned, the sound echoing from one end of the cave to the other. "Feels so good," he rasped, pushing his friend's mouth to the other nipple. "What else can this orifice do?"

Jesup looked up and grinned, the orifice in question now traveling southward, slurping its way from one steely ab to the other before gliding over a dense, hairy bush and then up, up, up Milton's fat prick. He downed it in one fell swoop, the turgid tool gliding down his throat, eliciting a happy, gagging tear that cascaded across his cheek.

Again Milton groaned, bucking his prick inside, his hands pushing down on Jesup's head as a million volts of adrenaline shot through his crotch and down his legs and up his now sweat-soaked torso. "A perfect fit," he panted. "What other pleasures can these joyful appendages administer?"

"Ah," Jesup ahed, sitting back up on his knees as he raised his friend's legs up and out, revealing a crinkled, pink, hair-rimmed hole that winked up at him. "See for yourself."

He slapped his prick up against the portal, teasing it inside, millimeter by millimeter, spitting down to slick up the action before gently sliding it home.

Milton sucked in his breath, clenched his ring, and then quickly abandoned himself to the onslaught. "Yeah," he sighed, the word drawn out as it ricocheted off the stone walls, his body twisting and writhing on the makeshift bed while Jesup rhythmically stroked his pulsing prick and pushed and prodded at his twitching hole. The feeling was indescribable, delight as he never could imagine, a force building up inside of him, eager, he felt, for release.

"Now watch," Jesup panted, picking up the pace on his partner's cock and ass, his massive prick pumping in and out, in and out, lightning fast, his wrist moving in sync, until every nerve-ending in both their bodies were ablaze.

Milton stared down through watery eyes, watching in rapt delight as his cock spasmed one last time before erupting forth in a flood of thick, hot cum, the sap splashing across his chest and belly, his moans and groans and sighs filling the space around them, quickly joined by Jesup's as the demon popped his prick out and jerked it until it too shot and shot and shot, the white fluid dousing the body below, dripping languidly down Milton's sides.

Jesup collapsed, his body landing flush on Milton's, their lips once more colliding, meshing, joining as one. "Wow," he sighed into his partner's mouth.

"Yeah, wow," Milton agreed. "Wow, wow, wow."

Jesup laughed, and with another kiss added, "And just think of all that's left to discover."

And so they moved on, finding clothes as they barreled forward, taking in all that the world of the living had to offer, not to mention the sins of the flesh, the joys of the senses.

But still they felt the evil drawing near, growing in intensity as their world continued to belch forth from the gate. Signs of this appeared on all sides: smiles turning without warning to frowns, love to murderous hate, green to lifeless brown, blue to black, dark black, black as tar and then darker than that. Hell on earth, and spreading like crackling wildfire.

Milton and Jesup, hand in hand, undeterred, traveled ever onward. The gate would close eventually. Satan would fix it. And by the time he did, the demons would be far, far away. Unfindable. Lost in a world of beauty and pleasure.

But Satan was not so easy to shake. Oh, hell, no.

Days past. Glorious days filled with splendor and wonder, days spent exploring the world and, of course, their perfect new bodies. When evil presented itself, Milton and Jesup turned and ran the other way. The humans, however, were still witnessing the terror of what Milton had unleashed; all around, the demons saw the horror on their faces, heard the misery in their speech, and smelled the fear as it wafted off their crawling flesh.

And then a new odor found them. A stench so powerful as to melt the very roads they traveled along. Evil so pure, so unadulterated, that even the holiest of the species began to sin unmercifully upon its approach.

The demons coughed as the foul aroma slithered and snaked its way through to their lungs. "I think I recognize this putrid scent," Jesup said to Milton, playing with the whiskers that now sprouted from his chin.

"You should," came the voice from behind them, shaking the very bones in their lithe bodies like dice in a cup. "After all, you sprung from me, demons."

The pair slowly turned to face the source. "Master," Milton groaned, bowing his head. "What brings you to this, um, awful place?"

Satan sneered. "Cut the crap," he warned. "You crossed over the portal."

The cowering twosome stared up. Satan, all eight feet of red, steely muscle, red as the broiling sun, with horns jutting out menacingly from his brow, stared down. Milton coughed. "Um, were we not supposed to, Master?"

Satan laughed, the sound like fingernails raking over a million chalkboards. "Look around you. What do you think?"

Milton looked around, as did Jesup. All had turned black. Foul, demented souls flew this way and that, filling the air around them with their despondent howls as the essence of evil permeated the landscape. "Well, there was no mention of it in my Evil 101 text," Milton tried, innocently batting his thick, ebony lashes.

"Rule number four, demon: Don't piss off Satan. And guess what?"

Again Milton coughed. "You're pissed off?"

"Gross understatement. You've set Hell loose upon the Earth, thereby emptying my realm."

Milton again looked up, his long legs quaking as he stood locked in place. "Um, can't you fix the gate and recall your world?"

Satan's scowl grew even wider across his hideous face. "No, demon. I hold no sway here. It is you who must fix this mess."

"I?" he asked, grasping Jesup's outstretched hand for support. "But, but how?"

Satan sighed, the force of his lungs trembling the ground as he did so. "When you crossed through the gate, all the evil within Hell was drawn to you like a magnet. See how it flows around us now, turning this place into a mirror image of the world below?"

Milton glanced from side to side, observing just what Satan had said and understanding what he was getting at. "So you're saying that I must go back in order to repair the gate."

"Yes, and to reverse what you have wrought."

Milton fixed his eyes on his lord and master. "But I, I do not wish to return. This world suits me better." He stood there and tried to squelch the terror that rose from his taught belly.

Again Satan laughed. "Brave little demon," he uttered. "But foolish, nonetheless. The longer you stay, the more this world will resemble the one you chose to leave. What you love about this place will disappear, and you will never witness it again. Return to your work and, at the very least, you will catch glimpses of what you so cherish."

The demon, now man, turned away and crouched down, collecting his thoughts before looking again to his master. "Will I be punished if I return?" he asked.

A sinister grin spread across the Devil's face, revealing jagged, yellowed, spike-like teeth. "You reside in Hell, demon. Is that not punishment enough? Now hurry along. You've done enough damage here. The souls must be returned and the gate fixed. This world, as you can see, is not meant for the likes of you and your friend here."

Milton smiled, crookedly, knowingly, holding on tight to Jesup's hand. "As you say, Satan. We will return to our world then."

And with that, the three of them walked back, evil following in their wake as the Earth, and, sadly, the demons themselves, reverted to their normal state. They crossed through Milton's portal, the gate at once righting itself, an inundation of souls flowing through in a massive tidal-wave of evil.

"Back to work, demons," Satan commanded, grabbing Milton by the scruff of his neck and sitting him down on his stool. "And no more travels to the world above." He then turned and stomped away, the sound of his massive hooves echoing loudly in all directions.

Milton, the coast now clear, hopped down off his stool. "Don't worry, Master," he said, winking at Jesup, a wry smile now appearing on his orange, scaled face. "We won't be doing any more traveling." He quickly planted in the ground what he'd taken from the world above, then added. "We won't need to." And with a satisfied sigh and a kiss on his lover's fiery red lips, he again sat down, staring contentedly at the little purple flower, which in time he knew would spread and spread and spread, not like wildfire but like love.

WHITBY
Jeff Mann

(for Angelia R. Wilson)

It's hard to name the color of his eyes, even in bright café light. They're brown from one angle, hazel from another. Now they're gray, as he cups his hands behind his head, arches his back, stretches hugely, and yawns. His thick biceps bulge, cresting like Highland hills. His T-shirt tautens over his chest, highlighting the curved meat of his pecs, the promontories of his nipples. Down the long length of him, he grins, staring at me over his ale. The bastard knows how hungrily I'm soaking him in. He's putting on quite a show.

I sip my pint of Tetley's bitter, stroke my bushy goatee, gone silvery since my last meal, and grin back. It's a tight grin, meant to hide lengthening fang-teeth. That's a surprise I'll save for later, once we're alone. My gaze rakes the dense ink of his twin tattoo sleeves – black, gray, and purple thistles and thorns – then returns to his chameleon eyes.

"How much?" I ask, as the waitress places before Robbie a steaming plate of fried cod and chips. He gobbles a good quarter of the fish in about ten seconds, wiping tartar sauce from the bearded corner of his mouth. "Two hundred quid an oor, mate," he says, before taking a big swig of ale and then munching a handful of potatoes. There's a tiny chip marring his right front tooth, a detail that adds to his overall air: rough-and-tough, yet boyishly endearing. "Normally one hundred, but extra since ye say ye like it kinky."

The iPhone my partner Matt bought me this last Yule has certainly proven handy in locating feasts during this most recent of my UK visits. It's found both this cheery restaurant, the Magpie Café, and this fetching Scots hustler. "Butch Glasgow Top. Hairy, bearded, built, tattooed. Age 30, horny and hung," said the profile, beside a tiny photo of Robbie grinning and flexing one burly, inked-up arm. Perfect source of warmth on this cold March night in northern England. I love the accent, that Glaswegian burr. I love the breadth of his shoulders, the dark fur foaming over his T-shirt collar, the trimmed brown beard, the long brown eyelashes. The boy's built like a fullback, considerably bulkier than I, with thick-muscled arms and torso and just the beginning of a beer-gut, all self-consciously and seductively displayed in a skin-tight white T-shirt. Exactly what his profile advertised, exactly what I'd hoped for.

I'm not even trying to hide my predatory stare. "Ye fancy ma look, eh, Mr. Maclaine?" Robbie's got more tartar sauce in his beard. If we weren't surrounded by noisy tables of diners, I'd offer to lick it off. He takes another big gulp of ale and finishes the first of the three pieces of fish.

"Yes, I do. You're even hotter than I expected. A physique like Hercules. How long since you've eaten, by the way? You seem ravenous."

"Ah, I'm always hungrysome. Ma dad calls me the locust." Robbie wipes grease off his lips with the back of his hand. "Mind if I order pudding? They have my favorite, roly-poly. It's verra fine here."

"I don't mind. Stuff yourself. You'll need the energy for later."

"I vow to plow ye fine, mate," Robbie says with a wink and a crooked grin.

"So you're from Scotland? I grew up on the Isle of Mull … a long time ago. How do you make a living, other than offering escort services for lonely gentlemen like me?"

"Auto mechanic," says Robbie. Lewdly, he tongues the tip of a chip, then slides the fried slice of potato slowly between his lips. "I'm handy with engines of all varieties. Yers need some attention tonight? Some lubrication, eh? Need me to drive ye home? Ile up your parts?" Another big swig of beer, this one leaving a pale smear in his moustache, foam he laps off with a leer and a flourish.

His clumsy double entendres and suggestive gestures make him even more appealing. Blue-collar vulgarity, it's a lagniappe. Reminds me of my sweet lover Matt and the other potty-mouthed country boys I've doted on back in Appalachia. As if a man this throbbing-hot needs to waste his energies on seduction.

"Let's just say that I'm mightily hungry and grateful you weren't already booked tonight. Someone like you is bound to make me feel younger." I can't resist a few double-edged expressions of my own. "Bound to satisfy."

"Ye'll get yer money's worth, Mr. Maclaine, I promise, though y'might be walking a wee bit crooked come the morn. I'm verra thick, if ye catch ma meaning." Robbie pats his thigh and arches an eyebrow. "Wouldn't want to hurt ye," he says, voice low and husky. "I'm too much for some blokes. Ye think ye can take me?"

I chuckle. "I'm sure I'll manage. I have no doubt you'll quench my thirst. But first, satisfy my curiosity. What's a Glaswegian mechanic doing in Whitby, other than making a little money on the side?" My eyes keep returning to the chunky curvature of his chest, the points of his nipples, the hair curling over his collar. The boy must be hairy as a bear.

"Ah! I'm gled ye asked!" shouts Robbie. He gulps the last of his pint, unzips the backpack resting on the floor, and jerks out a paperback. "*Dracula*! *Dracula*, mate! Part of it was set here, ye know! Whitby Harbor was where the vampire's ship ran aground after he left Transylvania! He lowpit off the ship in the form of a wolf! He hidit in the suicide's grave! Here he took his first victim in England!"

One minute a seductive hustler, the next an overgrown, enthusiastic kid. Robbie's so loud and excited that folks at several tables about us turn to stare before returning to their food. "Right," I say. "I remember. Lucy Westenra. He fed on her in St. Mary's churchyard, right across the river." Delicious. Exactly where I should take him later on tonight. It will be a literary lark. "But what does that have to do with ..."

"Ah, I'm a writer, mate! I'm here to research ma novel. Being a mechanic pays the bills, but writing's really what I do. Y'see, ma book's gaun to be a sequel to *Dracula*! It'll sell whappin big! Y'know at the end of the novel, they never staked him, right? They just cut his throat and knifed him in the hert. No wooden stake, y'see? So what if the bruit survived, eh? What if ..."

Robbie chatters for forty minutes straight, through the last of the fish and chips, through three more pints, a scotch, and an order of roly-poly pudding with custard. If he weren't so visually luscious, he'd be intolerable. Typical would-be author's attitude, this pure self-absorption. Perfect candidate for a ball-gag. His writerly ambitions, however, have given me an idea. Greed is so easy to manipulate.

Fairly well sauced by now, if his slurred burr is any indication, Robbie finally winds down. "And so what I nee's a bad dream. Like Stoker. Y'know he got his idea for Dracula from a nightmare? Ate too much dressed crab, he did, and dreamed of the count. So that's how this

..." Robbie waves the paperback at me "... got started! Fuck all! I just need ridden by a nightmare. For insp'ration!"

I choke back a snicker. Bending forward, I take a deep breath of him – some sort of woodsy cologne, olfactory patina atop his body's warm musk, and, bass note beneath that, his lifeblood. Below the table, I grip his knee. "I'd like to see the churchyard, Robbie. Why don't you give me a tour?"

# # # # #

We're both bundled against the damp chill of northern England, Robbie in a jacket of brown rawhide, I in my black Western duster. It's a cloudy night, with a sharp breeze off the North Sea. St. Mary's churchyard is a long walk from the Magpie – along the river, across the bridge, and up, up, up the 199 steps to the hilltop, where the church stands, and, behind it, the crumbling walls and Gothic arches of a ruined abbey. Young and well-built as he is, Robbie's panting by the time we reach the top, his breath fogging the night air, his gait a little unsteady on all that alcohol. He's too self-absorbed to notice that, despite the long and strenuous climb, my breathing is unaffected. Amazing stamina is one of several gifts I received that night in 1730.

All about the squat-towered church eroded gravestones jut. We wander among them before taking a seat on a bench. It's very dark up here, but below us are the lights of Whitby, spilling over the steep slopes of the valley channeling the river Esk, and the harbor, a widening where the river meets the sea. In the distance, the sheer Yorkshire headlands recede, breaking waves a recurrent gray against their feet. To our right, the churchyard's edge drops off into sea cliff. A good place to toss leftovers, were one to have a mind to.

"Here, I think," I say, resting an arm across Robbie's wide shoulders.

My delicious escort's mind is clearly stuck on Bram Stoker rather than tonight's assignation. He misreads me. "Aye, right, mate, Mina saw Lucy from over there," he says, pointing across the valley. "Lucy was in her nightgoun sitting on one of these kirkyaird benches and something daurk was bent over her. The count! Mina ran across the brig we just crossed and all the way up those bloody stairs, for fuck's sake! She saw the count's fauchie-pale face and glistering red eyes! She found Lucy here. The next day she noticed the bite on Lucy's throat. In ma novel, I think I'll ..."

"Did you bring lube?"

Robbie turns to me, thick eyebrows knitted. "Aye, in my jaiket."

"Good. It's time you shut up and strip," I say. "I want to fuck you."

Robbie shrugs my arm off. "Here? It's too cauld. And I'm the Top, ye recall. No, Mr. Maclaine, le's go back to ma hotel. Yer strappin, an eesome bonnie bloke, but you'll look even better with your lang shanks in the air. I'll stuff my briefs in your gab and haimer you till you sab, mate, I'll ..."

"No," I say evenly. "Here. Tonight I think you'll enjoy being the bottom. Surely a man as handsome as you has been ass-fucked before? And I don't think I'll need to pay you. I have something else you want more than money."

Robbie stands up, fists clenched, face grim. "Look, wanker, are ye mental? Are ye an eejit? Do you want a bleachin? We agreed ..."

If I were mortal, a man this large and angry might be intimidating. But as it is, I'm simply amused. I stand up, smiling. I could try to mesmerize him or I could simply overpower him, but this is more fun. It's always entertaining to turn a man's greed against him.

"Lucky for you that we met. I'm a publisher," I say, pulling out my wallet and producing a business card. "I own a publishing company in America. How'd you like to get your vampire novel published?"

Robbie's mouth drops open. He takes the card from me, peering at it in the darkness. "Too mirkie to read," he says.

"Trust me," I say. "Are you willing to forgo such an opportunity?"

"Ye'd publish me?" Frowning, Robbie folds his arms across his chest. He's shivering. Tight T-shirts are good for pec display but not too handy at keeping a man warm in England's late winter.

"If your book's any good at all."

"Why would ye do that?" Suspicious, dubious, hopeful. Delectable.

"Because I'll owe you. Because you're going to do exactly what I say now. You're going to please me all night in every way I require. Am I right?"

"Yer word, mate. I need yer word."

"You have my word. And my card." I slip it into his back pants pocket, then pat his big ass. "Now strip."

Robbie hesitates, still disbelieving. "I'm na sure. What if yer a psycho?"

"You aren't afraid of me, are you? A big-muscled man like you? The Glaswegian Hercules?"

Pride pricked, his frown deepens. "Afraid? No! But what if yer conning me?

"All right," I say, moving toward the path on which we came. "Good luck with that novel."

I've passed only five time-stained gravestones before Robbie shouts. "Wait, Mr. Maclaine! Come back. Aye, I'll do it! I … I'll do what ye say."

I turn. He's shucked off his jacket. By the time I've returned to his side, he's peeled his shirt off. He stands before me, bare-chested and trembling, hugging himself. My fangs lengthen again, beginning to throb. The wind picks up, rolling off the jet-black sea.

"All of it," I say. He sits on the bench, unlaces his Doc Marten's, tugs them off, peels off his army pants, then his skimpy briefs. He stands before me, clad now in nothing but white socks and a thick metal cock ring.

"Very fine," I say, licking my lips. "Put your hands behind your back. Keep still and keep quiet. Scenery this mouth-watering deserves some study."

Robbie obeys. Our eyes lock for a few seconds, but then he can take my gaze no longer. Shame-faced, he hangs his head. I circle him, taking in the details. Stocky as a barrel, thickset as an oak trunk. Sturdy arms entirely etched in ink. The dense chest- and belly-pelt I'd expected. Big nipples stiff and prominent with the cold. A broad, round ass, cheeks and crack coated with more delightful hair. And, between his substantial thighs, a short fat cock, standing erect in its pubic nest.

I laugh. "Hell, aren't you pretty?" I stroke his cock. Robbie shudders. "Seems like you savor submission all of a sudden," I say, thumbing a drop of pre-cum, smearing it over the head. "And I thought you were all Top."

"Mostly," he mutters. "Na always." He shuffles in the dead grass. He clears his throat. "Sometimes I bottom if the bloke's hot and butch and willin' to pay extra."

I drop his cock and step behind him. From my duster's pocket I fetch the cuffs. He jumps at the sudden chill of metal about his wrist, but before he can react further I have both hands locked together behind his back.

"No, no, mate!" my captive gasps. He tries to turn, to pull away, but I wrap my arms around his quaking frame, pulling him close.

"You're not going anywhere, Robbie," I say, holding him firmly against me. "A man as handsome as you needs bounding. My rapture requires it."

"Don't hurt me. Please, Mr. Maclaine. Don't ..."

I lick the fan of hair between his shoulder blades, the furry patches capping his shoulders.

"What? You're going to scream for help like some Victorian damsel? I won't hurt a man who does what he's told. All right?"

Robbie nods; his struggles subside. When I run my fingers over his hard nipples and torso-thatch, he gives a little groan.

"Suck me," I say, releasing him. Sitting back on the bench, I pull my very hard cock from my jeans. "Now."

Robbie needs no further direction. Dropping to his knees, he takes me into his mouth's hot grip. For a supposed Top, he's a surprisingly fine cocksucker, tonguing my slit, gently gnawing the head, deep-throating me till I begin to pump his face hard. He chokes and gags, then rediscovers his rhythm, his beard tickling my balls, his saliva moistening my shaft and dripping onto my lap. I sigh, looking out over the harbor, the dark and distant bluffs that drop so steeply into sea. I take Robbie's big pecs in my hands and knead them, tugging on the thick hair there. When I pinch his nipples, he groans around my cock, nods, and bobs with even more vigor on the stiffness stuffing his mouth.

"Like a little hurt, huh?" I chuckle. For long minutes I give him the rough tit-work he clearly relishes, his slurps alternating with excited sighs. "Now for your ass." Pulling my penis from his eager suction, I lift him to his feet. "You're the one getting fucked tonight."

"Ma novel? You swear?" he says. He staggers a little, beard dripping wet.

"Yes," I say, pulling a ball-gag from my duster pocket. "Now let's make you even more helpless."

His eyes widen. He emits a little gasp as I push the black ball between his teeth. "Umm umm," he mumbles in protest, shaking his head like a dog, giving me some fight.

"Behave, or the deal's off," I say. Instantly he submits, allowing me to buckle the straps behind his head with no further trouble.

"You were quite the chatterbox this evening," I say, leading him behind the bench, shoving him forward, bending him over the back of it. "I've been wanting to shut you up for a while now. In my considered opinion, men as hot as you should be kept naked, bound, and gagged most of the time."

Robbie shakes and grunts as I brush my silvery goatee over his ass-cheeks, then tug at the hair in his crack with my teeth. "You like your hole eaten?" I whisper, raking a fang gently across one cheek, then the other.

My hairy Scot nods. His groan is long and low, much like a foghorn, as I clench his broad cheeks, spread him, and work my tongue up inside.

He's opening now, like a pink peach blossom, and, if his happy nods and ecstatic grunts are any indication, he's having quite the fine time. I tongue-fuck him for a good while, savoring the tasty ass-amalgam of musky, salty, bitter, and sweet, nipping his cheeks every now and then.

"You ready to be ridden?" I say, running my fingers over his ass and down the wet cleft.

This nod's more enthusiastic than any before. The bigger and butcher the man, the hornier and hungrier the bottom, 'tis true indeed. So much for his Top pose. In a flash, I've fetched lube from his jacket, dropped my jeans around my ankles, greased us up, and am pushing my cock against his hole.

"You want me inside you, don't you, Robbie?"

He nods, fists clenched in the small of his back.

"Beg me to fuck you, Robbie."

He pleads and mumbles around his gag: unintelligible syllables, ball-muffled, spit-wet, compliant.

Robbie whimpers and winces as I work the head in, apparently hurting a bit, head tossing like a Highland pony. His is the kind of ass I love most: rarely used, almost painfully tight. Slowly he opens further, my brave boy. He keeps mumbling and nodding as, by slow degrees, I slide inside him and begin moving in and out, a rhythm of cresting sweetness. Soon, he's spread his legs wider and pushed back against me, driving me deeper into him, his flesh gripping me hard from inside.

"Does that feel good?" I growl, gripping him by his hair, pounding him harder. "Do you want more?" I can feel, tight around my cock, the throbbing of his blood, the racing of his heart. Cold as the night is, his back's growing faintly silver with sweat. "Uh huh!" he murmurs. "Uh huh!"

The bench creaks beneath us as I ride him. I stroke his gag-tautened lips, saliva smearing my hand. I fist his hard cock, dig my fingers into his nipples, grip his pec-meat and tug. I gaze out over the twinkling seed-pearl lights of Whitby, down at his broad back, his tattooed arms, his cuffed, fumbling hands, out again to the harbor and the sea. Beautiful man, beautiful vista. I can't recall a more pleasing combination.

Another few minutes of bucking and grunting in flawless unison and we're finished, I up his hole's snug sheath, he in my hand's tight stroke. I lie atop him, licking up sweat-beads along his spine. When he's caught his breath, I help him up. We sit side by side on the bench. Heavily he leans against me. I wrap my arms around him, lapping first drool from his beard, then semen from my hand.

"I'm going to take you back to your hotel room," I say, "and warm you up. I'm going to cuff your hands in front of you, tape your pretty bearded mouth shut, take you to bed, and cuddle with you all night. Just before dawn, I'm going to hoist your legs over my shoulders and ram your hairy ass again. Would you like that?"

Robbie nods, his breath slowing, his shivers renewed by the sea breeze.

"Say please," I coax, bumping his chin with mine.

"Pleh," he grunts. Bubbles of saliva fleck his lips.

I nuzzle his neck, lick the throbbing column of his carotid artery. Now that one hunger's been answered, it's time to sate the second. "Didn't you say you needed a nightmare? I'm ready to give you that."

Robbie has time only to lift one curious brow before I've bared my fangs. Gripping his hair, I yank his head back. His eyes go wide, twin terror stars. His frame stiffens against me. His scream's a well-dammed torrent.

My teeth sink into his neck. Against the rubber ball, Robbie keeps screaming and screaming. His thick body thrashes against me. I hold him close, gulping and growling, lips clamped to his neck. Within minutes his youth has flooded and filled me with its luminous liquid.

His blood's thick and sweet as wildflower honey; in it are the salt of Northern seas, the metallic tang of swords.

I pull away as soon as Robbie passes out, before any lasting damage is done. A few centuries of such supping has taught me that skill. Lowering my captive gently onto the bench, I sit by him, watching his broad, hair-dark breast rise and fall. A light rain has begun, falling upon my head and in my beard, upon Robbie's naked form and the old gravestones about us. I could lift him to me and drain him completely, fling his husk over the sea cliff, be on my way. That would be expedient, uncomplicated.

That would be weak. The world needs all the loveliness it can get. Droplets of rain are beading the matted fur of his torso, belly, and groin; the slow wash of rain thins out the blood oozing from his wound. With a fingertip I trace the thorny swirls of his extensive tattoos. It will be grand to own him.

Robbie groans. His long-lashed eyes flicker open. He stares up at me without fright. His glance is fond, familiar, acquiescent.

I help him sit upright. I unbuckle the gag, unlock the cuffs. "Thanks, mate," he mutters, listing limply against me. I rub the stiffness from his jaw, from his wrists. I lick the last crimson from his neck.

"What happened?"

"You fainted. Get dressed," I say. He does so, slowly, wobbly from blood loss. The rain thickens about us. Out on the sea, a mist creeps toward the land. The distant headlands grow vague. Far up the coast, a lighthouse flashes.

Clothed, he stands before me. "Robbie, you have a choice," I say, straightening his collar. "If you want, I can make you forget this night. Do you want to forget?"

Robbie gives a puzzled smile. "Yer hair and beard are black now," he says, stroking my face. "Na, sir, I don't want to forget ye. Who would want to forget such a royal plowing as ye gave me? And that fiery kiss?"

"If you invite me to your room, I'll hold you till dawn. Tomorrow night, if you choose, I'll come to you again, here among the graves, or by your bedside. Whenever I return to this land, you may serve me, be my boy, my slave. I'll care for you well."

"I need na choices, Mr. Maclaine." Robbie runs a hand across his rain-spattered brow. "Dinna understand it, but I know I'm yers now.

Come callin' whenever ye tak the mind. I'll be ready and eager. To open for ye, if ye catch ma meaning." He steps forward, wraps his big arms around me, and rests his chin on my shoulder with a sigh. "Sir, the room I'm lettin' is on Crescent Terrace. Help me back there, will ye? Seems I'm a wee bit dizzy. All this cauld and damp, I guess."

"On the way, let's stop for some single malt by a pub fire," I say. "That should warm us up till I get you naked again. Meanwhile, here's a little advance."

Pulling out my wallet, I peel off 1,000 pounds and lay the bills in his palm.

"What's this?"

"For your novel. Have you had sufficient dreams to inspire you?"

Robbie stares at the money. "Well, fuck me." He pockets it, then gives me a quick kiss. I can smell my own musk in his beard.

"First round's on me, mate, master, Mr. Maclaine."

The fog's reached the coast now, swallowing us in its deep chill. I grip Robbie's hand, leading him through the gravestones. He stumbles once, across a broken bit of statuary, but his stride has steadied by the time we reach the stairs and begin our descent, through the lowing of a distant foghorn and the thickening mist. Wrapping a protective arm around him, I help him down the wet steps, leading him from the dark hilltop of the dead into the warm yellow lights of town.

THE LAST DARE
Christopher Pierce

I was tied up and getting worked over by a crowd of men before I had second thoughts about taking my friend Chad's dare.

But, I never turned down a dare. No matter how dangerous they were, I always took any given to me. The more crazy they were, the more I liked them. My friends could never figure out if I was really brave or really stupid.

I figured I was probably both.

That was before I stopped taking dares. After what happened, I haven't taken any. I never will again. It was last year around autumn time, you know, the time when the leaves start turning bright and the wind whispers through the streets and back alleys.

That was the season I took my last dare.

New in town, it didn't take me long to find the leather bars. I'm a hot man, there's no mistaking that. I turn my share of heads when I walk into a place, especially with the nice tan and amount of skin I was showing in those days. Dressing like it was summer all year 'round was one of my trademarks, one of the things that made me a unique individual. Or just an idiot who didn't know enough to put on more clothes when it was cold, take your pick. Actually, that wasn't the only thing that made me a unique individual.

My fatal attraction to dares was another.

So there I was, decked out in nothing but a pair of tight gym shorts, army boots and a leather vest. I hit the bars every night after work, and soon enough I'd found myself a nice pack of leather friends. Bottoms all, we prided ourselves on being coveted by the tops. But, we mostly kept to ourselves, finding our camaraderie more fulfilling than one-night stands with nameless men who called themselves "Masters" but were really self-hating bottoms in disguise.

Anyway, one night when nothing exciting was going on, it came out in conversation that I was a dare-taker. I lamented the fact that I'd done everything worth doing, from skydiving to bobsledding to fire walking, and there were no thrills left to be had. One of my buddies, Chad, glanced at the others and then shot me a challenging look.

"Well, there is one thing you haven't done."

Joey looked alarmed and put his hand on Chad's arm.

"Don't, man ..." he started to say, but my third buddy, a big guy named Nick, put his hand over Joey's mouth.

"Shut up, Joey," he said good-naturedly. "Let him tell it. What harm can it do?"

I was intrigued. "What?" I said. "What're you talking about? What haven't I done?"

"Well," Chad said, taking a pull from his beer. I knew he was making me wait on purpose, stringing me along. He was as bad as a top. "I was just thinking, maybe we can give you one dare you won't take."

I grinned my biggest grin. "Try me," I said. His eyes met mine, full on, a smirk on his face. Challenge accepted.

"There used to be this bar downtown called the Meat Market. It was the wildest leather bar in town, you know, before the Dog Pound opened. The biggest names in town used to go there and do their thing. This was before AIDS, you know, so anything goes. There was nothing that didn't happen in that place. And, the owner was friendly with the Chief of Police, so it never got raided."

He took another drink from his beer and glanced at the others. Joey still looked worried, and Nick was watching me closely.

"Yeah? So what happened to the Meat Market? How come I haven't heard about it?" I said, impatient for him to get to the dare.

"You're still new in town, man. Nobody really talks about it anymore. It's kind of ... I don't know, bad taste to mention it because of what happened."

"What did happen, Chad?" I asked. "You're such a fuckin' tease ..."

For the first time he looked impatient. At least I had wiped that smirk off his face.

"One night there was a terrible fire, and almost a hundred men died."

"Holy shit," I said. This wasn't what I expected.

"The building itself was mostly metal, so it wasn't hurt too badly. But, most of the men there that night got trapped inside and couldn't get out. They died right there in the bar. The place closed

50

down after that. The leather community was hit pretty hard; it took a long time for everyone to recover."

"How do you know all this?" I asked curiously.

"It's history, man," he said. "Every leatherman in town knows about the Meat Market and what happened there."

A creepy feeling was building in my stomach. I didn't want anything else to drink. Glancing at my watch, I tried to sound casual.

"So, what does this have to do with me?" I said, watching Nick and Joey's eyes move from me to Chad.

"Well, the owner was so upset he's never let anyone build anything on the property. It's stayed just the way it was after the firemen left."

The creepy feeling was getting worse.

"No one I know's ever gone there, but people say the place is haunted."

"Haunted?" I said, searching my buddy's eyes for sarcasm, humor, any hint that he was making this up. But there was none. Chad believed what he was saying, and a glance at Joey and Nick told me they did, too.

"Yeah," he said, "by the spirits of the men who died there that night." Joey put his hand on my arm.

"Don't do it, man," he said. "You don't have to do it."

"Do what?" I asked. "What is it you want to dare me to do, Chad?"

"I dare you to go there tonight and spend the night there, tied up."

I grinned, hoping to break their serious mood, but their expressions didn't change.

"You're serious?" I asked. Chad nodded.

"That's all you want me to do?" I said, with more bravery than I felt. "That's nothing."

"Yeah, that's all," Chad said. "If it's nothing, then you'll do it, right?"

"What'll you give me?"

"We'll pay for all your beers here for the rest of your life," he said. I raised my eyebrows.

"Really?" I said. They nodded.

"Sure, I'll do it," I said, and Joey sighed, shaking his head.

"We'll help you," Nick said. "We'll take you out there and tie you up, and at an agreed time, we'll come back and let you loose."

"You promise you'll be back at the time we agree on?" I asked.

"Sure," Chad said. "We'll be there."

"Done," I said, and we shook hands.

# # # # #

Later that night, we parked Nick's Jeep and got out. We were downtown, in an old run-down neighborhood. It was dirty and ugly but didn't look dangerous. Chad, Joey and Nick led me through some buildings that were half-torn down into an area that was blocked off from the street.

There we found a blackened metal structure, the size of a large apartment. It stood by itself in the middle of the property. The place was really creepy looking. I followed the other guys through the ragged entranceway into the building itself. The metal structure was blasted and torn, as if the blaze had tried its hardest to consume it before giving up. Thick layers of dust and leaves covered everything, and spider webs lurked in the dark corners. Disturbed by our entrance, clouds of filth flew up into the air.

Chad stopped and pointed at something across the room.

"That's it," he said. "That's where most of the action happened."

I followed his outstretched finger and saw a metal table. Bolted to the floor, it looked sturdy enough to hold a man, and judging by the worn-off corners, it had done so many times. It was just as fire-blasted as the rest of the building, the blackened metal twisted and torn in some places. Ancient manacles for the victim's hands and feet had been welded onto the corners, so he could be bound spread-eagled.

It was almost like looking at a torture rack in a medieval museum. The thought of being bound there was appalling, and spending the night in this place where so many men had died was suddenly unthinkable. Maybe this wasn't such a good idea after all.

But, I had been dared, and I never turned down a dare.

"It's not too late to back out," Joey said. I glanced at him with a faint smile.

"You're not scared, are you, Will?" Chad said.

That did it.

"No, I'm not scared," I said. "Let's do it."

I started walking over to the table, hopefully looking braver than I felt. The floor creaked and moaned beneath my feet, as if it was protesting my being there. My friends trailed behind, and in seconds, we stood before the table.

Close up, it looked worse than a torture rack. It looked like a sacrificial altar to some demented cult's evil god.

"Will?" Joey said, as I stood there staring at it.

"Fuck it," I said, as I started taking off my clothes. Out of the corner of my eye, I saw Nick raise his eyebrows at Chad. Good, I thought. At least I surprised them. Doing this naked had never been part of the dare, but I wanted to show these guys I wasn't scared, that I could take whatever they dished out and more. When I was nude, I hopped up on the table and lay down.

I spread out my arms and legs, and my friends went to each corner and fastened the manacles around my wrists and ankles. The metal moaned and creaked as it was twisted into place.

"Okay, it's done," Chad said.

"You ready, man?" Nick asked me. I tried to move my arms and legs, and was unable to. "Ready as I'll ever be."

"Chad, are you sure he's going to be safe?" Joey asked.

"This is a dare, Joey," Chad said in a cold voice. "No one said anything about it being safe."

"Let's go," Nick said. "I want to get out of here."

They started to walk back to the door, and I raised my head.

"Guys, you'll be back, right?" I said. Chad looked at his watch.

"It's eleven pm, now. We'll be back at six in the morning. We promise." he said.

"Okay, I'll see you then," I said.

"Have a good time," Nick said.

Now what the fuck did that mean? I thought. But all I said was "I'll be lucky if I don't die of boredom."

At that, all three of them laughed. Even Joey giggled a little, uncomfortably. For some reason, that was more unnerving than anything else that had happened so far. With my neck still craning up, I watched them walk out of the place. The dust on the floor was so thick that they left very clear footprints. Now there were two trails of them, the first when the four of us came in, the second, leading out, was the three of them leaving now. I looked at the two trails of footprints for a long time before I laid my head back down.

I stared up at the ceiling. It was very black, from the fire I guessed. The old thrill came back to me as I realized what a great dare this was, how I was doing something that no one else had ever done, how much my friends would respect me and be in awe of me when it was over.

There was very little noise, besides the usual background din of the city. This place was so well hidden I had no fears of anyone finding me. Not even homeless people could have found their way through the wreckage to where I was now.

I was safe.

I would be okay, I knew it.

I was alone.

And with that thought, I must have drifted off to sleep.

I dreamt I heard footsteps coming, echoing and re-echoing back and forth between the hollow metal halls that led to the main room I was in.

Then the noises got louder, and whatever was making them entered the room. Very slowly, I became aware of other sounds, sounds like the creak of leather as it moved, the sound of boots scuffing on the floor, the sound of matches being struck.

It was as if a bunch of men had entered the room and were standing over me, looking at me, pointing and laughing. My vision was blurred. I could hardly make it out. Then I realized that my eyes were closed, that I had fallen asleep and was dreaming.

I opened my eyes, and it wasn't a dream.

The room was full of men, I couldn't even count how many. They were of all shapes and sizes and races, and they all were wearing leather. My sight was filled with them, my mind seeking out little details and fixating on them: deep piercing eyes, bushy handlebar mustaches, rough callused working-man's hands, tall black boots, clouds of cigarette and cigar smoke, pierced nipples, handkerchiefs sticking out of back pockets in all the colors of the rainbow, reflective aviator sunglasses, motorcycle gloves, biker caps, military insignias and sailor hats.

My mind was flipping back and forth on itself like a dying fish. How had they gotten in here? Who were they? What the fuck was going on? Then I grasped at the only answer I could imagine: it was a set-up, of course. My friends had sent these guys here to scare me, to make the dare more frightening. But I wasn't frightened; I was excited, and powerfully turned on by this crowd of hot men. These were the leathermen of every boy's dream, tall, dark, serious and intense. These guys meant business; they were the real thing. No dressing up here, these men wore these clothes all the time.

I could hardly imagine where Chad knew these guys from. I had never seen them at the bars in town. They must have been a bunch of friends from out of town or from an exclusive leatherman's club. How could he afford to pay them all to do this? But then again, I thought, I was pretty hot, maybe they wouldn't need to get paid ... yeah, I could picture it: Chad and Nick and Joey telling these guys where to go, saying "You'll find a hot guy chained to a table out there; go in there and scare him a little ..."

That's what they must have done, got these guys in on the plan with them, told them where to go ... I saw that the crowd of men had formed a circle around me. They surrounded me on all sides – even if I wasn't tied down, I wouldn't have been able to escape through this group. They stared down at me, those harsh faces with their broody eyes under furrowed eyebrows, mouths scowling or grinning under mustaches. There was something frightening in the way they looked at me. It was as if there was more here going on than I realized ...

For the first time, the idea that I might be in actual physical danger played through my mind. But that couldn't be true, no, and even if it was, there wasn't anything I could do about this. There was no way in hell I could break myself out of these manacles.

But, suddenly my feet were being taken out of the manacles, and many hands lifted my legs up, bending my knees so my asshole was exposed. I wanted to fight, to kick, but in these men's hands, my strength was impotent, gone, I could not resist them.

What the hell was going on? I had never agreed to any sex! Playing around with strangers had never been part of the dare. Who knew if they were going to use condoms? My mind frantically went over it again in my mind, and I heard Chad's voice again.

"I dare you to go there tonight and spend the night there, tied up."

That was it. No one had said anything about what might happen there if I did this. I saw the loophole now, and I had fallen right into it like a stupid animal being tricked by a hunter's trap. Someone jumped up onto the table, got between my legs and started to push something against my butthole. I craned my neck upward, trying to see what was going on. Clenching my ass muscles, I tried to prevent whatever it was from entering me.

"Okay, guys," I said. "The joke's over, I got it. Now turn me loose, okay?"

No one said anything. In fact, it looked as if they hadn't even heard me, they were so intent on staring down at the man who had gotten between my legs at the end of the table. He was big, like a football player, but with the evilly intelligent eyes of a mad scientist from a monster movie. From this angle, I finally saw what it was that he was using on me, a king-size dildo bigger than any porn star's dick that was pressing and pushing against my hole as if it wanted in and wanted in now.

"No, please," I said, trying not to sound frightened. "I don't want to do this ..."

Another push, this one more insistent, and painful.

"Don't, please!" I shouted. Now they heard me, and stared at me as if I had made some unforgivable error. Without a word, they went into action. The men down near my crotch and legs started slapping me hard, raining their open palms on the exposed flesh of my inner thighs, my semi-hard dick, my tender sensitive balls. It hurt like a son-of-a-bitch, and I started howling in pain. Two of the men at my head grabbed my jaws and held them open. Another shoved a handkerchief in my mouth. I tried to force it out, but the man slapped my face hard, and I couldn't resist anymore. In it went, and tasted like it had been soaked in sweat and beer. Someone produced a short piece of rope and tied the gag in place around my head.

Distracted by the slapping and the gagging, my asshole had relaxed. Too late did I realize how vulnerable I had made myself. Before I could tighten up, the man between my legs had forced the dildo up into me.

Now I really howled, screaming into the handkerchief as the intruder split me open. It felt as if it was going up past my stomach into my chest cavity and would come out my mouth it was in so far. I twisted and writhed on the table, hoping somehow to break free. But that was crazy, I knew. I tried to get a grip on myself, knowing I couldn't panic or it'd be curtains for me. Staying calm was all that mattered; I had to get calm somehow.

Suddenly, I felt magnificent pleasure course through my body. What the hell was happening? I craned my neck up again and was astonished by what I saw. My dick was totally hard. How was that possible? I was in a terrifying situation, at the mercy of and in the power of men I didn't even know ... and I was totally horny and turned on. The men were taking turns leaning over me, spitting on my upraised cock and then giving it strokes with their fists.

I felt something tight and hard go around my ball-sack. I recognized it: it was a leather thong. Those bastards! They'd gotten me stiff just, so they could tie off my cock and balls and keep them hard for as long as they wanted. The thong was tightly tied up around my equipment. They continued to spit on it and stroke it, making it feel incredible despite the pain of the massive dildo up my butt.

One of the other men came forward now, taking the position at the foot of the table between my legs. He was Aryan-looking, with fierce blue eyes and beautiful blond hair. Dressed totally in black leather, he was a sight to see. The Aryan pulled a riding crop from his belt, and ignoring the pleading in my eyes to not do it, he started swatting my bright red cock and balls. It was like little bursts of fire on my flesh every time he hit me with the crop. Somehow, my cock stayed hard through this, but the pain was so intense, I don't know why I didn't pass out. While this was going on, some of the other guys had taken up positions right above me.

I didn't realize what they were doing until it was too late, but I wouldn't have been able to do anything about it anyway.

My chin was roughly grabbed and forced upward, tilting my head at an extremely uncomfortable angle. The handkerchief was yanked out of my mouth, and suddenly it was filled by something else, something hard and hot and salty. I was getting face-fucked while being plowed by that monster phallus between my legs and the blond whipped my cock and balls. It felt as if I could die and go to heaven or hell, the feelings were so overwhelming.

Struggling to breathe, I did the best I could to suck the huge dick that was pressing into my mouth, boring its way into the back of my throat. If I gagged and threw up, I would probably choke to death, so somehow, I had to keep control of my breathing.

Before I knew it, hot jizz was shooting down my throat as the face-fucker released his load. Gulping spastically, I swallowed it down just in time to take another dick as it was forced into my mouth. As the men above me changed places, I caught a glimpse of them arguing about who would get to use me next.

A particularly hard stinging swat to my nuts brought my awareness back to my crotch. The Aryan had delivered his last blow, it seemed, and was stepping out of the way for someone else to take the position. My eyes widened at the sight of him, a big black bruiser with skin as dark as the night outside. His eyes glowed white like the moon as he pulled a many-tailed flogger off his shoulder where it had been hanging.

Grinning maniacally, the bruiser drew his arm back and lashed my chest with his flogger. I screamed, the noise muffled by the new dick that was filling my mouth. It felt as if each one of the flogger's tails was leaving a wake of pain as it streaked across my pecs. My torturer was an expert, twisting his wrist and varying his strokes, so I was never prepared for the hits, each becoming a hideous surprise.

But, I couldn't move. Even if my arms hadn't been manacled to the table, I was surrounded on all sides by men that were bigger than I and had their minds set on using me and using me well. My legs refused to do what I wanted them to do.

What seemed like quarts of cum were getting shot down my throat as the parade of face-fuckers went on and on. Somehow my dick stayed hard through all of it, as if the fear and pain and disorientation were only making me more and more excited. I was sure my chest must be covered with welts and slashes by the time the bruiser stopped flogging me. Grateful for even a moment's rest, I relaxed my flexed muscles, releasing the tension that had been building up for what seemed like hours.

Bad mistake. At that instant, the worst pain I'd felt yet tore through my body. Someone had grabbed hold of the dildo that was impaling me and yanked it out, with no warning or preparation. The sudden absence of the object inside me was even worse than the agony of its entry, and I howled against the cocks that were fighting to get through my lips. A man got up on the table, forcing himself between my legs. I was filled again, the pain easing somewhat. I cocked my head to the side, trying to get a look at who or what was fucking me.

The man that had taken the bruiser's place between my legs was dressed like an Army grunt. A sweat-stained brown tank-top covered his bulging chest, baggy camouflage pants were shucked down to his knees to expose his dick, dog tags jangled around his neck, and mirrored sunglasses hid his eyes.

He fucked me slow and sure, as if there was no hurry, and I wasn't going anywhere. His manrammer felt amazing inside me, so warm and alive after the rigid coldness of the dildo. Not a trace of a smile crossed the grunt's mouth. He hardly even seemed to notice me at all, I was just something to be used, the way he would use toilet paper or a beer can before tossing it away. I was nothing to him, just a hole to fill and get his rocks off in.

His jetting cock spurted its hot juice into my guts. The grunt pulled out as two dicks were forced into my mouth at the same time. The men had given up arguing, and now were taking me two at a time. I gagged and did my best to lick and suck the intruding organs, fighting to breathe. The grunt got down off the table, and another man replaced him.

My aching asshole was invaded again, this time by a man that looked like a leather god. Seemingly perfect in face and form, he was unreal in his nobility and attitude. His black leather harness perfectly enhanced his chest, his bearded face looking down on me as an eagle would look at a rabbit, his exquisitely sculpted crotch and legs encased in chaps that were as tight as his own skin. The cock that was entering me felt as if it was ice cold, shocking me with a hundred new sensations as it reamed and plowed my tormented butt.

My neglected dick was screaming for release by this time. And suddenly, the leather god took me in his black-gloved fist, holding my cock with a touch that was brutal in its tenderness. I was moaning and whimpering against the dicks that were in my mouth. Ecstatic with pleasure and the insanity of what was happening to me, I arched my back, actually lifting myself off the table. The air all around the table was electric, charged with an intensity that would explode at any moment. The cock in my ass was screwing me insistently, as if time was running out and it had to finish fast. Sweat from the leather god's body dripped down onto me as he claimed me, scorching me and freezing me with his power and strength.

Hot liquid flooded into my throat, gurgling down into me as I tried to swallow and catch my breath at the same time. The leather god pumped my dick hard now, all traces of his earlier gentleness gone.

My world seemed to have been filled with sensation now, only sensation. Thought had been destroyed, leaving only feeling. All the universe had become the sound of the men around me, the taste of their cum and sweat, the smell of their bodies, the sight of their raw masculinity and most of all the feel of the incredible cock that was fucking me harder and deeper and better than I'd ever been before ... then in a heartbeat, it all came together in an explosion of passion that seemed to split the air above the table. All sound became a roar, the roar of the leather god as he shot his load inside me, filling me with a tidal wave of heat and cold that ignited every inch of my body. The leather thong was ripped free of my cock and balls.

My vision blurred and flared, impossible images swimming into my brain. I thought I saw the men around me gather into a single mass and dissolve away like a candle's flame being blown out. I thought I saw the leather god change into a glittering column of light that burned between my legs for a moment before disappearing altogether.

My orgasm raged in me, and I closed my eyes against the visions and lost myself in pleasure. I must have lain there for five or ten minutes before I tried to get my bearings.

It was almost morning.

The air had gotten chilly and a breeze was blowing through the burned-out building, whistling ominously. What I had just been through was unbelievable. Who would have thought Chad and Nick and Joey could stage such an elaborate scene? I had been the focus of many group fuck-fests, but this night – this night would live on in my memory as the most spectacular by far. Where had they found those men anyway? They couldn't know that many hot guys, could they?

Then I stopped. I was alone right now, I was sure of it. When had they left? I must have been so out of it I didn't hear or see them leave.

Twisting my head to the side, I looked down to the floor. So many men would have left hundreds of footprints behind; the dust on the floor would full of them; but there were no footprints except the original few made when my friends and I had arrived. No others, not a one. The covering of dust on the floor was complete and undisturbed except for the two trails that had been there before my ordeal. Looking at the floor, you'd think no one had been here except Chad, Nick, Joey and me, and hours ago at that. But, the men had been there! I knew it! I looked down at my chest and saw the puddles of cum between my pecs. My hands were still bound to the table, I couldn't reach my dick – how had I come if the men hadn't been here? I couldn't have imagined it, the evidence was everywhere: the cum on my chest, the welts and lashes on my body, the gallons of jizz in my stomach and up my ass. Evidence was everywhere, that is, except on the floor, where it should have been most obvious.

And, my ankles were bound again.

I suddenly felt very frightened.

Just then I heard my friends come back. Chad called out to me.

"Will, you did it! I've got to hand it to you, man ..."

"He really did it," Joey said as they walked over to me.

"Let me out, please," I said breathlessly, staring up at their faces.

"Okay, okay, a promise is a promise," Nick said as he loosened the manacles and let my sore wrists and ankles loose.

"How did you pull this off?" I said as I rubbed my aching joints. So tired I didn't want to get up, I was still lying down.

"Pull what off?" Nick asked.

"How did you get all those men here? And how come they didn't leave any footprints?" They were staring at me as if I was a crazy man.

I sat up on the edge of the table and jumped down, stretching out as I did.

"I swear to God, Will, we didn't pull anything. The dare was for you to spend the night out here tied up. That was it."

I slowly looked back and forth between my three friends.

"You didn't get a bunch of men to come in here and work me over during the night?"

They shook their heads.

"Then who the hell were they?" I said, feeling hysteria building up in my stomach. What the fuck was going on? "And why are you looking at me like that?"

"You're white, man," Nick said.

"What?"

"He's not kidding, Will," Chad said, pointing at my chest. "Look at yourself."

I looked down and couldn't believe what I saw.

My skin had turned white. Not pale, but white. White as an albino. My tan had completely disappeared over night, leaving me with skin as white as the belly of a fish.

I looked up at my friends, my mouth falling open. Then I had a thought that almost made me piss myself.

"Guys," I said. "How long ago did the Meat Market burn down?"

"Twenty years ago ..." Chad said, "... last night."

Suddenly Joey sniffed and wrinkled up his nose.

"Do you smell something?" he said. Chad and Nick sniffed, too, and covered up their noses.

"It's awful," Chad said. "What is it?"

"Will, do you smell it, too?" Nick asked.

Hardly believing they could get side-tracked by an odor with everything else that was going on, I inhaled deeply.

I did smell what they smelled, and I recognized it, too.

It was a smoky old smell, a smell that held many others within it. It was the smell of fire, and within it, the smell of burnt clothing, and the smell of burnt flesh.

WEREBEAR
Logan Zachary

"Get out of the way, half-breed homo," the man with two missing teeth growled. His scruffy beard and unwashed smell made most people give him a wide berth, but entering the door to Cheyenne Crossing's restaurant and store, Buck Running Bear had little room to avoid him.

Buck pushed his way past. He usually wore his ranger uniform, but this was his week of vacation. Faded jeans and a worn T-shirt covered his muscled frame. His long black hair hung loose, just brushing his shoulders. At work, he usually pulled it back into a slick pony tail. His cabin at Wickiup Campground waited for his quick return, as he stopped by to pick up a few forgotten items.

"Use the back door next time, Squanto," the man's brother said.

Buck ignored them and headed over to the left where the café was.

"Off duty, Deputy?" Marilyn asked as she pulled out her order pad. She nodded to the man sitting at the counter. "Have you met Phil? He's the new owner of Cheyenne Crossing."

"Another fucking faggot from the city," the toothless man swore and stormed out the front door. A truck's engine roared and revved as tires spun out on the gravel drive. Small stones hit the side of the building, one even bounced off the large picture window.

"Earl is such an asshole," she said.

Phil turned his stool around and smiled at her.

"Sorry, boss. He gets me so angry sometimes ..." Her face reddened.

"No need to apologize. The former owner warned me about him and his brother Merle." He stood up and extended his hand. "He told me about you, too, Buck. Nice to meet you."

Buck took his hand and felt warm electricity flow from his skin. This man carried an energy inside that Buck hadn't encountered before. His father was white, and his mother was the eldest Lakota daughter of a Medicine man. His exotic good looks made it hard to see the Native American, easily having him being mistaken for Hispanic. While jogging shirtless one day in Custer State Park, a tourist thought he was Ricky Martin.

Phil's startled look told Buck he had felt it, too. Phil's white button down shirt was open two buttons, revealing a deep tan and a trimmed furry chest. All the hair was closely clipped to an even mat. A deep black mat of ....

Buck started from his thoughts and met Phil's deep blue eyes. His brown ones held the stare as his jeans started to tighten, a stirring in his loins.

"Did you come in for supper?" Marilyn broke the silence and the men released their hands.

"Ah, no. I needed a light bulb, some matches, and toothpaste. I forgot them at home."

"You staying at the campground?" she asked.

"Someone canceled their reservations for the Frontier, so the cabin's hot tub called to me for my week off."

"Frontier?" Phil asked.

"Randy and Helen Armstrong named each cabin. Isn't that cute?" Marilyn said.

Neither man said anything. They just stared at each other.

Buck nodded. "I should get going. Welcome to Cheyenne Crossing, Phil. Best of luck with the new adventure."

"I'm glad to know you'll be watching my back," he said as he extended his hand again. Buck shook it and thought, what a sexy backside to protect.

Buck started awake. His ears strained to figure out what woke him, but he heard nothing. Night had fallen, and the glow of the small furnace's fire sent shadows racing around the log walls. He had dozed off fully dressed on his soft bed. The covers were still in place. The warmth of the fire and peace of the night had lullabied him to sleep.

The cabin was one room: bedroom corner, table and furnace corner, kitchen corner, entryway corner. Buck walked over to the front door and glanced into the small closet bathroom to his right. He opened the front door and stood on the threshold, looking out. The full moon shone bright in the starry night. Streaks of heat lightning illuminated the sky. The small creek flowed to his left, the same side as the deck and the hot tub. Maybe he should take the lid off and jump in before bed.

A gunshot ended that plan.

Buck ran into the cabin and opened the closet. He pulled out his holster and checked his gun. He grabbed a flashlight and raced out into the night. He knew the shot had come from the North, so he ran around the cabin across the dirt road that connected the cabins and searched for a path into the woods.

Another shot echoed through the trees as he entered them. Thick clouds raced across the night sky and covered the moon. Buck paused for a second to let his eyes adjust. The Black Hills were named for the deep rich soil and the thick forest that didn't allow any light in.

He heard a bloodcurdling howling scream and started forward again. His gun was ready, and it led the way as he forged through the brush and spruce trees. The heat of the day radiated off the ground as the cool night breeze washed over him. The terrain sloped down into an opening in the trees. As he entered the clearing, a shape entered on the other side. It fell against a tree and crumbled to the ground.

Buck remembered his flashlight and slowly advanced before turning it on. He neared the shape and flipped the switch. His beam of light revealed a naked man's form curled into a ball on the fern-covered ground. Thick, red streaks of blood ran down one arm. Buck knelt by his side and gently rolled him onto his back. Phil's unconscious form lay in the center of the circle of light. Buck ripped at his T-shirt and pulled a long strip of cotton off the bottom. His tight six-pack abs felt the cool breeze run up his half shirt and sent a chill over his bronze body. He carefully looked at Phil's arm and found a bloody streak across the upper curve of his deltoid.

It looked like a bullet had grazed his shoulder. He wrapped the cotton over the wound and slipped it under his armpit. Hair brushed his fingers as he worked the cloth around and around. His eyes wandered, wanting to look over his chest, across his torso, down to his …

A branch snapped under a heavy footfall.

Buck held his breath and waited.

Nothing.

He switched off the flashlight, quickly finished wrapping the injury, and tucked the loose end into the bandage. His hands burned as he touched Phil's naked body. Buck carefully picked him up and bent his body over his shoulder. His arms wrapped around his muscular legs as he searched for a handhold. His fingers wanted to caress his furry butt, but getting out of there was more important. Poaching had increased due to the hard economic times. Phil's hands tapped Buck's ass as he walked through the clearing. He tried to find a wide path to limit the branches scratching his naked flesh.

Buck kicked open his cabin's door and walked in to gently place Phil on his bed. He pulled a blanket over him and raced to the bathroom. He threw two washcloths into the sink and opened the medicine cabinet. He found a few rolls of gauze and a Telfa pad. He carried the supplies to the bed and pulled back the covers to expose Phil's shoulder. He carefully unwrapped his crudely-covered shoulder and looked down. The gash was wide and raw, but the bleeding looked as if it had slowed.

Buck had seen many gunshot wounds, but none ever seemed to close this fast. Maybe it was a shallow flesh wound and had appeared worse in the panic and the dark.

Phil's breathing was even and constant, but no signs of waking up. Had he hit his head? Internal bleeding on his brain? He reached for his cell phone and flipped it open. No signal.

What should he do? He took one washcloth and folded it twice and laid it across Phil's forehead. He took the other one and wiped down his arm, cleaning the blood off his shoulder. He rinsed it off in the kitchen sink, then washed the rest of Phil's arm and wiped up to the new bandage. He rinsed again and started to clean along his neck and over his pecs. Less blood was sprayed over his hairy chest. The closely cropped hair tickled his fingers as he worked. His hand washed lower, over his pec. The half dollar-sized nipple rose from the warm rough washcloth. He circled it, and it popped up into a sharp point.

Buck wiped lower down Phil's well-defined chest, slipping down to his sculpted abs. He could see the muscle definition of his six-pack. The coarse hair seemed softer there. His hand worked lower, pulling the blanket back. He cleaned his navel and wiped over his hip. His hand continued down to his knee, and washed his upper thigh.

He rinsed the washcloth again, the water warmer now. He worked back up Phil's leg and gently grazed his low-hanging balls. Two smoothly shaved orbs hung low as his flaccid penis rested over them. Buck's fingers combed through the thick bush of black pubic hair. Phil took a deep breath, and his balls rose up as his penis seemed to swell with each breath, inflating as Buck washed. His fingers cleaned the short hair on his abs and worked lower. His hair seemed longer and softer. Maybe the water was making it appear that way.

Buck pulled back the curtain, and looked out the window. The clouds had blown away, and the full moon peeked in, a moonbeam flowing through the window pane and caressing Phil's naked torso. His hair seemed to grow even longer, softer, and thicker as the light touched it. Buck's fingers combed down through Phil's pubic bush and trailed along his rapidly growing penis. His hand left the washcloth on his abs and stroked his cock, his fingers wrapping around his length.

It swelled and rose up. As Buck's fingers neared the tip a small trickle of pearly fluid flowed out. He spread it over the fat tip as a low moan escaped from Phil. His hips rose up to follow Buck's hand, trying to maintain the skin contact. Buck's gaze scanned Phil's body, and he saw the hair pattern appeared even thicker, coarser, and longer. His other hand joined in caressing Phil's body. It cupped his balls and found that the orbs were no longer smooth and soft, but bristly and hot. The growing hair poked and tickled his palm. He pulled down on them, and a low moan rumbled deep down in Phil's chest in his throat.

Phil sat up suddenly, fully erect.

Buck held his cock and balls in his hands as he looked into Phil's deep blue eyes, but his eyes were changing, spreading apart, bulging out and getting bigger. Grandma, what big eyes you have, floated through Buck's consciousness. Phil's whole body started to quake and shiver. His muscles rippled under his furry skin. His nose pulled forward and open wide to roar.

Buck let go of the other man's penis and fell down on the floor in surprise and terror.

Phil's legs pulled back on the bed, and he assumed a four point stance on his hands and knees. He breathed in, and his back expanded and filled out. His arms and legs swelled as thick claws came out of where his fingers once were. His ears pulled back into small rounded ones, bear ears, grizzly bear ears.

Buck started to crabwalk backward across the floor, but his feet were unable to find purchase on the cheap linoleum. He flipped over on his hands and knees and crawled to the cabin's door. His fingers curled around the knob and twisted as he felt thick claws grab and pull his leg. He hung onto the knob and pulled the door open. His body was lifted off the floor and fell back down as soon as he released the knob.

Phil released his leg and walked over his body. As his mouth opened to roar, hot drool poured out and dripped along the back of Buck's neck.

Buck braced, waiting for the back of his neck to be ripped out. When he looked up and out the cabin's door into the campground, he saw Merle and the tooth-missing Earl poised with guns aimed at him.

A shotgun blast hit the door as the other one took out a corner of the door frame.

Phil roared, sniffed Buck once, and bolted out the door. His claws dug into the gravel road as he chased after the brothers. The men ran before they were able to get off another shot.

"Don't run!" Buck shouted after them, but realized how stupid that sounded. He pushed himself onto his feet and ran back to the table to get his gun. He slipped an extra clip into his pocket and ran off into the night.

Buck tried to follow their path through the woods, but the underbrush was too thick. He heard a few gunshots and a few screams that made his blood run cold, but helped guide him through the woods.

After about forty-five minutes, Buck entered a secluded grove. He shone his flashlight and discovered a secret patch of marijuana. The plants were evenly cultivated into rows, and he knew this wasn't from Mother Nature.

"Drop the gun and don't make any sudden movements," Earl commanded from behind him. Buck started to turn around, and the butt of Earl's shotgun slammed into the side of his head, and the night went black.

His head throbbed as the forest swam back into view. The double vision fuzzed for a while and then became one image. Buck felt the ropes that secured him to the tree. The coarse fiber cut into his skin as did the tree bark into his back. His shirt and pants were gone. Only his thin underwear covered his cold body. Something wet flowed down the naked flesh of his arms and legs. At first, he thought it was dew, but this fluid was thicker.

Blood?

He rubbed his fingers against his thumb and felt a gritty thick substance. He inhaled deeply. Underneath the humidity and rot of the forest was a sweet, candy-like smell, and his body went rigid.

Honey.

His body was covered in honey. He licked his lips and tasted it. The brothers were baiting the bear with his body. He pulled frantically against the ropes, and only felt them cut deeper into his skin. Nothing budged or relaxed. He was tied to stay.

A low grunting and crunching sounded in the underbrush. Buck held his breath. In the moonlight, he could see the hulking form slowly moving toward him.

His heart pounded against the inside in his chest. Would they kill the bear, before it killed him? Or would they kill him, too? What was their plan? He doubted they would let him live after he had seen their cash crop. The bear sniffed the air and stood up on his hind legs. His long claws glowed in the moon and appeared to be six inches long. It roared once and dropped back down to all fours and continued toward Buck. He tried to free himself, but the ropes were too tight. The bear sniffed at Buck's feet. One sock was still on; the bare foot sparkled in the moonlight. The bear licked its lips and brought his mouth down on his bare foot.

Buck's ankles were tied in place. He wasn't able to kick the bear away.

The bear tasted the honey and licked up his calf.

Buck's native genes made his legs smooth and hair-free. His bronze skin took on a healthy glow in the moonlight, and he wondered how long that would last. The bear's tongue moved up his leg and worked around his kneecap, making large circles with the rough wet surface.

Despite the fear racing through his body, Buck's penis started to become erect. The honey wet the thin cotton, showing the detailed outline of his cock, balls, and a triangle of black hair underneath. The bear's tongue was warm and wet as it worked up his leg. It was the same thing he had wanted to do to Phil's naked body earlier but didn't get the chance. Now it looked like he never would. The bear licked across his cotton-covered balls.

"Now the faggot's into bestiality," Merle's snickering laugh cut through the forest, followed by the metallic click of a bullet being forced into the chamber.

The bear heard the click and reared up onto its powerful hind legs.

In the past, Buck was always amazed at how quickly a bear's bulk moved. He had fired many warning shots to scare them away. But somehow, this bear was different.

The shotgun exploded, a white flame shot out of the barrel in slow motion and took out a chuck of Buck's tree. The rope that held his arms hostage snapped and his hands were free.

The bear dropped down and charged.

Merle tried to aim, but the raging ton of anger bore down on him.

Earl shouted, "Shoot!"

But, Merle's body refused to move. The bear was on him and grabbed him around the neck with his massive mouth and around his portly body with his huge paws' claws.

The gun discharged harmlessly into the ground, as the bear's jaw clamped shut with a loud final snap. Merle's body went limp as the bear shook his head from side to side, his arms hugging the body close to him.

Earl screamed and pulled the bolt back on his gun. He slipped behind a tree and chambered the next round. "Merle?" he called with a shaky voice. He raced behind the tree where Buck was trying to untie the rope around his neck. He pulled the trigger and an explosion deafened Buck's right ear.

Buck felt the heat of the blast and the flash of light by the side of his head.

The bear threw Merle's body to the side, discarded as it spun its hulking body around. Buck stared into its eyes, seeing the red rage that burned deep inside. He doubted Earl's shotgun would stop it when it charged him. He closed his eyes and tensed his body for the impact. Earl appeared on the other side of the tree and readied his gun. The explosion sounded.

Buck felt a heavy weight fall down at his feet. He swallowed hard as he felt the wet fur roll over his bare foot. His fingers clawed at the rope around his neck. Could he escape before Earl shot him? Earl tentatively peeked out from behind the tree and stepped toward the bear. He kicked its nose once and readied his gun.

Nothing happened.

"Got 'im," he smiled his tooth-missing grin and leveled the gun at Buck. "Say your prayers, injun."

Earl's finger touched the trigger, and then his whole body was raised up from the ground until he was hanging upside-down from the bear's claws.

The bear roared in his face as Earl screamed. The veins in Earl's neck bulged out against the skin, just as the bear's head surged forward. The gun fired. A sickening crunch sprayed across Buck's face, and all went quiet.

The bear dropped Earl at Buck's feet and waddled behind the tree. It extended his claws and scratched deep into the wood. The rope around Buck's neck tightened for an instant, then went slack. Another tug pulled around his ankles and then his legs kicked free. Buck fell to his knees as the first pink of sun appeared in the distance.

Spruce needles, chucks of tree bark, leaves, and dirt clung to his sticky body.

As his breathing returned to normal, he pushed himself up onto unsteady legs and looked down at Earl. He didn't have to check his pulse to know he was dead. He swallowed hard and slowly peeked around the tree.

The bear was gone.

A naked man lay curled in a ball.

Buck slowly moved over to him. He knew this body, all too well.

Phil.

He reached down to feel for a pulse. A healthy one pumped in his neck. No dark pool of blood spread out from under him.

"Phil?" he said, softly.

His eyes fluttered and slowly opened. Deep blue looked into his.

"Are you okay?" Buck asked, helping him to his feet.

Phil's legs threatened to collapse, but Buck held him up.

"Let's head back to the cabin." Buck held onto him and took a few steps. He saw his discarded clothes and gun tossed into a pile. He picked up them up, as they made their way through the woods.

"Why don't you shower first?" Buck offered. "That way I can check over your injuries."

Phil slowly stepped into the metal shower stall with the white plastic curtain. "I think we can both fit."

Buck looked down at his filthy body. He pushed down his briefs and threw them into the garbage can. He stepped into the shower as Phil turned the water on.

A cold blast of water startled them as they huddled together. Slowly, the water warmed and flowed over their cuts and bruises. Dirt and leaves washed from their bodies. Spruce needles swirled in the drain.

After they were soaked, Buck reached over to the small shelf and grasped a small bar of white soap. He rubbed it on Phil's chest and watched as the lather started to form. The creamy white foam contrasted against the black hair that covered his body. He scrubbed over one pec and then moved over to the other. He could feel the nipples rise and harden under his touch. His fingers combed through the hair as they worked lower. The hair grew longer and thicker. His hands brushed against his semi-hard erection.

Phil turned his back to him in the small space, and Buck started soaping up his shoulders. The open wound on his shoulder appeared as a pink scar, completely closed and healed. Buck worked down his broad shoulders, down the arc of his lower back, and paused above the curve of the perfect bubblebutt. The fleshy orbs screamed to be touched, and Buck lathered them up. His fingers slipped between and explored their depths.

Phil moaned as he pressed back against him and spread his cheeks wider.

Buck's fingers drilled lower and found a tender opening. He soaped and explored as Phil rode back and forth on his hand. He reached lower between the muscular legs and grasped the dangling sac below. Covered in hair, no longer shaved smooth, he rolled the fleshy orbs around and around. Lather swirled down his hairy legs and circled the drain. Phil turned to face him with a raging hard-on.

Buck stepped back.

"Your turn," Phil said as he took the bar of soap from his hand. He brought his head back and tossed it from side to side, letting the water rinse his hair. He rubbed the bar over Buck's smooth chest and met some resistance.

"Honey," Buck said.

"A pet name already?" Phil asked.

"I'm covered in honey."

Phil leaned forward and stuck out his tongue. He licked along the side of Buck's neck and down his shoulder. "Sweet. I hate to waste it." His tongue worked its way down to Buck's nipple and pulled it in. He drew down hard on it, sucking it clean. His teeth rolled it back and forth. Buck threw his head back as the pleasure radiated through his body, adding to the warmth of the water. Phil dropped down on one knee and worked his mouth over Buck's body, the bar of soap forgotten in his hand. He moved over his chest and down the line in the center of his chest. His tongue explored his belly button. He stopped and spit out a chuck of bark. "Maybe I should …" he raised up the bar of soap. He stood and started to lather up his hands. Once they were covered with foam, he massaged them over Buck's chest. He cleaned his chest and moved lower to his torso.

Buck could feel himself swell as the water and soap washed over him. His smooth skin made the cleanup easy.

Phil dropped down to the stall's floor and scrubbed Buck's legs. The honey took elbow grease, but the soap and the heat helped him with his task. Buck turned to face the corner of the stall and Phil started up the back of his legs. Little honey covered the back, so his progress was faster, working up to Buck's shapely bottom.

Phil's hands cupped each cheek and polished them. Squeaky clean, he pushed them wide and dove between, his tongue exploring and tasting. Buck's whole body stiffened as the tip sought entry. He pressed back, relaxing and allowed him in.

Phil's tongue circled and probed, circled and probed, spreading Buck's tight opening wider. He stood, washing Buck's back, as his erection replaced his tongue. Soapy and wet, it easily slipped in, filling Buck to its hilt. Buck's body swayed in time with Phil's, matching him stroke for stroke. Buck could feel Phil's low-hanging hairy balls slap against his with each thrust.

Water cascaded over the men, sending the last of the dirt and honey down the drain. Phil's pace quickened, as Buck's body tensed. "Let's move over to the bed. We'll have more room," he suggested.

Phil slowed his pace and turned off the water. Reluctantly, he slipped out of Buck and back out of the stall. He picked up a scratchy towel and handed it to Buck. He picked up another mismatched one and dried himself. Their bare feet padded across the old linoleum, leaving quickly-disappearing wet footprints on it. The covers were still pulled back on the bed and Buck dove in. He rolled onto his back and spread his arms wide, welcoming Phil.

Phil jumped on top of him as his mouth found Buck's. They kissed deeply, tongues dueling as their erections rubbed along side each other.

The weight of Phil's body comforted Buck. The warm furry skin, the soft caresses, the passionate kisses soothed the rope burns on his neck, wrists, and ankles and the blow to his head. Buck's hands rubbed over the damp pelt of fur that covered Phil.

Moans of pleasure washed over the men as they rubbed against each other. Pre-cum oozed out of both their cocks, mixing together.

The clean smell of soap and water mixed with an earthy, manly scent. The crackle of the fire sent shadows dancing in the early morning hour.

Phil reached down and pulled back Buck's foreskin. Pre-cum gushed over his hand as he slicked up Buck's cock. He grabbed his own penis and lubed his eight inches, slightly longer than Buck's but not as thick. Buck tipped his pelvis back and his erection slid under Phil's hairy balls and poked between his legs. Phil sat back and felt it slip between his cheeks, up and down along his crease, its tender hooded tip seeking entry. Phil teased it, letting Buck think it would slide in, but pulled back and away. After several attempts, he crawled lower on the bed, his bare ass pointing to the ceiling, and he found the wanted invader, taking it into his mouth.

Buck's body went limp.

Phil's fingers re-tracked the foreskin, and another wave of pre-cum oozed down his girth. He swallowed him whole. Phil's hand milked Buck's testicles, pulling them down, stretching them as far as they could go. His rough tongue circled the raging hard-on. He sucked on it, drawing it down his throat, trying to swallow all of Buck. He pulled it out, drawing the foreskin over the fat mushroom head, then rolled the small flap of flesh between his teeth. His tongue probed the fleshy tube and tickled the tip.

Buck spun his body around, so his head was between Phil's legs. His tongue licked his furry balls and drew one into his mouth. They were too large to both fit in at the same time. He slid his tongue along the shaft and watched it bounce up and down as he worked his way to the sensitive end. His lips kissed the bulbous tip and pulled it in.

Phil bucked his hips and drove his cock into the waiting mouth. He sucked Buck's cock into his mouth and held him deep inside. They plunged back and forth, in and out of each other as their excitement grew. Buck let Phil's cock escape and returned to his balls. Phil slowly sat up and reached across to stroke Buck's cock as his back straightened. Buck's tongue worked up his balls and slid up to his crease. He used his hands to spread his cheeks wider as his tongue licked the tight opening.

Phil pressed down on Buck's tongue, forcing it to enter him.

It swirled around and around, drilling the hole, forcing the muscle to relax. Saliva dripped off his balls and trickled between his hairy cheeks, pooling on Buck's chin and chest. Phil rode his face, jacking his and Buck's cock at the same time. Soon enough, he couldn't take it any more, and he rolled onto his back, pulling Buck on top of him.

"I want you in me," Phil said, "hurry."

Buck spun around so he was face-to-face with Phil again. "Are you sure?"

Phil pushed a pillow under his hips and spread his legs. "Yes."

Buck reached over to the bedside table and retrieved a condom and a bottle of lube, then positioned himself between Phil's legs. He spread lube over Phil's cock as he slipped his penis between his cheeks. Its tip touched his opening and circled it.

Buck stroked Phil's cock and massaged his balls. He pressed his hard-on against the tight muscle and held it there. Phil rocked his hips back and forth, relaxing his butt and enjoying Buck's long strokes on his cock. He pushed down and felt his bottom relax.

Buck's penis slipped slowly in and stopped, its girth preventing further entry. He gently rolled his hips and pressed forward, increasing his stroking on Phil's dick. He withdrew and applied more lube to his cock. He added more on Phil's and started again. This time he slipped in deeper, but Phil was tight.

"Take a deep breath," Buck suggested. He pulled his hips back, but as Phil started to inhale, he drove forward and entered him with one big push. Phil gasped as his ass was filled. The painful pressure eased and soon disappeared. He held still as Buck worked deeper into him. The motion became pleasant. His body welcomed each thrust. He pushed his cock harder into Buck's hand.

Their rhythm increased as their pleasure doubled, their breathing came as quick gasps as sweat broke out over their clean bodies, adding to the ease of their motion.

Buck's balls bounced off Phil's bubblebutt as his hooded tip tapped his prostate. Waves of electricity tingled through their bodies as their excitement grew. Buck took a deep breath in, and his cock swelled with the intake of oxygen.

Phil's butt clamped down as his cock threatened to explode. "I … I … think …"

Buck felt the pressure rising in his balls as they pulled up along side his shaft. "I … know," was all he got out before the first wave hit him. He plunged in to the hilt and held his penis there.

Phil's ass tightened and clamped down on his cock.

Buck pulled back against the contracted muscle as the explosion ripped out of him, filling the condom.

Phil's balls released at the same time and white hot cum flowed out of his shaft and streaked across his hairy chest. Wave after wave of white cum shot out across his black hairy torso, emptying his balls. Buck continued to pump into Phil, draining his balls in the process, orgasm upon orgasm racking his body before it collapsed on top of the other man. Phil shot another load of cum as Buck's body flopped down on top of him.

The men lay breathing heavily as their bodies slowly returned to normal. Sweat and cum trickled over their bodies. Buck reached above the headboard and opened the window. The scent of man and sex and sweat mixed with the spruce and the morning breeze. The babble of the creek and the song of the morning birds welcomed their day.

Phil slipped from the bed and wiped himself off with a hand towel, which he tossed to Buck. He walked over to the window that looked out over the deck where the hot tub sat. He looked at the closed lid and said, "At least there's only one full moon a month."

Buck sat up in bed and enjoyed the view of his furry bubble butt. He swung his legs over the edge and joined him at the window. His hand caressed the fleshy orbs. "I think there'll be a full moon every night." He squeezed Phil's tight muscles.

Phil turned to face him, pressing his penis against Buck's quickly rising flesh. His hands reached around and cupped his butt, pulling Buck even closer. "No, I think there will be two."

And he kissed him deeply.

THE VAMPIRE HEART
Wayne Mansfield

Night had fallen. A chill wind whistled through the branches of the forest trees as giant shadows cast by the full moon behind swiftly-moving clouds reached out like grabbing fingers across the snow-covered fields. At the edge of the forest, where the great oaks met the meadows, a field mouse scurried from a hollow in one tree toward another a short distance away. Suddenly, an almighty screech tore through the night. After a flurry of beating wings, a high-pitched squeak and the sound of flapping wings fading into the darkness, the mouse was nowhere to be seen.

Edvard had witnessed the whole incident from a window in the upper-most level of a small dilapidated chateau he had taken for his own.

"The night remains savage," he mumbled to himself as he turned and padded across the room to the dressing table. "It never changes."

He sat down in front of the dull mirror and looked into the reflection of his pale blue eyes and then at his hair, which hung down to his shoulders like a length of black silk. He admired his high cheekbones and his full, sensual lips. Yes, he was handsome, but what good was beauty when there was no one to appreciate it? How many centuries had he roamed alone, full of love and passion with no one to share it with?

He put his hands to his face and sobbed, tears of blood streaking the pale skin of his face before spilling off his jaw and onto his defined chest. But as he lamented his lonely existence and his tears continued to fall, he heard a strange noise outside, which immediately drew his attention.

He crept to the window, wiped away the condensation and looked out into the bleak night at a man who was alighting from his automobile. With preternatural vision, he studied the details of the stranger's face in the moonlight noticing that his jaw was strong and shaded by bristles. His nose was straight and looked finely sculpted, and his lips were sensual and pale due to the temperature. The man wore a woolen beanie that covered his ears, but he could see from his sideburns and trimmed moustache that he had light brown hair.

Edvard stepped back from the window. His heart was pounding. His eyes stared into the shadows as he tried to decide whether this turn of events was a good thing or a bad thing. His presence in the chateau had been a secret. The building had been vacant for longer than he could remember, and it had fallen into such disrepair that only the ravens bothered visiting him. Should he make himself known to this man? Would he become a friend, a lover, or his executioner? He ran to listen at the door, but the distant footsteps stayed well away from where he cowered.

Week after week for two months, Edvard hid in his private chamber, tortured by the sounds of carpenters, stonemasons and electricians performing their duties on the lower two floors. The screaming of drills and the endless pounding of hammers nearly drove him mad and kept him from sleep. It was sweet relief when they finally finished their renovations and drove away for the very last time.

One night after Antonio, for that was the stranger's name, moved in, Edvard flew into the night earlier than usual. He found a victim within the hour, drained him of the warm blood so vital for his survival then hurried back to the chateau. This night, however, instead of returning to his chamber, he crept along the narrow corridor to the room where Antonio slept. With his ears pricked, he listened at the door and could hear quite clearly that the man was snoring just a little. There would be no danger of being detected should he choose to enter the man's room. Still, his heart beat wildly within his chest.

Throwing caution to the wind, he placed a hand carefully on the doorknob, turned it and slipped into Antonio's bedroom. Despite his nerves, he managed to push the door shut with such dexterity that it hardly made a sound. He turned and surveyed the room, easily spotting the bed with the object of his curiosity lying motionless in it. He hurried across the room and, in the filtered light from the window, gazed down at the stranger who was even more handsome up close.

He pulled a small upholstered stool to the bed and sat down, not once taking his eyes from the sleeping man. For a while, he was content to watch the flare and fall of Antonio's nostrils as he inhaled and exhaled, but soon that wasn't enough. He leaned over, hovering not more than three centimeters from the man's face, and breathed in the scent of his warm, masculine body. He closed his eyes and drew Antonio's manly aroma deep into his lungs.

When Edvard finally opened his eyes again, it was to gaze again upon Antonio's ruggedly handsome face. He smiled, then realized that his hand was moving slowly through the air towards the man's face to touch it, to stroke it. He held his breath. Even as his trembling hand neared the man's cheek, he knew he was about to do something forbidden, but his heart had become the master of his body. Gently, he brushed Antonio's unshaven jaw, thick with bristles as it always seemed to be. He shuddered. How he longed to put his cheek against Antonio's cheek, to feel the roughness his skin against his own soft skin. But he daren't. He would have to save that pleasure for a future time.

Between his legs, he felt his cock stiffen, straining the fabric of his breeches. He lowered a hand to his crotch and rubbed the erect muscle hidden beneath the fabric. As his eyes gazed longingly at Antonio's slightly parted lips, he felt his cock twitch. The pale redness of the man's lips against the dark shadow of his unshaven top lip and jaw and the hint of white teeth behind them was drawing him nearer until he could have almost kissed them. Yet again, he restrained himself.

Instinct told him that morning was approaching. He'd been so lost in his desire for Antonio that the imminent sunrise had nearly caught him by surprise. He arose, not once taking his eyes off his sleeping prince, but as he turned to leave, a sudden and powerful urge gripped him, compelling him to kiss Antonio's gently parted lips. He leaned down, and as his lips touched Antonio's, the man stirred slightly, though did not wake. Satisfied, at least for the moment, Edvard hurried out of the room and returned to his own chamber, locking and bolting the door before climbing into the wooden crate he slept in and lowering the heavy lid into place.

As the days of winter dragged by Edvard found himself becoming more obsessed with Antonio. Of course, he had to hunt every night or he would die. He needed blood just as Antonio needed oxygen. But, the hunt was always swift. No longer did he search for the perfect meal. He was beginning to make mistakes, feasting on villagers instead of travelers; leaving bodies where they could be easily found instead of taking them to the forest where their deaths would be attributed to wolves or bears.

His carelessness had led to the local villagers organizing a vigilante group.

One night, shortly after returning from the hunt, there was a banging on the front door and some commotion on the front steps. Edvard, who had been maintaining his regular nightly vigil at Antonio's bed, leapt onto the canopy of the bed and watched as Antonio hurried from the room.

Taking his chance, Edvard jumped to the floor and ran to the window. He could hear the angry mob demanding to be let inside to search the chateau and felt nauseous when he heard Antonio give them his permission.

"What are you looking for?" he heard Antonio ask.

"Vampire," came the curt reply.

"A vampire? You must be joking!"

"'Tis no joking matter when family and friends are being sucked dry."

Edvard fled to his chamber and lay mortified in his crate. Hopefully the large, dusty tapestry which hid the entrance to his small room would be overlooked. Somehow, Antonio had overlooked it all these weeks. And if by chance they did find the door, he hoped the motley collection of dusty antiques left there by a former occupier would deter them from searching the space too carefully.

He could hear the men coming closer; hear the sound of their boots running up and down the short corridor outside. Someone lifted the tapestry, and Edvard held his breath, but whoever it was didn't take the time to investigate further and soon the men left altogether.

Edvard stayed hidden in his crate for the rest of the night and throughout the following day, only leaving the safety of the chateau the next evening when his gnawing hunger grew too fierce to bear. Moving like the wind through the forest, he hunted further afield this time, taking a drunken man who had fallen asleep in the snow in a village many miles from the chateau.

When he returned home, he crept as always to Antonio's bedroom door, listening as he approached for the familiar sounds of sleep. He turned the knob and made his way silently to the man's bedside. He knelt down next to the double mattress and gazed at Antonio's face, so peaceful and calm. He kissed Antonio's lips at first lightly and then again, letting his lips linger. He felt the blood rushing into his cock, swelling it and making it firm. His desire, made more potent by the erection he now sported, set his mind racing with ideas of how he could appease that desire.

Despite being aware of the danger, Edvard climbed onto the bed next to Antonio, and for the first time lay beside him, daring to put his hand on Antonio's before closing his eyes to savor the warmth coming from it.

"I know that when you look at my pale face, untouched by the marks of time, that you will see a monster," he whispered. "However, I pray that I am wrong and that when you open your eyes and see the man who has kept you company all these long nights that you will recognize love."

He leaned over and brushed his lips against Antonio's cheek, barely touching it but feeling the warmth of it. The smell of blood was strong in his nostrils, though this was the only soul alive that was utterly safe from his fatal bite. In a whirl of black cloth and hair, Edvard turned and disappeared from the room.

The following night as Antonio slept, Edvard hunted and returned as soon as he could. His only thoughts had been of Antonio and the way his warm body had felt beside him. Tonight, he had decided, he could not, would not, hold himself back. For too long he had dreamed and fantasized. Tonight, caution would be thrown to the wind.

When he returned to the chateau, he went immediately to Antonio as he slept and gazed at his face as was his habit. But tonight, his gaze was purposeful. He hoped that within the beauty of Antonio's face that he might find an answer to the problem which haunted him like a thorn in his side; he might see within its striking features a solution which would allow them to be together. For an hour, he stroked the man's hair softly and waited for an answer.

Too soon he felt the approach of morning. It was a great distance away, but time was nevertheless of the essence. He removed his clothing before climbing under the covers next to Antonio to kiss his cheek, leaving his lips to linger upon the warm skin, so they could savor the salty taste of the mortal's living flesh.

Antonio stirred in his sleep, but the movement did not deter Edvard. His kisses grew more and more passionate, and as he felt his own cock stiffen he also felt Antonio's grow hard. He reached down, feeling the warmth radiating from the swollen member before he even touched it. When finally flesh touched flesh, he felt his own cock quiver and the muscles of his arsehole contract. Slowly, he cupped his hand around the thick cock and slid the palm along the entire length of the shaft, feeling every vein and the spongy, engorged cock head at the top.

His tongue slipped inside Antonio's mouth and was surprised when Antonio's mouth closed around it, sucking on it.

"That feels good," said Antonio, his voice deep and low.

Edvard gasped.

"Do you think I am that stupid? That I don't know what you've been up to?" asked Antonio. "I know you come in here to gaze at me in the night. I know what you are and where you hide. I drew the villagers away that night they almost discovered that dark room where you rest during the day."

"But why did you not say anything?" asked Edvard.

"I wanted to see how long it would be."

"How long what would be?" asked Edvard.

"How long it would be before you could no longer control yourself, before you had to give in to your urges."

"Tell me, was it easy for you to wait?" asked Edvard.

Antonio chuckled. "Of course not, though I have jerked off many times thinking about how our first time would be."

Edvard smiled and kissed the man whose lips were firm and fleshy beneath his own.

"Hold me," he said.

He felt Antonio wrap his muscled arms around him and felt the man pull him close. Antonio's hairy chest was scratchy against the smooth porcelain skin of his own chest, but it was a feeling he liked. Together they held each other beneath the sheets, their bodies as close together as they could be – mouth to mouth, nipple to nipple and cock to cock.

"I want to feel your fat prick inside me," whispered Edvard. "I want to feel that thick cock fill me up."

Without a word Antonio flipped him over and pinned him face down onto the mattress. He heard Antonio rummage around in the drawer of his bedside table and the click of a lid being opened before feeling something cold and wet smeared over his tight arsehole. He opened his mouth to ask what Antonio was doing, but was silenced by the sensation of Antonio's cockhead pushing against the puckered skin of his arsehole.

He gasped.

"How do you like it so far?" he heard Antonio ask.

"Better than I could have imagined," replied Edvard. "Push it in. Push it all the way in. I have waited too long to feel you inside me."

He felt Antonio place his arms on either side of his body, and a short, sharp explosion of pain at his arsehole as the thick eight-incher was pushed inside him. He closed his eyes and clenched his teeth for a moment, but in seconds the pain had gone to be replaced by a soothing warm feeling.

Antonio thrust only a handful of times before stopping.

Edvard looked over his shoulder.

"Spread your legs for me," Antonio said.

Edvard spread his legs open and felt Antonio move in between them and start thrusting again.

"Ahhhh that's it," moaned Edvard. "Fuck my tight arse."

"Oh I'm gonna fuck it all right!"

Antonio thrust down, spearing his prick deep inside Edvard. Again and again, he pumped his hips against the twin mounds of Edvard's fleshy butt cheeks, using the bounce of the mattress as leverage to get his cock further into the pale, slender vampire. As the mattress bounced Edvard up, he would thrust down and his big, full balls would slap against Edvard's groin.

Edvard's arsehole was glowing. There was a glow to it he had never experienced before. His tight arse had been stretched taut by Antonio's large prong, and the heavy pounding he was getting created quite a bit of friction. The slap, slap, slapping of Antonio's bull balls was mesmerizing, and for a time, he focused on the sound, imagining what it would feel like to have them emptied into his bowels.

Then he felt Antonio's full weight on him. The man was lying down flat on top of him, his hips still driving his thick meat into his hole. He felt Antonio's lips kiss the back of his neck and the sweat from Antonio's brow dripping onto the back of his head. Simultaneously, Antonio's arms came up from under his armpits, gripping him, so he could drive his organ in with a force that had the whole bed rocking.

"Fuck your arse feels good," Antonio grunted into his ear. "Gonna cream your vampire hole and gonna cream it good."

Edvard smiled then twisted his head around so that his lips met Antonio's. It felt good to feel Antonio's warm breath on his face, in his

83

mouth, as the man's large cock was slamming into his arsehole. With his preternatural senses everything was magnified – the radiating warmth around his arse, the smell of sex, of sweat and arse juice in his nostrils, the warm splash of sweat on his naked flesh and the taste of Antonio's mouth on his.

His tongue probed Antonio's mouth. His lips sucked Antonio's lips. If he could eat the man he would have.

"Oh yeah," he muttered. "Oh yeah. Just like that."

Antonio's breathing had become deeper. It was exploding into his mouth in short, sharp bursts. Behind him he could feel the man's hips slamming relentlessly into him, and he noted that he could no longer hear the sound of slapping balls.

"I'm gonna come," Antonio grunted. "I'm gonna fucking seed your vampire hole."

"Do it," said Edvard. "Do it now."

Antonio grunted a few times and then let out an almighty cry. His hips pounded into Edvard once before he lifted himself up onto his arms and slammed his hips in again.

"Oh yeah," he cried out.

Edvard closed his eyes as jet after jet of thick, creamy man juice erupted into his guts. Each splash hit the sensitive tissue lining his bowels, feeling like a waterfall of warmth inside him. He wanted it to never end. It felt so good to have Antonio's jizm inside him at last.

Antonio finally collapsed on top of him, panting.

"How was that? Three day's worth up there."

Edvard opened his eyes and smiled.

"Unbelievable," he replied. "Better than I could have imagined."

Antonio rolled off and Edvard turned over onto his back, a small dribble of cum trickling down his thigh as he did so.

"Thank you," said Edvard. "Thank you for being my lover. If we never make love again then I will have this night for eternity."

Antonio slapped him playfully on the thigh and let his hand rest there.

"You going somewhere?" he asked.

"No, but I meant that if you …"

Antonio laughed. "I knew I had a houseguest. I knew it long after I moved in to tell the truth. You're welcome to stay for as long as you need to."

Edvard beamed. "Thank you."

"But what about you? You haven't come yet."

"I don't mind," he said. "It was enough ..."

But before he could finish his sentence Antonio had grabbed his still hard cock and was slipping his lips over the pink, swollen head. He swallowed the entire length down his throat and then came back up again, lingering at the top to tickle Edvard's piss-slit with the tip of his tongue.

Edvard shuddered.

"You've done that before," he said as he brought his fingers up to his nipples and started twisting them.

Antonio didn't reply. He kept his mouth on Edvard's cock, taking it down the back of his throat as far as it would go before coming up again for air. And while one hand gripped the base of Edvard's cock his other hand disappeared between Edvard's legs. When his fingers found Edvard's arsehole he poked one, then two fingers in, pushing them right inside until the tips were pressing against Edvard's prostate gland.

Edvard twisted the nubs of his nipples between his fingers and writhed as Antonio's fingers slid in and out of his arse, lubricated by the ample quantity of cum the man had just pumped up there. But it was the action of Antonio's mouth on his cock that had his body quivering. Antonio's mouth was firm but gentle around his shaft, and it was well-lubed with spit so that his tongue and lips were like velvet against the sensitive skin of his cock.

Several times, Edvard could have blown his load, but he wanted the sensations he was experiencing to continue. Yet, he knew that was not possible. He also knew that he could not hold back for much longer. The more Antonio's fingers massaged his prostate and the harder he sucked, the closer he came to emptying his balls into the man's eager mouth. And when Antonio's head began to bob up and down faster and faster Edvard knew it was to time to let go.

"Get ready," he groaned.

The words encouraged Antonio to keep going as he was. His fingers pistoned in and out of Edvard's arsehole, and his mouth sucked even harder on the seven-inch uncut cock that was swelling in his mouth.

With a long, loud wail, Edvard exploded, sending a great gush of creamy vampire cum into Antonio's mouth. His cries continued as he fed Antonio the entire contents of his balls. Again, he shuddered, his whole body awash with such pleasure that he couldn't remember when last he had been made to feel that way. And still Antonio continued to suck until the pleasure became a little too much like torture.

Edvard pushed the man off his cock and smiled as he winked at him.

Antonio, a considerate lover, placed his lips over Edvard's and as he returned Edvard's cum to him, he withdrew his fingers from Edvard's arse. Soon their lips were slick with the thick jelly of Edvard's sperm, though Edvard still got to swallow most of it.

"That was delicious," he said. "Thank you for sharing."

Antonio smiled at him, his tongue running over his own lips to lick the last of Edvard's cum from them.

"My pleasure. I haven't tasted cum so sweet for a very long time."

Edvard smiled. "Feel free to sample it any time you want to."

Antonio pecked him on the lips and then fell back onto the mattress.

"Tell me," he said, "why did you wait so long to kiss me? Not tonight but all those other nights."

Edvard blushed.

"I guess it was fear."

"Fear?" said Antonio. "A vampire who is afraid?"

Edvard felt a slight fire in his cheeks.

"And what do you know of vampires?" he asked defensively.

"Only what I have read," he replied.

"Well I can tell you that most of what is written is fiction, the results of very imaginative writers. The reality is far less glamorous. You saw how angry those villagers were. They would have killed me without a second thought if they had found me cowering like a mangy dog in that tiny room. Is that not enough to make anyone frightened?"

Antonio rolled onto his side and propped his head up with his hand.

"You're right," he said. "I had no idea. Of course that is frightening. I'm sorry."

Edvard ran a hand over Antonio's hairy pectoral muscles.

"Think nothing of it."

He let his hand fall between their naked bodies and silence descended over them for a few minutes.

"So tell me," said Antonio, "how did you come to be a vampire? When did it happen? I hope you don't think I'm being nosy."

"No," said Edvard. "You have every right to ask, but I will tell you later. I don't want to spoil tonight by dredging all that up. I understand how it might be intriguing for you, but for me it is a memory that I would rather faded away."

From outside the window, Edvard heard the first chirrup of the dawn chorus.

"By the devil!" he exclaimed leaping out of bed. "The new day is nearly here."

He pulled his clothing on and flew through the air to the door.

"Very impressive," Antonio called out after him. "Same time tomorrow night?!"

"Of course. I'll count the hours."

THE LOOPHOLE
Michael Bracken

I'd seen a few demons in my time – usually after bouts of heavy drinking – but I had never before had one appear in my office in the middle of the day.

This one materialized out of thin air, completely bypassing both the law firm's receptionist and my hardnosed secretary, and it took a moment for the smoke to dissipate before I could see him clearly. He wore a sharply tailored black suit over a white shirt and crimson tie, and he stood in polished black wingtips made of Italian leather. Coal-black hair combed straight back from his forehead hung to his shoulders, and he was clean-shaven, with a cleft chin and a square jaw. To call him handsome would be an understatement, but he wasn't without imperfection. His smooth, unblemished skin trended red rather than flesh tone and the pupils of his yellow-tinted eyes were more feline than human. His cologne was heavy on the brimstone, and it stung my eyes and caught in the back of my throat. I coughed before I spoke. "Do you have an appointment?"

He laughed – a deep, throaty laugh of genuine mirth – before he spoke. "You people slay me. You make us an offer and are then surprised when we arrive to collect."

I stared at him across the top of my desk. "What offer?"

"Last night you said you would give anything for one night of memorable sex," he explained.

I'd been drinking with Jeremy. I might have said anything, and an oral contract such as the demon described would not be unimaginable given the dismal state of my sex life. "And you've come to provide it?"

"It would be my pleasure," he said. "More importantly, it would be yours."

"Will I need to light some candles, draw a pentagram, sacrifice a goat, anything like that?"

"The candles would be nice," the demon said. "Makes for a romantic atmosphere."

"So what's the deal?"

He removed a tri-folded piece of parchment from the inside breast pocket of his jacket and smoothed it on the desk in front of me. The language was remarkably straightforward for a deal with one of the devil's minions: One night of memorable sex in exchange for my soul.

I pricked my finger in the expectation that the demon would later finger my prick and squeezed out a drop of blood. I signed my name to the contract. As the demon retrieved the parchment, a duplicate appeared before me. He folded the original and returned it to his jacket pocket. I slid the duplicate into a folder to be filed later.

"Nine o'clock," he said. "Be ready."

Then he disappeared.

I spent the rest of the morning and much of the afternoon completing my due diligence on the Everson eviction case, and I felt certain that no harm would come to my client if I presented an ultimatum to opposing council during our meeting that afternoon.

We met in my firm's boardroom. On my side of the table with me sat two junior partners, three paralegals, and my secretary. On the other side of the table sat a young man fresh out of law school, employed by one of the storefront legal firms that do pro bono work for those unable to pay a successful attorney's hourly rate. His clients – an elderly couple who were the last remaining tenants of a building my client planned to demolish – were refusing to move, even after receiving a legal notice of eviction and my client's cessation of electric and water service to the building.

After we exchanged pleasantries, I presented the ultimatum. "Demolition begins Monday."

"My clients won't move."

"Doesn't matter."

The young attorney had exhausted every legal channel earlier in the week, and the only card he had left to play was pity. "They've lived in that apartment for forty-three years."

"And?"

"They have no place to go."

"Not my concern."

"They'll be homeless."

"Many people are."

"What about their cats?"

"They'll be homeless, too."

The young attorney narrowed his eyes and glared across the table at me. "Have you no soul?"

I closed the folder before me and said with a smile, "Our work here is done."

Jeremy and I had once been lovers, but discovered we were better friends than sex partners. One of the reasons Jeremy and I are no longer lovers is because he let himself go, adding weight and losing hair in equal proportions, while I was in great shape despite creeping middle age. Regular workouts at the gym, a little nip-and-tuck for the eyes, regular application of Just for Men, allow me to pass for several years younger than I am.

But we still had much to talk about. He'd made his money arranging adjustable-rate mortgages for people who could barely afford their house payments before their mortgages reset, and he'd made even more money selling short the stock he held in many of the banks that held those loans, and I liked his attitude of win at all costs.

We met for dinner and drinks at our favorite restaurant. Over filet mignons and shots of Jack I told him, "I made a deal with one of the devil's minions this morning."

"A minion? You didn't even get the senior partner?" Jeremy asked. "You've chewed up and spit out so many opposing councils that even the devil should know not to send underlings to your office."

"My demon certainly looked successful," I explained, "but anybody can dress the part. He made a rookie mistake, so I'm guessing he's fresh off the hell-bound train."

I gave Jeremy the complete story, from the moment the demon appeared in my office to the moment he placed the contract on my desk.

"And you signed it?"

"Without hesitation," I said with a smile. "What do I have to lose?"

By nine o'clock that evening, I had showered, shaved, manscaped, and prepared myself for the evening ahead by slipping into blue boxers. I was sitting up in bed, enjoying the feel of freshly laundered red silk sheets against my skin, had a trio of candles burning on my dresser, romantic music on the CD player, a fresh tube of lube on the nightstand, and a copy of my favorite pictorial magazine spread across my lap. I was planning to use the lube one way or the other.

At seven minutes past nine, the demon arrived in my bedroom with the same flourish of smoke as before, and he wore the same clothes he'd worn earlier that day. Luckily, he'd replaced the brimstone cologne and, unless I was mistaken, was wearing Heaven – the demon's idea of a joke, perhaps.

I closed the magazine and placed it on the nightstand. "About time."

"I apologize," he said. "I was finalizing an agreement with a Republican senator."

Except for the wet bar, my bedroom is simply furnished – queen-size bed, pair of nightstands, single dresser, and a chair in the corner. The demon sat in the chair and removed his custom-made Italian wingtips, revealing not feet but polished cloven hooves. Then he stood and removed his jacket, tie, and shirt, placing them carefully over the back of the chair. His broad, hairless chest tapered down to six-pack abs and a trim waist, and I felt my cock twitch in anticipation.

I asked, "Care for a drink before we begin?"

"A Bloody Mary," the demon said as I flipped back the sheet and slipped out of bed. "Hold the tomato juice, hold the consommé, hold the vodka, hold the garnishes."

That left Tabasco sauce, horseradish, and cayenne pepper. I mixed the demon's drink and prepared Jack and Coke for myself. While I sipped from my tumbler, he knocked his truncated cocktail back in one swallow.

While I finished my drink, the demon removed his slacks and I realized three things: he was completely hairless from the neck down, he had a prehensile tail at least three feet long, and, as if to compensate, he had a flaccid penis barely an inch long. I almost laughed at the sight of it. I could not anticipate any way that little nub was going to provide me with a night of memorable sex.

But I was wrong. His little nub grew on me, clear evidence that the demon was a grower, not a shower. The demon stepped forward, hooked a hand around the back of my neck, and held my head as he covered my lips with his. He thrust his tongue into my mouth, and it felt thick and hot and forked.

He shoved his free hand between us and slid it under the waistband of my boxers. He wrapped his hand around my rapidly inflating cock and tugged at it until it reached its full potential. My erect cock isn't the largest I've ever grabbed, but it's much more than a handful, and the demon had his work cut out for him as he stroked up and down the length of my stiff shaft.

As he jerked me off, he kissed his way down my neck, down my chest, and, as he dropped to his knees, down my abdomen, leaving behind a hot trail of saliva. He peeled my boxers down my thighs, revealing my turgid cock, and let them drop to my ankles. He took the swollen head of my cock in his mouth and painted the purple head with the tips of his tongue. As he cupped my heavy ballsack in one hand, he wrapped his forked tongue around my cock shaft and ran it up and down the length. He took my entire length into his oral cavity and his breath felt hot against my neatly trimmed crotch before he drew his face back.

As I began face-fucking the demon, I looked down and realized his tail was snaking back and forth between his hooves. I didn't have time to think much about that as his bifurcated tongue did things to my cock that I couldn't have imagined, and I began pumping my hips back and forth.

He still held my scrotum in one hand, and he squeezed my balls together, kneading them and roughly tugging on my sack. I tried to restrain myself, but I couldn't. I grabbed the demon's head and felt the nubs of his horns hidden beneath his hair as I thrust into his mouth one last time. I emptied my balls against the back of his throat, and he swallowed every drop.

He didn't give me a chance to catch my breath. He released his oral grip on my cock while it was still spasming, and he stood. He grabbed my shoulders and spun me around, bent me forward, and pressed the thick head of his flaming red cock against my sphincter. I hadn't seen him reach for the lube, but he must have because his cock was slick, and he rammed it into me like a hot poker through butter.

His cock was longer and thicker than any I'd ever had before, and it seemed to grow within me. When he drew back and pressed forward it felt as if it was at least twelve inches long. He grabbed my hips, his fingers turning to talons that punctured my skin. I couldn't pull away from him even if I had wanted to for fear that he would shred my skin.

Then the demon's prehensile tail snaked down between his thighs and up between mine, coiling around my flaccid cock and quickly bringing it back to life. He fucked my ass like a demon possessed, slamming into me hard and fast and without end. His tail jerked me off as it stroked my cock with a steady rhythm.

I came first, firing cum across my carpet, but he just kept fucking me harder and faster, drilling into me until my knees were so weak they couldn't support my weight. The only thing that kept me upright was the demon's powerful grip on my hips and his enormous cock in my ass.

I wanted to cry out the demon's name, but he had never given it to me, and I had to content myself with expletives and repeated commands to fuck me harder and faster.

When the demon finally came, he came hot and hard, slamming his massive cock into me one last time before erupting within me and spewing cum like a volcano spurting molten lava. He howled, and the sound curdled my blood and made the hair on the back of my neck stand at attention.

When he finished howling, the demon asked, "Do you smoke after sex?"

Three years earlier I'd given up cigars at the advice of my physician. "No."

"I do," he said. "Do you mind?"

"Go ahead. Light up."

When the demon released his grip on my hips and pulled away, I fell onto my bed, rolled onto my back, and looked up. Smoke rose from his entire body as if he'd been aflame and had just had the flame extinguished.

I felt hot enough to start smoking myself and wanted nothing more than a few minutes rest, but the demon wasn't finished with me.

By the time dawn peeked through the bedroom curtains, we had fucked so many times and so many different ways that I had lost count.

After the last time, after an orgasm that had me howling, the demon calmly dressed, adjusted the knot of his tie, and looked down at my spent body sprawled across the tattered red silk sheets.

"Was it memorable?"

I knew I would never forget it. Out of breath, I said, "Yes."

"Then I kept my part of the bargain?"

"Yes."

"Someday I will return to collect my part," the demon said.

Then he disappeared, leaving behind only memories and a thin haze of smoke.

I met Jeremy for a late breakfast and told him about my night with the demon. I even showed him the ten puncture marks on my hips where the demon's talons had gripped me. I knew no man would ever please me the way the demon had, but I accepted that because I knew I had gotten the best of our deal.

The devil should never have sent an inexperienced demon to negotiate with an experienced lawyer because the demon had failed to perform his due diligence. If he had, he would have known that the best attorneys – and I am the best – are born without souls.

I smiled.

Poor demon.

His senior partner was certain to be raking him over the coals.

THE RENFIELD AFFAIR
Gregory L. Norris

In a place with a name like Insomnity, you're bound to cross paths with all types of outcasts. Renegade investment bankers, most of them on the lam from wealthy clients they've fucked over financially and one bad dip of the stock market away from blowing their number-crunching brains out. Wannabe musicians with nifty little Van Dykes who've run out of sofas to crash on, who stare at their espressos with glazed, forlorn expressions. Even the occasional creature of the night.

Me, I'd stopped sleeping right around the end of August. It was the damn novel. My old schedule – days commencing at sunrise, writing until sunset while savoring my one-pot-a-day habit of Kona blend – just wasn't working anymore. In three weeks, I hadn't slept so much as dropped from exhaustion since discovering the all-night coffee bar at the farthest end of my neighborhood block, but at least I was closing in on completing a draft of the literary millstone around my neck.

Him, his name was Flebotte. I gleaned that sliver of intel soon after camping my ass on one of the luxuriously comfortable upholstered chairs at a table in a dark corner, safe from the limelight. Flebotte's manservant, his Renfield, never called him by his first name. It was always 'Mister' or, on numerous occasions, 'Master.' Most nights, Flebotte sat in a jaunty pose on the big camelback sofa, beneath a garish painting of lilies in a vase that exuded a funereal quality. So fitting for him.

I discovered Flebotte lived at Insomnity. Not over it, in one of the converted brick mill's loft-style apartments, but underneath, in the basement. He would disappear down there with a different Ms. Right Now every night, or the occasional Mister. All of his admirers would return before sunrise clutching at their necks, with the dopiest lust-filled grins on their faces. But none of them, apparently, told Flebotte that the whole bleached blond spikes look stopped being trendy while Slick Willie was still in charge of running a mostly-unbroken world.

While writing at a fevered clip or laboring through a cruel transitional sentence, I'd catch Flebotte staring at me, as though trying

97

to make sense of what he was seeing. I didn't really fit the norm of Insomnity's abnorm; even I felt like something of a freak sitting among the attractive fruitcakes having conversations with the ice cubes in their glasses and Flebotte, who I guessed wasn't entirely human late one night while in the middle of Chapter Twelve. Unlike so many of the coffee bar's clientele, I didn't work on a laptop. I wrote old school, with an antique fountain pen, an inkwell, and pads of lined white paper. This wasn't entirely by choice – going back to the basics was the only method that got me out of the block that drove me to Insomnity to begin with.

Maybe it was the charm of such a concept, writing by fountain pen in an era hopelessly addicted to keyboards and text messaging, that earned me my private audience with him. Part of it, I'm sure, was that he sensed I was immune to his magnetic charm. The whole wanting that which we can never have sort of thing.

Oh, I'd felt the pull of his mind from across the room several times, usually at the worst possible moment. Case in point, Daphne in peril at the hands of the sinister warlock, and Byron about to sweep into the tower room just in time to rescue her, body and soul. You always conclude a novel chapter on a cliffhanger, whether it be an emotional one or action-based. Get the reader to turn the page. Flebotte seemed consumed with my presence right at the most-intense of those page-turners. Perhaps it was the rush of energy he detected, the gallop of my heartbeat. All that adrenaline pulsing through my blood vessels as I lived the words and tears tugged at my eyes. I am and always have been a silly romantic at heart.

Flebotte, however skilled at head games, would never put one of those hypnotized grins on my face. The mere sight of him turned my stomach. He wore ascots in a variety of pale colors, cinched at the side, and a kind of suit and slacks that would have looked more appropriate on Willy Wonka or a past incarnation of Doctor Who. And, please, spats. He carried a walking stick capped by a goose's head with glittering blood-red rubies for eyes. Thumb rings. Christ, I hate thumb rings. And that hair.

In addition to being a romantic, I've also always been attracted to men, but men of a certain quality. Men who don't primp excessively, who can roll over, pull on the same clothes they left at the side of the bed the night before, and still look like a million bucks with zero effort.

Men like Flebotte's Renfield.

Now that guy, let me tell you … he was the kind of man who inspired romance writers to pen novels about handsome, tragic heroes, because he was one himself. Tall, somewhere past the six-foot mark, I pegged him as being in his mid to late thirties, though indentured servitude to Flebotte had put a few hundred extra years on him, in evidence around his twin sapphire eyes and the lines at the edge of his perpetual scowl. He wore his dark hair short and neat, in the cut of an athlete. Blue jeans and T-shirts, old hiking boots on his giant feet. His upper arms sported perfect muscles, not overly large, strong without being showy. There used to be a tattoo on the right one. The tattoo would have once poked out from just below the cuff of his shirt before it got burned off his flesh. A cross, judging by the shape of the jagged gouges.

Writers are observers yes, but you didn't need to be one to notice the Renfield straight away, and I had. A man so handsome, with such presence, demands attention. But over the course of my three weeks of nights at Insomnity, I observed other, finer details that a less-intuitive person might have missed, like the scar. And the look of contempt I sometimes caught in the Renfield's magnificent sapphire gaze when Flebotte escorted the latest of his conquests down to the basement, and his protector assumed guard duty in front of the door.

And, a few wondrous times, I caught that poor, painfully handsome soul looking in my direction, and my heart ached for him as much as the rest of my sex organs.

He approached me, silent, brooding, the wounded look on his face testifying to tragedies I could only imagine. What had Flebotte done to him in order to force such complete devotion? It didn't matter now because my love for his manservant was stronger.

I reached for his belt and unbuckled it. Even more boldly, I passed my hand over the tent in the front of his blue jeans and cupped the impressive swell of his cock. The Renfield's erection pushed back. I lifted his T-shirt, baring the ring of dark hair around his belly button. Coarse fur ran in a line along the top of his underwear's waistband – boxer-briefs, black, I discovered after hauling down his zipper.

His legs were as breathtaking to behold as I'd imagined, long and hairy, muscled like his arms, the legs of a hockey player or baseball god. White socks, one bunched atop a shaggy ankle. Salivating, I licked my lips in anticipation of freeing him from those socks and sucking his toes, one at a time, as if they were ten smaller versions of his cock.

There would be twenty total, because I planned to do the same to his fingers. Those long, strong fingers that once swung a baseball bat, that scratched his balls and jerked his dick and were presently raking my hair, guiding my face closer to his maleness.

I pressed my nostrils against the dark cotton, that last barrier between my mouth and his cock, and inhaled. A mix of masculine smells, soap and sweaty balls, mostly, hypnotized me further.

I tugged at his underwear. He raised his T-shirt the rest of the way over his head, exposing an impressive chest and the T-pattern of hair superimposed over his muscles, the lush fur under his arms, and that ugly, jagged cruciform scar ripped out of the meat of his bicep. He stepped out of his boxer-briefs. His cock snapped up at full mast, thickest in the middle. The lone eye of its fireman's helmet wept cloudy tears. The Renfield's balls hung loose and full in a hairy sack that dangled halfway to his knees. I placed a hand on his leg to steady myself and felt him tremble.

"The blood is the life," he growled.

"No," I said, squeezing down on his thickness. "The cum is, dude. Your cum."

I wrapped my lips around the head of his cock and sucked as much of him down as I could take without gagging. Alternately, I tickled his balls, an action that sent him to the tops of his sexy feet. The Renfield's grip on the back of my head tightened, and he started to thrust into my mouth. The movement quickly turned furious, near violent. Struggling to match his rhythm and loving the bounce of his balls against my chin, I wondered how long it had been since he'd received a blowjob. Hell, how long since he last came, or was allowed to. Judging by the grunts and the weight of his nuts gonging against my throat, it had been some time. Like the scar, I knew this too was Flebotte's doing.

The realization launched my enthusiasm to pleasure him to the next level. I reached around and gently raked my fingers down his firm, athlete's ass. I then gave his balls a yank. He fucked harder, driven into a frenzy by the pressure, the passion.

His grunts died behind clenched teeth, though I sensed what he really wanted to do was let forth with a blue streak of expletives, howling them to the limit of his lungs. But Flebotte had stolen his voice, imprisoning it along with the rest of him. At one point, as I pondered the truth and pulled on his nuts, a gasp escaped his lips. His cock, steadily painting my taste buds in salty-sour ball juice, erupted, soaking my tonsils in what felt like a gallon of whitewash. I swallowed.

Before he stopped unloading, he pulled his squirting cock out of my mouth, dumping more of his sperm across my cheeks and the bridge of my nose. Then he dragged me up to my feet and crushed his lips over mine. The part of me loving his taste caught fire in the knowledge he loved it, too, and wasn't ashamed to recycle his own junk.

He set me on my back, on the bed, after tearing off the little clothing I still had on. His tick-tocking cock remained fully swollen. Cum dripped down those amazing balls, which never tightened and were as loose now as they had been at the start of our love-making. There would be very little making love in what was to follow, I thought, overjoyed. Once that cock entered my ass, he'd pound one hole as ferociously as he had the other. And it would be the best sex of my life. And –

"I love you," he growled, towering over me.

I glanced up into his twin sapphire eyes and knew that I had fallen madly in love with him as well. Then I jolted awake, having humped my first wet dream into a mattress in over twenty years. Late afternoon sunlight, orange and dusty like a layer of smoke, hung across the bedroom.

"I love you," I whispered.

But the words were inelegant, galumphing on my lips, submerged in the phantom taste of his dream-spunk. I pinched my wet eyes, adjusted my package, confused about some things while clearer than ever on others.

One thing was for certain: I planned to free the Renfield from Flebotte, or die trying.

# # # # #

A coy smile was all that it took to set the plan in motion. That, and antacid to settle my stomach – as previously stated, Flebotte was the kind of man who pushed my buttons the wrong way. Not that he really was a man in the fully-human sense.

I felt his eyes wandering over me while my fountain pen scratched its way through Chapter Seventeen. I was so close to the end of my longhand draft of the romance novel that had transformed me into an insomniac that it was becoming easy to smile again, to exude the pheromones of happiness and creativity. It was also easy to see the clear path to the end, both with the book and with Flebotte's Renfield, that handsomest of men, because I did love him, so much as one stranger could be in love with another.

Three nights later, Flebotte sent his manservant over.

"Master Flebotte wants you to join him for a drink."

All the snarky comebacks I'd rehearsed instantly drained out of my gray matter at the sound of his voice. Staring into the Renfield's wounded blue gaze, I relived numerous masturbatory fantasies at breakneck speed: me sucking on his sweaty toes; licking the alphabet into his hairy asshole – both upper and lower cases; taking his cock inside me, kissing him passionately while he ground and humped. And the two of us lying together in the shadows of the night, sleeping like normal people, all curses of insomnia and indentured servitude ended.

"Okay," I said flatly, simply.

The handsome slave picked up my valise and carried it over to the camelback sofa beneath the lilies, a gentlemanly gesture I hoped owed more to him than his master.

"We meet at last," Flebotte said in that uppity voice, flashing a cocky smirk that showed a section of sharp teeth. His slender hands rocked on his goose-head cane.

"We haven't yet," I said, a level of sarcasm creeping back into my voice. I told him my name.

"Charmed," Flebotte said. "Mine is, as I'm sure you might have already heard while scribbling away in your little corner, Duke Flebotte."

"Duke?" I snickered. "Not 'Count'?"

"Ha ha," he said dryly. "So tell me, my chubby little scribe ..."

Boy, that Flebotte had a way with words, not to mention fantastic people skills.

"... what is it you've been working on so furiously, night after lonely night?"

I forced a smile. Seeing the tall man at my periphery helped keep it fixed on my lips. "A novel about love and the eternal passion between two tragic hearts who overcome great odds to be together."

"Two men?"

"A man and a woman in this case. It's for my New York publisher."

"Color me impressed. Though love is love, whether between a man and a woman, two women ...or a man and another man." Like he would know. I could tell that the only person Duke Flebotte ever truly loved was himself. "Or multiple, polyamorous combinations, which can also be quite fun."

I accepted a frosty glass from the Renfield's warm hand, tried not to glance at the prominent bulge at the front of his blue jeans looming at eye level, or those magnificent sapphire eyes. "Sorry, I'm not really the orgy type. I prefer my romance to be one-on-one, if you know what I mean." I winked, sipped.

Flebotte's mouth puckered into a taut, unattractive reverse-asshole. "I think I do. There's something about you, a kind of energy I haven't seen much of in recent years. Certainly not among these poseurs." He tipped his sharp chin toward the caffeinated crowd of musician wannabes and bean counters. "The passion that infuses your blood, I can almost taste it."

"Kinky. It must be my love of the romance genre."

"I want to taste it."

"Perhaps you shall."

"That you work with a fountain pen and a tablet of paper ... it's positively Victorian. I love it. Reminds me of the good old days. Not that all of them were very good, mind you, but I look back on them nostalgically with a degree of fondness."

"It's just one of my quirks," I said, reaching into my valise for the pen, holding it seductively the way I might his manservant's dick – and had, in so many passionate dreams.

Flebotte's expression tightened. "We should discuss this love of romance you have in private."

I followed his beady black eyes toward the basement door. "Are you suggesting ...?"

"It will transcend your wildest dreams of love and passion." He flashed a toothy smile.

"So they all say," I countered, unimpressed.

The grin on Flebotte's face sagged. "I could have you dragged down there, you know."

"That's not very romantic," I said. "Let me guess, you and your barista, the tough guy over there." I tipped a nod at the Renfield.

"My boy here, this colossal penis with feet ..." He snapped his fingers and the tall man looming at the edge of my line of sight plodded closer. The movements, however, seemed forced, as if Flebotte's slave wanted to resist but was powerless against his master's will. "He can be quite convincing, you know."

Yes, he can be, I thought. I held up my hand. "There will be no need to strong arm me, Count."

"Duke!"

"I go quite willingly to your little subterranean love nest because it's exactly what I want. The chance to experience unrivaled passion. To create a connection that sparks an effulgence like the one that gave birth to the cosmos."

"Huh?"

"I only have one stipulation." He shot me a look. "Okay, a request, my dear Duke."

"Perhaps," he hissed through his incisors.

"Please, I'm at a bit of a block in my novel. Let me record our synthesis with this antique fountain pen of mine that so intrigues you. Let me write while we make love so that the experience is recorded."

Flebotte's eyes narrowed. "I'm not so sure about that."

"While also paying tribute to you for all my readers to enjoy, of course. Unlike those poseurs you mentioned, I'm legit. Once this goes into print, our lovemaking, too, will attain a level of immortality. Well, except for those copies that get remaindered or returned, that is."

"Immortalized again, in print," Flebotte said, a dreamy smile breaking across his face. "I like that. You have my permission. But first …"

It was a scene I had quietly witnessed on many occasions, only now I was the one being frisked for religious artifacts, sharp wooden coffee stirrers, flasks of holy water, and concealed stakes. I did my best to ignore the heat of the Renfield's powerful hands as they traveled over my chest, down my spine and buttocks, and when he patted down my crotch and legs. The minty scent of his breath and a hint of his sweat tempted me to roll my eyes in ecstasy, to gasp aloud in surprise. Somehow, I resisted.

"He's clean," the Renfield growled, releasing me.

"Excellent," said Flebotte. He extended a hand and its hideous thumb ring toward the door. "After you, my sweet."

"Thank you," I said. Beneath my breath, I added, "My sour …"

I passed through the door and down a staircase whose walls were upholstered in black velvet. A galaxy of glow-in-the-dark stars glittered against this canvas. The image would have charmed me, had those stars been set in the heavens by any hand other than Duke Flebotte's.

The stairs descended to an oblong room outfitted in gaudy décor: lava lamps on noodle-shaped acrylic tables, thick red and black velvet curtains on every wall, an old Victrola in one corner, a Wurlitzer bubbling away in another. A round bed decked in leopard print dominated the center of the space. The air smelled exotic though slightly bitter; some expensive, musky cologne disguising an underlying fetor of rot and cemetery earth.

"Where's the coffin?" I asked, kicking off my shoes.

"This is the coffin. I'm claustrophobic, love."

Shuffling toward the bed, I felt the squish of dirt beneath the carpet through my socks. "Gotcha."

Flebotte set down his cane and moved toward the Wurlitzer. "Any preferences?"

"You wouldn't happen to have this great little number by the Critters, Mister Dieingly Sad?"

Flebotte's face grew serious in a theatrical way. "I love you," he said, stabbing at buttons on the console. As the elegant, otherworldly ballad began to play, he added, "I must say that you and I were meant to be together."

I unbuttoned my light cotton top and exposed a nipple. "Do tell."

Flebotte licked his lips and snarled, baring his fangs. "Oh, my tasty, rotund little novelist, I am going to show you a kind of passion all mortals dream of, but few ever experience firsthand. A love that will consume you. A fire that will ..."

"Show it to me," I interjected.

"Show you what?"

"Your dick, Duke. Whip it out. I want to see it."

Flebotte smirked. "You are as naughty as you are rare." He hastily kicked off his silly spats and his sillier attire, exposing slender, hairless limbs stretched in sallow skin.

"Please leave the socks on," I said. Mercifully, he complied.

Not so, the same deal with Flebotte's underwear, a breechclout of striped purple silk that matched his stockings. The erection jutting up from a trimmed Hitler's mustache of blond pubes was wiry and slender. The testicles hanging below looked like two caramel candies.

Flebotte mistook my aghast expression for ardor. "You like?"

I blinked myself out of the trance and beckoned him over with an exposed length of throat. "Get over here, you."

He and his veiny erection were on top of me in a flash. Flebotte furiously humped my still-clothed leg while slathering my neck with repellant kisses. "I'm so horny for you," he said.

So close up, his stink was even more pronounced; cologne slapped on by the bucketful to disguise skin that smelled brinier than deli pickles. "So I see."

I patted his back. Fangs brushed my jugular.

"Wait," I protested. "Let me get out my notepad and pen."

"Yes, yes, hurry up, dammit! I want you so desperately, my sweet, sugary treat filled with such energy and cholesterol and literary-fueled passion! Hurry!"

I set the paper against his bony chest and began to scribble, reciting the words as I wrote them.

"He was a man impossible to miss, a man with presence …"

"Ooh, nice!" Saliva dripped down his chin.

"A man living under the shadow of a terrible curse, forced to serve the darkness and the night …"

"Oh, baby!"

"The one who loved him promised to free him, and then they could be together …" I ceased scrawling and turned my pen around, nib-side-down. "Oh, Duke?"

His eyes, rabid with lust, met mine. "Yes?"

"This fountain pen of mine …"

"Yes, my sweet?"

"It's made of rosewood."

I drove the pointy handle into the waxy flesh beside his sternum, and in as far as it would go. Through Flebotte's high-pitched screams, I heard a loud, liquid pop, then a hiss of escaping air reminiscent of a deflating balloon. Hatred replaced the glaze of sexual hunger in his eyes. He clutched at my throat, but that deflating balloon carried his carcass off me and sent it flying around the room, crashing into the nearest wall before careening off the rest.

The pulpy mass continued to ricochet, knocking over lava lamps and leaving a bloody spider's web on the Wurlitzer, killing the music with a jarring screech. On its final spin, Flebotte's corpse nearly decapitated me. Then it pounded a lone, hollow knock against the basement door and skidded down to the floor with my fountain pen still lodged in it.

I was only given a second or two to study the gory result of my crime because someone answered that knock. The door burst open, dragging a smear of blood across the carpet, and the Renfield stormed in.

I stood and unconsciously pulled the two halves of my shirt together. He quickly swept the room with his sapphire gaze, absorbing the remains on the floor and the telltale evidence of my fountain pen at the center of the mess. Chest heaving, nostrils flaring, he focused upon me, his angry expression both inexplicably attractive and terrifying to behold.

"What did you do?" he growled.

For an instant, all I could think about was his voice, so deep and masculine, and how it would sound in bed, freed from Flebotte's curse to bellow in happiness without restraint. But then he stormed across the room, grabbed me by the collar, and backed me against a section of black velvet wall. I had slain his master. Was I so naïve to think there wouldn't be retribution, spilled in blood? My blood.

"What I did was set you free, my love," I said.

The Renfield's wounded eyes darted nervously around before again greeting mine. There, they remained, and hope replaced my fear.

"You ... you did this for me?" he asked, his tone less gruff. He choked down a heavy swallow that knotted his hairy Adam's apple.

I nodded. One of his giant hands moved from my collar to my neck. The other wandered over my chest, settling atop a nipple. The barest of smiles broke on his mouth. And then he kissed me.

RUNNING WITH THE PACK
Mark James

People think of New York, and they picture a big city, lights everywhere, underground trains kicking up a racket, and buildings so high their elevators could take you to Heaven. That's the skin of the city; the part I'm gonna tell you about, that's different.

It's what you'd see if New York was a man, and you ran your hands down the smooth muscle on his chest, then hooked your finger into his waistband and pulled it down, and got on your knees, and looked up at him.

And now you're getting a little scared, 'cause he's bigger than you thought, and when he picked you up on the street, thirty stories down, he told you he liked to use a boy's mouth real hard.

My name's Zak, and I'm gonna tell you about New York from the bottom up.

Dezmond found me on the street I used to work. He walked by real slow, like he didn't see me. Now I know better. He saw every inch of me.

I needed one more trick for the night. It was late, rent was hounding my ass; calendar countdown said three days to pay up or get gone.

I got in his way, like I'd bumped into him, and asked for a light. He smiled, and even back then, that first time, I thought he had a few too many teeth. It was going on three in the morning, Weirdo Hour. When I saw all those teeth, I backed off, told him I'd buy a lighter.

He grabbed my wrist, not tight, but tight enough so I knew I wasn't going no place 'til he let go.

"How much?" he said.

I looked at him again, calculated dollars, weighed common sense. Hotel was just around the corner; thin walls. He couldn't get up to nothing too weird. Then his eyes caught mine, and out of no place, I was harder than I'd ever been.

I wanted to get on my knees right there on that filthy sidewalk. Hell, I wanted to be on all fours. I wouldn't have cared if the grit and

109

grime turned my hands and knees black, as long as he was behind me, giving it to me. I know it's hard to believe, but with just a look, he had me short of breath.

"You seem distracted, boy."

I pulled my eyes away, then he was just a customer again. No, that's not right. Sometimes, there's these customers, they're so hot-looking, you don't know what the hell they're doing on the street buying ass. He was like that. I got back to business, told him my price, plus twenty-five bucks, 'cause of rent coming up. My landlord was one of my regulars, but he still wanted half his rent.

"And you pay for the hotel," I said.

"I have my own place nearby."

Shit. Rule one of surviving the city at night: Go nowhere with no one after midnight. "I don't get in cars."

"Then let's walk, shall we? And you can tell me of yourself."

He let go of my wrist, bowed a little, swept his hands out in front of him, like a fancy waiter saying after you. It should have made me laugh, should have looked stupid; but on him, it looked just right.

"You don't talk like you're from here," I said

"And you don't walk like a city boy."

"How's that?"

"As if with each step, you expect the ground to be soft, like grass. And you're bitterly disappointed that your feet find only hard, unyielding cement."

In two seconds, this guy had summed up my life for the past two years – caught in a place where I didn't wanna be, trapped in miles and miles of a concrete maze. I almost turned back – and fuck all with the rent – when he said that. I didn't like the feel of my past breathing down my neck.

"That's pretty good," I said. "You should do the cards or something."

He pulled me close, tilted his head, looked at me as if he was deciding if he should do it now or later. I had no idea what 'it' was.

I should have been scared.

I wasn't.

We'd stopped walking, two men, one much bigger than the other, facing each other in the cool darkness between streetlights.

Up close, I noticed the rock solid bulk of his body. When he ran his fingers through my dark hair, I felt the raw strength he held back, felt his untamed hidden side. His sensual mouth, his black eyes, his long black hair – glossy like silky fur – only added to the feeling that I was facing some exotic creature that was only half-tame.

His fingers in my hair felt so good. Like his unimaginable strength sandblasted my past, blew away every customer who'd fucked me hard enough to leave me in tears, then left an extra twenty. His touch made me feel as if the things I'd let the city grime and filth bury inside me were back, shiny and brand new.

"If I read the cards about you, what would I see?" he whispered.

"Nothing," I said. And I was whispering too, looking – no – falling into his eyes. "Just a boy who wants to go home."

He kissed my forehead. "Then why not come home with me, Zak?"

His lips on my skin felt cool, soothing. His touch made me forget to be scared he knew my name; made me forget it was Weirdo Hour, the hour when street boys dropped out of sight forever.

"Yeah," I said, so low I couldn't hardly hear myself. "Take me home with you."

"And you'll be mine?"

Without hesitation, without any hint that I was leaving everything I ever knew behind, I said, "Yes."

# # # # #

I know we talked on the way to his place, but I don't remember any of it. Later, I asked him. He said, with a soft yellow glow in his eyes (that's what Wolfs do when they're messing with you) that perhaps at twenty, my memory was failing, since humans are such delicate, fragile things.

He lived on the top floor of a brownstone, looking over Central Park. I mean the whole floor. He owned it. All of it. In the city, that's like saying he was rich enough to own a thirty-five bedroom mansion on fifty acres of land. Inside, his brownstone was like a museum – pictures, paintings, drawings – and all of them, everywhere of wolves. Big wolves, little wolves, baby wolves, giant wolves; even some cave drawings.

His bedroom wasn't a room at all. Somehow, here in a brownstone just off Central Park, someone had built a cave.

The walls were rough, unfinished black stone. A pile of animal furs big enough to hold him and me and maybe three others stood in the middle. There were drawings on the walls. I didn't know you could draw detail on stone like that; all of them wolves fucking, humping, going at it hard. Instead of being built into the wall, a fire burned low in a pit in the floor. I felt like I'd slipped back in time – way back – to a time when men did what the wolves on the wall were doing, just grabbed whatever they wanted, and took it and used it 'til they were satisfied. It made me rock hard.

That night was like a dream. Not because it was so good – it was – more because it was like living in a dream. Music came from nowhere, filling the cave. It was a lot of drums but underneath, if you listened real close, you could almost hear the wild sounds of animals fucking, tearing at each other, snarling, grunting. The flickering firelight from the wide pit set the animals in motion, made it look like we were surrounded by animals in heat, fucking and heaving at each other. A bathtub was in the far corner. It was a round hole, dug into the stone. He turned on the copper pipe and reached into a stone bowl on the lip of the sunken tub and threw in a handful of leaves.

Dezmond talked to me while his sure, strong hands undressed me. God. His hands were everywhere, caressing me, soothing me when I got scared, saying how I was his now, and I was safe. Then I was naked, and he lowered me into the warm water. The most incredible scent surrounded me, sharp and sweet at the same time, filling my mind with the wild musky scent of a man's sweat, his balls, his cock, his hot cum when it's dripping from your ass. It drove me wild.

He undressed, never taking his eyes off me. Then he was sinking down behind me, pulling me into his strong arms.

He reached between us and guided his cock to my ass, and I never wanted anyone as bad as I wanted him. I looked up at the pictures of the animals around us, fucking, humping, and I pushed back, wanting him to take me, fill my ass. He slid into me, so thick and hard, and it hurt like hell. I cried out, tried to pull away, but in the water, in his strong grip, I was helpless.

Dezmond murmured soothing things into my ear, stroked into me, slow, letting my ass open to him, but not giving me any room to pull back and take it at my own pace. He made me take it, until I relaxed, and let him have me.

"Good boy," he whispered. His deep voice thrummed through me. "Give yourself to me."

After that, his hands were all over my body, and his driving strokes never broke rhythm. You understand? Never. That's impossible; but I didn't think of that 'til after. I pushed back, grinding into his driving cock. I wanted more, wanted him to fill every inch of me. He grabbed my hips tight, so I couldn't push back, and held me like that, then let go and kept his hard cock in me, utterly still. I was breathing hard. My whole body teetered on the edge of coming, but I didn't, couldn't.

It had been so long since I'd come with a man inside me, let my load shoot just because it felt so damn good. He ran his hands over me, kissing my neck, my throat, turning my face, so he could kiss my lips, as if he knew somehow that I was holding back. Then he pulled me tight against him and fucked me in short, quick thrusts.

"I want it all, boy," he said. His hips drove into me, hammering my mind, demanding my surrender. "Give it to me."

He kissed my neck roughly, pulled at my skin with his sharp teeth. And then, I couldn't believe what I was hearing. He growled into my ear, but not like a man growls when the fucking's real good. No. This was more like a low animal sound; and it didn't stop, like he didn't need to breathe to do it. That low sound shot through every nerve in my body, and I pushed back hard on his cock, holding onto the sides of the tub, and shot the biggest load of my life.

"Oh my God, Jesus," I said, panting. "What are you?"

His answer didn't surprise me. I'd fucked a whole lot of men, and no man could do what he'd done.

"A werewolf," he said, and kissed my throat. "Did you enjoy serving me?"

His cock was still in me, still hard. "Yeah," I said. "Who's not gonna like getting it like that. But – dude – you're not human."

He stroked in and out of me a few times. "Is that a problem, Zak?"

#

It should have been a problem. I should have jumped out of that stone tub and ran out of there naked and screaming.

I didn't.

Not because I was scared of Dezmond. I can't explain it any better than this. I wanted to stay, wanted to be with him, wanted to feel that little thrill I got when he called me 'boy.'

"No," I said, signing myself up for a life I couldn't have dreamed of back then, "it's not a problem."

Then an awful, terrifying thought struck me. "You don't change into a wolf and – you know – with humans, do you?"

Dezmond laughed, a rich deep sound that started in his belly, and rolled out his wide, sensuous mouth. "No. You break too easily for that. We only use boys in our human form."

He got out of the tub, lifted me up as if I weighed nothing, and set me down at his feet. When I tried to get up, he pushed me back down to my knees. I thought he wanted me to service him.

"No," he said, pushing my mouth away gently. "You'll start learning tonight. When I'm done with you, kiss my feet."

I did. It felt right with him. No one had ever fucked me like that. "If I stay, I'll be like, your servant?"

He ran his big strong hands through my hair. "You are staying."

It should have frightened me, the way he said that, as if I didn't have a choice now that I was here; now that I knew his secret.

It didn't.

"You'll be what humans call a slave. Wolfs call it …"

He made a low guttural noise that didn't sound as if it could come from a human throat.

"What does that mean?"

"Wolf boy, roughly – one who gives pleasure and is cared for."

I met his eyes. "I want you to take care of me."

"I know."

He pulled me close, and I licked his balls softly.

Dezmond jumped back, as if I'd bitten him.

Oh God, my first good gig in forever, and I was already fucking it up. I looked up at him. "I do something wrong?"

"It's difficult for us to have pleasure with humans," he said, smiling as if he were telling only half a secret. "We must control ourselves, or we could hurt you with our need."

I looked at his cock. He was still bone-hard. "Don't you …"

"Yes, but not often. And hardly ever in a boy's ass. We mostly use a boy's mouth to ease our needs. Easier to control."

I kissed his balls softly, hoping I'd get a load down my throat. "My mouth's not busy."

"No, but my mind is. It wouldn't be safe for you." Dezmond went across the stone floor to the furs; the way he moved – lithe, graceful – made me want him all over again.

I trailed after him. "Do I call you Sir?"

"Only in front of other Wolfs. When we're alone, it's not important."

He pulled me down onto the pile of furs. It was softer than any mattress I'd ever slept on. I asked Dezmond if he'd fuck me again. When he refused, I pleaded and begged. When that didn't work, I slid down between his muscled legs and took him in my mouth.

Laughing, he grabbed my arm in an almost painful grip and hauled me up. It happened so fast. One second I was between his legs, the next, he was on top of me, kissing my mouth, my face, my neck and I was under him, writhing and begging.

"Didn't I leave you sore, boy?"

"Yeah. But I still want you to fuck me again. It was so good. I'm so fucking hot for you."

He kissed my throat, bit me softly. "No." His mouth found mine, kissed me. "Not until I'm ready to have you again." He rolled off me, held out his big arm. "Come to me."

I snuggled close, one of my legs over his, my head on his broad chest. He curled his thick arm around me and pulled me even closer.

His long fingers drifted slowly over my body. "I enjoyed you very much."

My ass was warm and tingly. There was this warmth seeping through my body, like I'd knocked back a shot of high end Scotch. "You were amazing," I said, saying nothing but the truth.

"Do you know what Alpha Wolf means?"

"Head of the pack, I guess."

His fingers explored the gentle slope of my back. "Yes. I'm the first Wolf to have you. Now you're marked with my Alpha scent. If I were human, I would be President and you would be wearing my collar."

I snickered at the thought of the stodgy President having a slave boy to warm his bed at night. "A red white and blue collar?"

He kissed the top of my head. "Perhaps." I heard the smile in his voice.

I don't remember falling asleep, but I must have, my head on his hard chest, his long fingers drifting slowly over my body.

# # # # #

Jethro lived on the third floor, just a flight of steps down from Dezmond. Wolfs owned the whole building. They did that when they could, without being too obvious. Wolfs don't like to scare humans. They don't like us to notice them. Except Jethro. He loves to put a good scare into a human, when he can get away with it.

I saw him for the first time the next morning, in Dezmond's kitchen. Wolfs don't eat cooked food. They live on the prey they hunt during the Change. But Dezmond, for some reason, loved to cook. His kitchen was a gourmet chef's wet dream. He'd gone out to get eggs and other things he said I'd like. He'd told me not to get dressed, that Wolfs liked their boys to be naked. I was in the kitchen at the window (only the top half of me showed to the street), waiting for Dezmond to come back.

I was thinking how it was strange to hear so much quiet in the city. The brownstone wasn't high enough from the street to cut off the city sounds, but the kitchen was nearly silent. The cars made only a low thrum of sound on the street four stories down. I wondered if the walls were super-thick or soundproof.

"You must be my brother's new pet," a deep voice said behind me.

I turned so fast, I nearly tripped over my feet. Looking at his long dark brown hair, his dark eyes, the way his smile had a few too many teeth, I knew he had to be a Wolf. He had on a black leather jacket, black mirror shades, and black biker boots.

He slid his shades up into his hair, looked me over as if I was a new kind of snack.

The kitchen was as big as most small apartments in the city, and he was way on the other side from me. Without seeming to take more than two steps, he was across the white tile floor and two inches from me in seconds. He ran his long fingers over my lips. "Very nice."

"Leave him alone, Jethro."

I was never so relieved to hear anything as I was to hear Dezmond's voice.

"Just making your new boy feel at home." Jethro paused, his eyes taking in every inch of my naked body. "I bet you enjoyed the hell out of him last night. You still sore, boy?"

"What do you want?" Dezmond said.

"Orders for The Haunt. Need your signature," Jethro said. "And the Hunter Pack's got a Petition."

"I already denied it."

Jethro shrugged. "Left them on your desk."

Dezmond shoved the brown paper bag of groceries in his arms onto the wide counter next to the stove. "I'll bring them down."

"Why don't you send him instead?" His dark eyes fell on me. "You wanna come see my place, boy?"

My heart pounded. Jethro's sleek body was so different than Dezmond. He moved with the calm confidence of a seasoned hunter, used to bringing down his prey without a fight. I forgot I was naked, and even if I got only a little hard, it would show. Jethro looked down between my legs. "Looks like me and your new snackmeat could have some things to talk about."

"Leave," Dezmond said, in a voice that was half-threat, half-irritation.

Jethro's eyes flashed a mellow gold that went through me, made me warm all over. In that moment, I knew all I needed to know about Jethro. He liked to play hard, and he loved to win. But more than winning, or even the game, was the thrill of the hunt.

I was sure, if Jethro was in his Wolf form, his pink tongue would be hanging down between his sharp fangs. I backed away.

Jethro turned his back on me, like he'd decided to hunt something easier to bring down. "Later, brother."

Then, with that liquid speed Wolfs have, he was gone. My legs felt wobbly. I sat at the kitchen table.

"Don't let him frighten you," Dezmond said. "You're mine. He knows if he lays a paw on you, I'll rip into him so bad, his fur will go grey."

"He's different than you. Like a Hell's Angel."

"A what?"

"You know – a man who rides motorcycles."

"My brother rides whatever he can grab and wrestle to the ground."

"You two don't get along?"

"He's my younger brother. Blood runs thick with Wolfs. He knows his bounds with me, but he likes to overleap, see how far I'll let him go."

I laughed a little. "He likes pushing your Wolf buttons."

"Something like that." Dezmond came closer, stroked my naked body, kissed me, cupped my ass, and just like that I was hard and throbbing.

I wrapped my arms around him. "Please, Sir, can breakfast wait?"

He pulled away from me easily, smiled. "Come help me. You must be hungry."

# # # # #

The next three months went by in a blur. Dezmond took me everywhere. I was a tourist in a city I'd lived in for two years.

The best part was not being afraid; afraid I wouldn't make the rent; afraid my landlord would come by and I'd have to give him my ass or go look for some other dump I couldn't afford; or scared some guy would fuck me and beat me up so bad, I couldn't work for days.

It was good like nothing had ever been good for me.

Then we went to The Haunt, where I learned I could tumble out of the Wolf world as easily as I'd fallen in.

# # # # #

Jethro loved to tell me about the Wolf world. After that first time in the kitchen, he still tormented me, but mostly he was pretty decent. He and Dezmond owned The Haunt together. Jethro ran it day to day. Dezmond did the financial side – approving orders for food, liquor, things like that.

The Haunt, Jethro told me, was neutral ground. All the Packs – Hunters, Warriors, Breeders – knew they could go there, drink, rent a pretty boy for the night. As Alpha Wolf for the Warrior Pack, Dezmond heard Petitions there, settled disputes between Packs. His word was final. To go against him, Jethro said, was to die.

"Even you?" I asked.

We were in Dezmond's living room, on opposite ends of a leather couch wide enough to seat ten; at least it looked that big. Jethro was looking out the window, staring at the leaves trembling in the light breeze outside. I thought he hadn't heard me, and I was about to ask again, but his low, cold voice stopped me dead.

"Our world's different than yours." He got up, walked to the window that took up the whole wall. "Dezmond's Alpha Wolf. If I fuck with him, he'd be real sorry to do it, but he'd rip out my throat."

I was horrified. "But you're his brother."

Jethro whirled from the window; his eyes sparked – a hard red glow. "And he's Alpha Wolf."

That scared me pretty bad, 'cause I started seeing how much I didn't know about Wolfs.

# # # # #

The first night Dezmond took me to The Haunt, I was nervous. No. I was scared to death. I was terrified about being in a place with that many Wolfs.

"Are they gonna think I'm lunch?" I asked Dezmond that night in the car.

He drove more carefully than a nun on probation. "More like a midnight snack."

I saw the way his eyes glowed a second when he looked over at me. His eyes flashed like that with real soft yellow light when he was messing with my head, or when he was in my mouth and coming real good. We parked in front of a warehouse. It was spooky like hell. The docks in New York were no place to be in the middle of the night. People didn't just die in that neighborhood in regular New York muggings gone wrong.

The abandoned buildings were a favorite of the street gangs to string up people on hanging chains, and use chainsaws and blow torches to prove a point. I almost said this to Dezmond, but I knew it wouldn't do any good. He wasn't afraid of anything in the human world. There was nothing around us except giant warehouses, big enough to hold two or three oil tankers, side by side. I sat in my seat gripping my seat belt, maybe the way a man might after the business flight to Boston turned to an ice water swim with the sharks. I was determined I wasn't getting out of the car. Not me. No way.

Dezmond came around, opened my door, undid the seat belt and pulled me out as easily as I would have pulled out a kid eager to go to Disneyland.

I should have hauled ass back to the car.

I didn't.

He took me in his arms, kissed me – a long kiss that made me hard instantly. He rubbed his hard cock between my legs and pushed his strong hands up under my T-shirt, exploring my smooth chest.

"What are you afraid of?" he whispered against my lips.

His hands slid down to my ass and squeezed. God, he felt so good. I wanted to get on my knees right there in the dark and take him in my mouth and –

His laughter broke into my thoughts. "Still afraid, boy?"

I blushed. "No, Sir."

He kissed me again and put his strong arm around my shoulders. "Then let's go."

We walked halfway down the sidewalk and turned into a dark doorway. I nearly pissed myself when a Wolf jumped out at us, snarling at me. Before I knew it, we were surrounded by a ring of Wolfs, all of them so big, their heads came almost up to my waist.

"Oh fucking hell." I tried to turn back, even though I knew those monster Wolfs would pounce on me, tear me between them for a midnight appetizer.

Dezmond's hand clamped down on mine, and pulled me real close. "Stay next to me."

"Dezmond – Sir – please, let's go back."

He held his left hand to a Wolf, who sniffed it, then nudged his hand aside and pushed his nose between Dezmond's legs, scenting his crotch. He seemed to decide that Dezmond didn't smell like special delivery late-night dinner, and padded toward me.

"Oh shit," I said soft and low.

"Stay still. Open your legs."

Breathing hard, holding Dezmond's hand in a death grip, I spread my legs and looked down at the Wolf's huge shaggy head between my legs, sniffing, snuffling at my crotch. He sneezed – a delicate sound that almost made me laugh – then he padded away into the darkness, claws clicking on the cement. The other Wolfs followed.

"Jesus," I said, when Dezmond walked us across the big echoing cavern of a space, "was that security?"

"Yes," he said. "You're not to leave The Haunt without me or Jethro."

I glanced back, saw their red eyes glowing in the depths of the warehouse. "Don't worry."

120

On the other side of the hangar-sized room, a platform was set into the floor. Dezmond stepped on, then pulled me on next to him. A big black bar with two buttons hung down from somewhere. He grabbed it, pressed a button; the platform screeched and lurched to a start, taking us down.

# # # # #

When we sank below the security checkpoint, it was like a submarine diving into the ocean. Darkness pressed all around us. The platform was exactly that – no walls – just a piece of floor that went down.

I'd spent two years on city streets by then, but after feeling that Wolf's muzzle between my legs, after my balls being that close to teeth that could rip me apart like I was a Sunday chicken dinner, I was scared as shit in the dark. I was so close to Dezmond, it was as if I was trying to melt into him. He didn't mind, just wrapped his big arm around me, and caressed me all over with his other hand. He lifted my face, so he could kiss me. Then I wasn't just close to him 'cause I was scared, I was moving against him, writhing, feeling his hard cock between my legs, and oh my God, how did he do that? How did he make me want him so bad?

I was breathing hard, his tongue in my mouth, my hands on his chest, feeling all that hard muscle, when a voice behind us said, "Enjoying your meat prize, brother?"

I leapt back at the sound of Jethro's voice. Dezmond grabbed me, so I didn't slip off the edge of the platform.

"If you kept them longer than five minutes, you'd know the pleasures a boy like Zak can offer."

"I like variety." Jethro tossed his long brown hair over his shoulder. "How's it hanging tonight, boy?"

Dezmond had told me that most Wolfs at The Haunt wouldn't speak to me or even acknowledge me. He'd taught what to say if they did. I tried it out on Jethro. "Evening to you, Sir."

"You been teaching him manners. Good."

That seemed to end Jethro's favorite game – Zak's Torment – for the night. He fell in step beside his brother, and they talked in low voices. Even though they were right next to me, I couldn't hear them. Wolfs can do that, talk so low, that only their ears pick it up. All humans hear is a faint murmur.

I heard the roar of The Haunt before I saw it. Loud pumping music surged around the corner with the overpowering feel of a surf coming in on a rough ocean. The music had a kind of animal quality to it, like if you listened really good, you'd hear the sounds of animals clawing and ripping at each other, while they fucked like mad.

"You taking him up?" Jethro said, loud enough for me to hear.

Dezmond stroked the back of my neck lightly. "It'll be a good experience for him,"

"Then you better fucking make sure he knows what he's supposed to do. I don't want any trouble with the Packs over meat on a stick that don't know how to act right."

"I know what to do," I said quietly. I only had the guts to say something because it was Jethro. He came so close I could feel his breath on me, then he ran his fingers slowly down my cheeks. "Stay out of trouble snackmeat. I don't wanna have to hurt anyone 'cause of you."

He disappeared around the corner, going on ahead of us.

# # # # #

We went around the corner, and I bumped into a wall, except it was breathing. I looked up and saw the biggest, blackest mountain of a man I'd ever seen. His naked chest was like polished, chiseled ebony. His eyes were deep, deep blue. Rastafarian dread locks hung down to his waist in thick red ropes the color of fresh blood. I fell back a step. A Wolf.

"Bossman Two come, now Bossman One," the walking mountain said in a voice deep enough to come from inside a volcano. "Bossman One's sweet piece," he said, looking down at me.

He had a soft island lilt to his words – Bahamas maybe, or Jamaica.

I tore my eyes away from his, knowing I'd already messed up. Never look a Wolf in the eye. It's an invitation, Dezmond had told me over and over. And what was I doing? Looking right into this Wolf's eyes as if I was inviting him down my pants and up my ass. I glanced over at Dezmond. He gave me a hard look, and something else might have happened if the Wolf hadn't sprung to my defense.

"Bossman One should maybe go easy on his boy. Never seen a Wolf like me before."

Dezmond squeezed the big Wolf's shoulder. "Been keeping my brother out of trouble, Stone?"

"Bossman One be crazy thinking Stone can keep Jethro from hunting down all the trouble he can find."

"Don't be telling my secrets," Jethro said, materializing out of the darkness. He looked from my frightened face to Dezmond. "If you think he's gonna be a problem up there, let him spend the night walking the floor with me. I'll watch out for him."

See? Told you. Jethro could be pretty decent when he wanted.

"He'll be alright," Dezmond said. "Zak learns fast."

Jethro looked out over the dance floor where some Wolfs were mixed in with the humans. "I'm staying down here a while," he said. "I'll be up."

He left and melted into the gyrating crowd. Stone stepped aside and let me and Dezmond climb the narrow steps.

At the top, it was a different world. The Wolfs were all shirtless, and the Wolf boys were all naked. Some Wolfs turned to look at Dezmond; a few raised their hands, but most went on with what they were doing. Even though nobody got up and bowed or anything, a kind of quiet hush followed us, the way it might if the President walked through a room crowded with men who worked for him.

A boy came and kissed Dezmond's feet. "Evening to you, Sir. A drink?"

"Scotch," Dezmond said.

I followed Dezmond to a table that was on a kind of balcony jutting out over the main club below. The lights were so dim, that from below, it probably looked like a midnight world, with moving shadows in the shapes of men.

"Your clothes go in here," Dezmond said, pointing to a drawer built into the long leather seat that ringed the table.

I looked around, reluctant to undress, even though I was the only Wolf boy wearing clothes. "Do I have to get naked, Sir?"

"Yes."

When Dezmond answered like that, short, without explanation, I knew he was serious. I stripped out of my clothes, while he watched with a small smile. Naked, I bent over and put my clothes into the drawer. He ran his hand over my ass in a soft caress.

"Come, sit with me. You'll get used to it."

I sat beside him, but he drew me onto his lap, so I was straddling him, facing him. And of course, I could feel his hard cock between my legs. Without thinking, I started moving, grinding into him, the way I always did when he let me sit on him like that. For a second I forgot we were out, and leaned into him, kissed his neck, ran my hands over his chest.

"Take off my shirt," he said, his nostrils flaring, inhaling the scent of my arousal for him.

I unbuttoned his shirt, helped him out of it. And it felt so good to lean my naked body against his bare chest, rub against his muscled body. He grabbed my face, kissed me, ran his hands over my ass, slid a finger inside me. I was writhing and wriggling, humping his hard cock and about two seconds from coming.

"If you want it, boy, get up on the table, ass up."

I froze. I'd whored a lot, but never done anything in public. "Is that an order, Sir?"

He ran his hands over my back, down the split of my ass, teasing me, making me want him. "No," he whispered in my ear, "just an offer to slide my fat cock up your tight little hole and make you come real hard." He kissed my lips softly, looking into my eyes. "If that's what you want."

I thought about it. Being up on the table, with Dezmond's cock up my ass, fucking me, writhing on it like I knew I would, every Wolf seeing me take it.

I didn't think I could do it.

But he was making me so fucking hot.

"I want you to fuck me, Sir," I said, wriggling all over him. "Please. Can't we go some place?"

"On the table," Dezmond said, "or I won't use you for days." He kissed me. "I'll do everything to you, except use your mouth or your ass." He slid his finger in and out of me. "Won't let you come."

Oh my God. No. I knew he'd do it. "No, Sir. Please. Don't."

He let me go. "Then get your ass up for me, boy."

I slid off him, breathing hard, and climbed onto the table, bent over, spread my legs, cringing inside at the thought of Wolfs passing and seeing me like that. But I wanted Dezmond so badly, wanted to feel his hands on me, feel him guiding his fat cock to my hungry hole. But the hands I felt on me weren't Dezmond's. I tried to turn around but it was a Wolf. He flattened my face into the table, way too strong for me to fight back. "Stay," a low guttural voice said.

"You're dead, Leon. The moment your hands are off my property, I'm going to gut you and make you squeal like a pig." Dezmond's voice was calm, but it was rage distilled, a low growl, barely words. What the hell was going on?

"We Petitioned you, but you wouldn't listen to reason," the voice behind the hand on my back said. "We waited. Now you're back. Now you listen."

"Hands off my boy, and I'll consider ripping out your throat, give you an easy death," Dezmond said.

There was a scuffling sound, low growls and snarls, then Jethro's voice. "Any one of you sorry Wolf rejects wanna live past the next twenty seconds, get the fuck out of my club."

I heard a low, heavy growl like the idling engine of a monster truck, and I knew that had to be Stone. Whoever it was would be crazy to go up against the big black Wolf. The hand holding me down was snatched away, and in a second, Dezmond pulled me off the table, and onto the bench next to him. "Lie down," he said, pushing me back 'til I was flat on the leather. "Stay."

Then he was gone, and a ring of Wolfs with their back to me was guarding the table. Their broad muscular backs were a barrier between me and the rest of the club.

I heard snarling, grunts and a few screams of pain. Then I saw Dezmond go sailing off the top floor, into the crowd below. As he fell, he Changed into a Wolf with sleek black fur and fangs as big and thick as my little finger. Jethro jumped down after his brother. Then the air was full of falling, snarling Wolfs.

I expected to hear the crash and screams of broken bones, but instead, I heard Jethro yelling, "Get the fuck out of the way!"

I recognized Stone's long red dreads, touched his back. "What's going on?"

"Hunter Pack making trouble. Like always. Bossman One and Two gonna make them bleed bad this time. Shouldn't of touched Bossman's meat."

A boy looked out from behind the solid-looking bar, and I looked up at the mirror over the bar. From my angle, the mirror showed about fifteen heads, all of them down, all of them still. They'd been herded behind the bar like cattle.

Three Wolfs were on the bar, pacing back and forth, and while I watched, first one, then the other two Changed. They paced the bar's surface, their mouths hanging open, their great shaggy heads moving from side to side, licking their chops, like they were hoping something juicy would come along, so they could have a late night meat treat.

I sat there, behind the circle of Wolfs, looking out into the darkness.

Dezmond scared the shit out of me, flying down from no place, landing right in front of the Wolfs guarding me. He'd jumped up from the floor below. Before I saw the blood dripping down his chest, I had time to think, my God, how strong is he?

"Are you alright, Sir?" I said.

Before Dezmond could answer, a boy was on his knees, offering him towels. He took them, and wiped the blood off. Jethro landed two inches behind him, grinning ear to ear. "Ain't had that much fun in a way too long time." He threw back his head and howled. "The way you went after them brother, that was fucking sweet."

The Wolf guards melted into the dark. Dezmond sat down, pulled me onto his lap. "Where were we, boy?"

Seeing him jump up like that, and feeling his strong body so close to me, holding me, running his big hands over me, oh my God, I almost squirted all over his pants. He kissed me, twisting his thick fingers into my hair, mashing my lips.

When he pulled back I was breathing hard. "Please, Sir. Oh fuck. Please. Take me home. I want you so bad."

"No, boy. Here. I'm fucking ready for your ass."

I'd suddenly lost my nerve to get fucked in public. Seeing him and Jethro go after the other Wolfs like that had scared me bad. I wanted to be home, in Dezmond's furs, with him fucking me. Not here, in a crowded club with Wolfs watching me.

"Please, Sir," I said, "take me home."

I was caressing his broad chest. He grabbed my wrists, rougher than he'd ever touched me.

"You're mine. After what I've done tonight, the Packs have to see that. Here. On the table, or you'll be back on the street where I found you."

My heart bumped and tripped and skipped a couple beats at the thought of going back to the street, back to being afraid everyday of my life.

"Do it, boy," Dezmond said. "I don't want to give you up, but it's the Wolf way."

For a second, I saw the same hard red glow I'd seen in Jethro's eyes the day we'd talked about how his brother was Alpha Wolf.

Oh God. Oh fuck. Jesus Christ in a sideways cart to Hell. "Yes, Sir."

When Dezmond all but threw me on the table, I didn't resist. I couldn't go back to working the street. I needed to be his Wolf boy, maybe like a hardcore addict needs his stuff.

He grabbed my hips, rubbed his cock up and down and around my hole, getting me slick with his pre-cum, then he leaned over me, whispered, "I'll make it the best you ever had from me."

Those words blew every other thought out of my head. Better? How? Dezmond was the best fuck I ever had.

When he slid into me real slow, I lifted my ass, spread my legs.

He humped my ass in a rough rhythm; I took every stroke. It was the first time Dezmond had ever used me like an animal, riding me, fucking my hot hole deep and hard, and oh shit, it was Heaven. I gave myself to him completely. Dezmond pulled me closer so my ass was right up on him, and on every stroke he ground his hips into me, fucking every inch of my ass hole. I pushed back, humping his cock, whimpering. "Please Sir … oh God … please …"

"Go on, boy," Dezmond said, pumping my ass. "Fucking come. Show the whole fucking club who owns your boy ass."

I groaned and grunted, my hips spasmed, jerking hot streams of cum all over the table. Dezmond rode me like a bucking bronco, never missing a stroke. Then, I couldn't believe it, he pulled me really close, dug his fingers into me, and shoved his cock so deep, I screamed, then he was coming, the biggest, hottest load I ever got up my ass. He held on to me, groaning, his cock pumping hot cum into me, and I moaned with every spurt I felt up my ass. Then he let me go, caught me before I collapsed to the table, and pulled me down next to him, kissing me long and deep.

A circle of Wolfs had gathered to watch. They made low sounds, almost like big cats purring; a sound of approval, satisfaction. Then they slipped back into the dark shadows. A boy came with towels and cleaned the table. He left a couple clean ones. I grabbed them and cleaned Dezmond before I cleaned myself. He leaned over and kissed me, pulled me onto his lap. I rested my head in the hollow between his neck and his shoulder.

He stroked the back of my head. I'd never felt his touch so light, so gentle. "I'm sorry I frightened you, boy."

It didn't matter that the other Wolfs had seen me get fucked 'til I screamed, that I'd come hard all over the table, squirming on Dezmond's cock. Didn't even matter that Jethro would torment me endlessly about it. All that mattered was that I was safe, in Dezmond's arms.

"I love being your Wolf boy, Sir."

He stroked my back. "I love taking care of my Wolf boy."

"I can't wait to hear all about it." Jethro slid onto the leather bench opposite us.

"Jethro ..." Dezmond said in a low, warning voice.

"Come on, brother, I just wanna know how he likes it better – squirming on the furs or on a table. I'm thinking a table's gotta be harder on the knees."

I laughed a little.

Jethro reached over, tousled my hair. "You did good, boy. You run with our Pack now."

"Where we go, you go," Dezmond said.

It felt like going home.

Now you know about New York, from the bottom up. If you're ever in the city, on the docks after midnight, and you get a taste for a man who's way more than a man, walk the narrow side streets, look for The Haunt. If you're lucky, a Wolf will find you, and bring you in.

THE EIGHTH
H. L. Champa

He was such a liar. I could always tell when people were lying. Maybe it was because I was such a good liar myself. No one could hold a candle to me when it came to fibbing. I could spin a tale with the best of them. Even when it wasn't important, lying seemed to be my standard operating procedure. Little ones, big ones, it didn't matter. I loved it, and more importantly, I was good at it. No one ever doubted me. If I said I was at the movies, I was. No matter what I was really doing. Truth be told, I hadn't been to the movies in years. But, what else would you expect from someone evil, someone who tempts the good into the darkness and the pious into sin. Lying rather comes with the territory.

He wasn't supposed to lie. But, he did. I saw his eyes go down as the words tumbled out of his mouth. I knew his words were untrue. I could practically smell it on him. The sweat across his brow, the looks to the left, the avoidance of eye contact. It was a laundry list of telltale signs. I should have felt sorry for him. After all, it was my fault he had turned into such a liar.

He truly was dreadful. As one would hope, being a pastor and all. Lying didn't exactly fit with the job description. Neither did wanting to fuck thy neighbor, but that hadn't stopped him so far. As he stood up there at the altar, talking about the virtues of truth and the scourge of bearing false witness, I had to stifle a chuckle.

His lying, even under such circumstances, was a minor offense, but the hypocrisy bothered me nonetheless. Just like the sermon he was going through right now. It was as clichéd as any, but the subject matter was what was getting me. It was all about how terrible it was to be something you weren't. How lying had a way of trapping you, and the only thing that could set you free was God and the truth. I mean, come on. Even the most devout in the crowd had to be cringing at this one. But, as I looked around, I saw only admiration beaming towards the good pastor. The blind trust that came with a black shirt and a starched collar. In a way, I was jealous. That kind of trust was something even I could never experience. Even at my devious best, there was always the tiniest shred of doubt. He was destined to always be believed and respected. God, he didn't have to rub it in my face. It was hard enough for entities like me to recruit. Sure, badness and sin always sounded good at first, but soon the guilt would take over. It was bad for business, all the shame he peddled.

Pastors were some of the most trusted people on earth. No one wants to believe they are capable of human foibles or flaws. Even though we all know they are. Being close to God is supposed to grant you some kind of free pass, some kind of special knowledge that keeps you from sin. But, this pastor was no better than a lying demon like me. I knew the truth about him, I saw the real him. Truth really was relative, and like beauty, was in the eye of the beholder.

Our affair had started innocently enough. Wait. That was a lie, too. The truth was I chased him, pursued the ultimate and unattainable good guy. Imagine my disappointment when I found out how easy he was to get. He was practically salivating when I told him I wanted to suck him off while he was behind the pulpit. It was the first real thing I ever said to him. I sat quietly in that church for months, never doing anything more than smiling at him. Fantasies had grown in my head, but I had never made a move. One day, I decided to up the ante. The first time I opened my mouth, right after the small talk, I let the filth flow. That was all it took. After that, the breaks in his perfect façade were bigger than the cracks in the ceiling of the old church where he preached. Deliberately saying something crazy was my way of testing him. I was trying to make it harder for myself, to make him run. But it had the opposite effect. So very disappointing. Usually you have to work to corrupt souls forever. He practically gave it away on the first day.

I wanted the game. Something forbidden to spice things up. Turning a pastor was a real feather in the cap. But, after my bold behavior, he started pursuing me. The chaser became the chased. Apparently, the visual of me licking all over his cock while he preached the good word pushed him straight over the edge. I started getting notes in my coat pocket, a single flower sent to my office with a card simply saying, "Please." His ability to turn on so quickly surprised me. It seemed strange that he was willing to walk down the road of sin so easily. Sin was supposed to be the enemy, the thing to avoid and resist at all cost. However, he went so willingly. It would have been tragic if I had cared at all. He didn't even try to save me when I propositioned him. He clearly didn't care about my soul. Maybe he knew I was long gone. And, happily so.

In the time that passed before the inevitable, I felt his eyes devouring me from up on high. His stares at me got longer, just like his handshakes after the service. His large fingers would massage my palm as he struggled to think of anything to say to me, just to keep me in front of him a bit longer. I started to feel a bit sorry for him, his longing so consuming and so wrong. His desire for me grew, and my desire to torture him grew right along with it. I knew I had him, but now I wanted to take him down in the most fun way possible. I wanted his fall to be complete and total. It would be hotter that way.

Soon, it was me sending notes and tokens to his office. I took the power back, gone back on the offensive, started chasing again. The notes were never as explicated as I wanted them to be, for fear of his reaction. I needn't have worried. His writings in response were downright filthy, like the floodgates of taboo had opened and spilled out over the pages. I started attending services whenever they were available, positioning myself front and center. After several weeks had passed, I knew he couldn't take much more. So I decided to test him right in front of the rest of the congregation.

I picked my moment, one of the most important of the service. Even as I stood up for communion, I didn't know exactly what I would do. I didn't want to be too obvious, not with so many eyes on me. I just needed a lasting impression. We moved towards the front of the church, each one of us kneeling in turn. I felt my face grow hot with delight. He saw me coming, his hand tensing around the chalice of wine. We locked eyes, and suddenly there was no one else in the room. I lowered to my knees, never breaking my stare into his intense eyes. His hand holding the wafer lowered to my waiting mouth. I extended my tongue slowly, pausing to sweep it over my thick bottom lip. As he set the host down, I tasted the saltiness of his finger. I expected him to pull back right away, but he didn't. I closed my mouth around the tip, letting my tongue swirl around it for just a moment before pulling back. I couldn't resist a wink before I stood up and walked back to my seat. God, if the rest of them only knew. He propositioned me that day, practically begging me to meet him after the service.

Instead of indulging him right away, as he requested, I simply disappeared. Pushing the torture to a new level, I made myself scarce, knowing full well that my absence would do nothing to quell his desire for me. Thinking I had him on a string was half the fun for me. I knew his very livelihood depended on his discretion, but I hoped the draw of having me would put that right out of his head. My need to have him, to have him betray himself overwhelmed me. I wanted to prove a point and add another unattainable soul to my collection. And, to get off. All this build-up had to be for something. It was time for me to push him right over the cliff, right down to hell with the rest of us bad people.

The note came as expected, his desperate plea for me to meet him. I knew it was time. His office sat off the sanctuary. It was tiny and cluttered filled with books and papers. It smelled like cheap incense and dust. The sun streamed in through the stained glass, the only attractive feature in the room. I knew he would be there soon, his routine was well documented. I sat on the desk, running my fingers over the pages of his next sermon. The door creaked and I snapped my head around to see him framed in the entry. His face was a mix of anger, fear and delight. I overloaded his brain with my mere presence. The power shot straight to my cock, which was already hard with anticipation. The door closed, and we were alone, silence surrounding us. I smiled, but he seemed too unsure to return one to me. He walked around the desk, pulling out his chair. Ignoring the fact that I was perched on the edge of his desk, he seemed to go on with his routine, opening drawers and putting things away. It was only the tremble of his fingers that gave him away. He was always calm, but this little shudder spoke volumes.

"Miss me?" I said as innocently as I could muster.

He cleared his throat but didn't respond. I turned myself until I was facing him, his chair right in front of me. He looked into my eyes, the dark blue swimming with confusion. I slowly stood up and started to open my pants. His gaze dropped, the gasp telling me he noticed I was stiff and ready. Torn between wanting me and his last chance to stop the madness, he hesitated. With a quick look to the sky, a silent apology perhaps, his resigned eyes fell back on my now fully-exposed cock. He stood up, his body now closer to mine than it had ever been. I looked up at him and felt his hands running up my legs, from my knees slowly moving towards my thighs. It felt so damned good, his touch on my bare skin. I could feel the heat of his hands; his tentative movements growing bolder. Wrong had never felt so right before. This was going to be epic.

"I did. I didn't want to, but I missed you. I need you. God help me, I need you."

"Tell me, Father. Tell me what you want."

"You know what I want."

He traced a finger down towards my dick, stopping just short of touching my curls.

"I want to hear it. Say it, or I'm outta here."

"I, I want you to fuck me."

The words came out in a hushed whisper, but I still heard him loud and clear. There was no hiding from it anymore. Words on a page could never substitute for the power of speech. My smile returned, knowing that I had won, beaten him and his godly resolve. His mouth lowered to mine, his kiss more chaste than any I had experienced in years. But, after my tongue dove into his mouth, his demeanor changed. His desire had finally wrestled his conscience to the ground. I wrapped my legs around him, bringing him closer to me. His hands couldn't stop touching me all over, with no attempts at slow seduction. It seemed beyond him to slow down, to control himself for another minute. My shirt was off, his fingers fumbling over my tight nipples. His trembling told me he was scared, and his fear fed my desire to break him. I smiled at the thought of it all, and at his teenaged style of teasing. I wondered if his wife was his only lover. I reached out for his belt, his erection pressing into the fly of his chinos. As my hand stole into his briefs, another shudder ran through him. He let me tease him for a while, his cock getting harder by the minute. Slipping to my knees in front of him, I locked eyes with him as I slid his shaft into my mouth.

He was used to having people in front of him on their knees, taking the bread and wine of communion every other Sunday. He looked down at me with more reverence than I had ever seen in the sanctuary. This was more my kind of worship. It didn't take long from him to start fucking my mouth, his hands pulling my mouth deeper onto his cock as it bucked and twitched. Taking back power, I stood up. Watching him, I expected more embarrassment or maybe even some shame. But, I didn't find it. His eyes gleamed with heat, and he pushed me back on his desk. The fumbling was gone, his tongue now masterful on my cock, licking the juice from my slit with abandon. I could feel the papers containing his sermon sticking to my sweaty back. Fingers now free of fear jerked me, teasing me closer to the edge. As much as I wanted to bathe his face in my juices, I knew it wouldn't be enough. I wanted to pound his ass into submission, into the ultimate surrender. He didn't know what I was yet, but he would soon enough.

I pulled him up and turned him around, pushing him onto his sloppy desk rougher than I needed to. He grunted as I pulled his ass cheeks apart, teasing his puckered hole with the barest tip of my finger. It didn't take more than a minute for him to start pushing back onto me, trying to get more of my digit inside. I spit right onto his asshole, working the saliva inside him as he babbled incoherently against the fake wood. Lubing up my cock with more spit, I was more than ready to have what I wanted.

"This is your last chance to save your soul."

"I don't want to be saved. I want you. Please, fuck me. Please."

I almost chuckled at his words. He thought I was being metaphorical when speaking of his soul. But, this sin wasn't merely an abstract concept. This sin was as real as it got. As I pushed inside him, the hot, incredible wash of power swept over me. It made my cock swell as I pulled back to thrust into my helpless pastor repeatedly. As good as his body felt moving and writhing underneath me, his undoing, right there in the church, felt even better. I loosened my grip on his hips and watched with delight as he pushed back against me, fucking me all on his own. Leaning forward over him, I yanked his head back, biting his earlobe before whispering in his ear.

"You're mine now. All mine."

His eyes were open wide and for the first time he understood what it all meant. The light from the stained glass fell across his face, a mixture of deep blues and reds. It was at that moment that he broke, the gravity of what he had become was finally clear. His eyes closed and a look of deep shame replaced the ecstasy that had been there moments before. It was so hot. My orgasm crashed into me like a voice from below, heat and hellfire surging through me as I came into his damned ass. I saw the light of the window on my own skin, its colors changing my flesh to a golden hue as I collapsed spent onto his back.

At that moment, I knew the game was over. This would be the only time we would ever be here with each other. My need to have him was satisfied. It would never, ever be the way it was in this moment. It could never be recaptured. His soul belonged to me now, and no amount of praying could get it back.

As I got up and got dressed, I saw the sermon on the desk, wet and crumpled. It was about how unexpected moments can change our lives; make us see things in a new way. I would have to remember to show up for that one.

WILLING
Xan West

I slam him against the wall. Bring out my knife. Whisper words across his skin, the steel teasing, tempting. Kick his legs apart. The blade ripping through his shirt, tormenting, aching to slice him open. Up close breathing on his neck, teeth almost breaking skin. Step back slapping, leaving a handprint on his cheek. My knife at his throat. My hand covering his mouth. My eyes on his. Feeding on his helplessness. Feeding on his fear. A slow smile creeping across my face as I begin. My fist driving into his pecs. My gloved hand slapping his face. His nipple twisted between my fingers, hot under my teeth. Turned over, face against the exposed brick of the wall. My fist on his back, methodical. My boot ramming into his ass. My open hand menacing him with slaps. My cock throbbing hard as I press into him and bite down on his shoulder, holding back, yet feeding on his pain. I ride with him as I pull out my tools, laying into his back ... until I am ready to thrust the pain home with my quirt. Driving welts into his back, we will soar together, gliding on his pain, his helplessness, my power, our pleasure. And when we are done flying, he will be on the floor at my feet, tongue wrapped around my boot.

It will do. The beast inside me calls for flesh, for pain. He is demanding and relentless, and I barely keep him in check. It's better if they choose it. Want it. It adds a certain something that is indescribable and yet has become necessary to the meal. So I keep him sated with sadism, feeding on fear and pain and sex and helplessness. Once, I was waiting for the willing. That illusive willing boy I might call my own. I no longer hope for him. He does not exist.

Now, I find boys at The Lure. Boys like this one, who want to open themselves to my tools. But sometimes that is not enough to take the edge off. Sometimes it just stokes the hunger. When the urge for blood becomes incontrollable I return to Gomorrah, looking for those hungry eyes, the pulse in a boy's throat that shows he wants it. It's hard to keep a straight face here, amidst the pretenders, the elitist pseudo-vampires, the Stand and Model version of SM, the Sanguinarium, the followers of the Black Veil. So it's a last resort, this feast of image and fantasy. When the beast must feed and pain is not enough.

I stride to a shadowed corner and watch for food. The rhythm of the music brings a booming to my brain as my eyes slide along the flesh exposed, watching for that look, that swiftly beating pulse in his throat.

Whispers begin as I am glimpsed by the regulars, and I know all it will take is a crook of my head and a smoldering gaze. It's too easy here. I am not seen. I am simply a fantasy come true, made all the more fantastic by my refusal to be showy in dress or demeanor. A growl of disgust rolls through me. I choose my meat, a tall broad-shouldered goth boy with long black hair and a carefully trimmed beard. I draw him to me, and lead him out to the alley. He thinks this is a quick fuck, and drops to his knees. My hand grips him by that delicious hair and yanks him up, tossing him against the wall. I want to savor this meal. He needs to last.

I pull out my blade and show it to him. His eyes widen and he whispers, "My safeword is chocolate." I am surprised. Most who frequent the fetish scene know nothing about real BDSM. That these are the first words out of his mouth shows that there may be more to this boy than I thought. I stand still, watching him. He is older than I had first surmised, at least 24. The little leather he wears is well kept, his belt clearly conditioned and his boots cared for by a loving hand. He is motionless, knees slightly bent, shoulders back, offering me his chest. His pulse is not rapid, but his eyes eat up the knife and his lips are slightly parted, as if all he wanted was to take my blade down his throat.

His brown eyes stay fixed on the knife as I move toward him. I tease his lip with the tip of it and then speak softly.

"How black do you flag?"

His eyes stay on the blade. He swallows.

"Very black, on the right, Sir."

"Is there anything I need to know?"

"I am healthy and strong. My limits are animals, children, suspension and humiliation, Sir."

"And blood, hmmm?" I am teasing. I know the answer. It is why I found him here, and not at the Lure.

"Oh please, Sir. I would gladly offer my blood."

"Why?"

138

He takes a deep breath, closes his eyes a moment, and then opens them. The pulse in his throat starts racing, but his voice is calm, and matter-of-fact. I tease my blade against his neck.

"I have been watching you a long time, Sir. I have seen how you play. I see the beast inside you. I know what is missing. Those boys at The Lure don't know how to give you what you really need. They don't see that they are barely feeding your craving, and not touching your hunger. The boys here don't see you. They just see their own fantasy. They are simply food. I am strong, Sir. Strong enough for you. I can be yours. My blood, my flesh, my sex, my service. Yours to take however you choose, for as long as you want. To slake your hunger. I would be honored, Sir."

I take a deep breath, stunned, studying him. This boy who would offer what I never really thought was possible. He has surprised me again. That alone shows this boy is more than a meal. He just might be able to be all that he has offered.

I almost leave him there. I am ready to walk away. Fear creeps along my spine. With the centuries I have lived and the things I have seen, this boy is what scares me. There is nothing more terrifying than hope. I rake my eyes over him. He is standing quietly. He looks as if he could stand in that position for hours. He has said his piece; he is content to wait for my response. Oh he is more than food, this one. What a gift to offer a vampire. Can I refuse this offering when it's laid out before me? I step back, looking him over, and decide.

I breathe in possibility, watching the pulse in his throat. My senses heighten further as I focus my hunger on him, noticing the minute changes in breath, scenting him. I want to see him tremble. I want to smell his fear. I want to devour his pain, without holding back. Forget this public arena. If there is even a possibility that I might truly let go and move with the beast inside my skin, his growl on my lips and his claws grasping prey, I know exactly where I need to take this boy.

I put the knife away, pull the black handkerchief from his back pocket and wrap it around his head, covering his eyes. He cannot see the way to where we are going. He has not earned that much trust. I grip him by the back of the neck and lead him to my bike. When I start the engine, it's growl answers me, echoing off the walls of the alley. I take the long way, through twists and turns of the back streets, enjoying the wind on my face and the purr of the bike.

139

We are here. I ease him off the bike and lead him by the neck down the stairs into the lower level of the brownstone. It is a large soundproof room. There are no windows. It is one big tomb. Every detail is designed for my pleasure, down to the exposed brick wall installed for the simple gratification of slamming meat against it. This room is where I sleep, and where I take my prey when I want privacy. Private play means I let my hair down, and roam free, claws unsheathed. I leave him in the doorway, and ready myself, breathing deep, and freeing my hair. I strip off my shirt so I can feel it brush my lower back. It is my vanity, and I have worn it long for centuries, no matter the current fashion.

I keep him blindfolded, and throw him against the wall. There is a ritual about it, beginning with a wall and a knife. It communicates the road we are on. He is trapped, nowhere to run. He is pressed against the wall, and going to take any impact into his body, through it to the wall, and back again, driven in a second time. He is facing danger, sharp edges. He could be torn open. He is pressed against something rough and hard. He is still. I am moving. He cannot see what's coming. My knife breaks the unspoken rules of knife play, and goes to places that feel forbidden and fraught with more danger than expected. And my knife shows my need. You can hear it in my breathing, feel it surge through my body. It travels the air in electric bursts of energy.

I play with it, toying with him, ramping my need up through his fear. I slap his face with the large blade. I run it along the top of his eye, just under the blindfold, teasing it against his eyelid, so he knows just how easy it would be to burst the eyeball. I fuck him with it, thrusting the tip under his jaw, not breaking skin, just teasing my cock to hardness at the thought of thrusting it deep. His breath is catching as I draw his lower lip down and slide the blade along it. My mouth swoops in out of nowhere and bites down on that lip, just barely breaking skin. This is a test of my control, as I slowly lick the fruit I have exposed, and growl deep in my throat. He is hypnotically delicious, his blood electric in a way that is familiar and yet surprising. I grip his throat in my hand, constricting his breath, watching his face, his mouth. It is true. He has surprised me again. I tuck my new knowledge and my surprise away, knowing that I can do my worst. Folks always said that his kind make good boys for us. Perhaps, I will be able to test that tonight. I release his throat and watch him breathe deeply. I grip his hair and tilt his head back.

"Keep your mouth open and still."

I start to tease it in, watching the large black blade slide into his throat. I exhale loudly. He is motionless for me, breath held, taking my knife. My cock jumps at the sight, as I start to fuck his throat. Mine. This incredible wave of possessiveness roars through me as I thrust into him. And I want to see his eyes. I tear through the blindfold with my teeth, the blade still lodged in his throat, and meet his gaze. His eyes are shimmering, large, and full ... full of what? I thrust in deeper, watching his pupils dilate with ... is that joy? I can feel his heart race, see him struggle as he realizes he needs to breathe. He must exercise perfect control, and not move his mouth or throat as he exhales and takes his first breath. Fear fills him. Not because he is afraid of the knife. Because he knows that it would displease me to draw blood when I don't intend to, and his whole being is focused on pleasing me. He works to do it perfectly, and contentment washes over his face as he succeeds. I thrust deeper in appreciation, picturing his throat muscles working to avoid contact with the blade. Oh this will be fun. I slide out of his throat.

I want my claws on his chest, now. I want to rip him open, expose him to my gaze, my teeth, my hunger. I want his blood on every tool in my possession. Now. I want to feast on him. I can feel the beast roll through my body.

Not yet. I want more pain to draw it out. I want to see if it's true. I want to know he can take my worst and still want more. I want to see his strength. That is worth delaying my feed. And postponing it will only make it sweeter.

I breathe deeply, focusing my senses as I walk slowly in front of him, inspecting him from every angle. He straightens his posture, easing into a position he can hold. I move close, and grip his shirt, tearing it swiftly from his chest and tossing it onto the floor. That's what I want first. I throw my shoulder into the body slam, and feel the electricity of our skins' contact. I trace my fingertips along the horizontal scars on his chest, and then grip his nipples, twisting. I am so close, I cannot resist sinking my teeth in and teasing myself. I bite deeply, barely avoiding breaking skin. Building connection. Making my cock throb. Drawing out my beast. I lift up and bite down, feeling his body shift with the pain, laying my mark on him. I claim him like this, first. Begin in the way you wish to proceed. With fear and pain and teeth and sex all rolled together. I can feel the blood pulsing just at the surface, calling me. I bite down hard and thrust my cock against him. My low growl mixes with the slow soft moan that escapes his lips. I lift my head to meet his eyes and see that he has begun to fly.

I step back and begin my dance around him. Heaving my fist into his chest. My boot into his thigh. My open hand slamming down onto his pecs. I move rapidly, layering and shifting, gliding around him. Thrusting pain into him in unpredictable gusts of movement. Upping the ante. Ramming my boot into his cock, grinding the heel in and watching his eyes. He is twirling high in the air, lips parted, offering himself to me. His eyes entreat me to use him. And I do, exercising minute control, I coil into him, watching as he floats. This is just the beginning. I constrict his breath, cover his mouth and nose and thrust my teeth into his shoulder, feeling his heart against my tongue.

I lead him to the table and tell him to remove what he must to give me access to his ass. He takes off his pants and socks, folding them neatly and stacking them on top of his boots in the corner. He is wearing a simple leather jock. I order him face down onto the table. He is quivering. Mine, I think. And catch myself. I watch him, building on his fear, and remove my touch. There is only the knife sliding along him, forcing him to remain still. There is only the knife, as silence lays on him like a blanket. I step away, moving quietly, and leave him alone. We will see how much he needs connection, how much fear I can build. We will see, I think slowly to myself, how much distance I can tolerate.

My play is usually about connection. About driving myself inside. About opening someone up to my gaze. My tools are up close and personal. Play is my source of connection, and I usually hurl into it, deep and hard. I don't want to show myself yet. This must be done slowly. I want to see what he can do. I want to wait, before I commit myself to what I have already thought. I will come to that on my terms, in my time.

I collect my favorite canes, needing air between us. Needing that sound that whips through the air and blasts into flesh. Needing controlled, careful cruelty. Canes are a special love of mine. It takes a lot for me to risk thin sticks of wood, easily broken to form deadly weapons. Canes are about my risk, too. Their simple existence menaces. Their joy is unmatchable.

I line up my weapons on a nearby table, carefully. Thinking ahead, I select another item and place it on the table softly. I am ready.

I step back, allowing the necessary distance, and begin from stillness. I place my stripes precisely, just slow enough for him to get the full ripping effect of the bite. I lay lines of piercing sting, not holding back my strokes, saturating him with an invasive assault. There is nothing like the sound of a cane mutilating air, and he shivers at it. I can feel the fear rising off him like steam and breathe it in as my due. I am unforgiving. It will never end. I can loom over him, layering slashes on skin, for eternity. I am breathing deeply. This is meditative. And I realize though there is air and space between us, I am attuned to his breathing. My cock swells at the almost-imperceptible sounds he makes. We are connected. There is no breaking that. I know that he could be halfway across the country, and I would feel the pulse of his blood. I smile at the thought, accepting it. I am ready. Ready to rent his skin with my teeth and tools. To break him open and take a good long taste. To unleash the beast roaming in my skin.

I feel an incredible calm at the roaring in my blood. A new calm. I can fully be who I am in this room, with this man. He is strong enough. And I trust him enough to risk. I pick up my belt, and begin.

There are few tools I have a deeper connection with. I have had this belt since the nineteenth century, and cared for it well. It is a part of me. An extension of my cock and my will. Nothing brings out my beast like my belt. Which is why I keep it at home, and only use it on prey I am going to devour. Until now.

I explain this to him, watching him tremble.

"Please use me, Sir," is all he says.

Mine. Possessiveness washes over me. I double the belt and start slamming him with it, the welts rising rapidly. Vision begins to blur. This is all about sound and movement. My body senses where to strike. My blows hammer him into the table. I can feel a growl building in my throat as his scent shifts. My cock swells, as I hurl the belt into his back in rapid crashing surges.

"Mine," I growl. "Mine to hurt. Mine to use. Mine to feed on. Mine."

The possessiveness rises in me, a tsunami cresting and breaking over him as I blast the belt into his back, rending his skin. Welts form on top of welts, and break the surface. He is moaning as I howl, the beast fully in my skin and oh so hungry. I lay the belt across the back of his neck and crouch on the table above him, eyes focused on the gashes opening his back to me. I drop on top of him, rubbing my chest into the blood on his back.

I breathe the scent of him in and growl happily, "Mine."

I free my cock, swollen to bursting, and shed my pants. I will savor the first real taste. Right now, it's enough to smell it and feel it against my skin and know there is more for the taking. I rub it onto my cock, stroking it in as I close my eyes. I want inside, now. Want to rend him open. Thrust myself into him, bloody and hard. I want to tear his back open with claws and teeth, and feast.

I describe this to him, and he moans his consent.

"Please, Sir," he says softly. "Please."

He is all want and need and craving, and where his hunger meets mine we will crest. Mine. The word fills me, taking me over.

I thrust into him, my cock smeared in his blood, ramming into his ass for my pleasure. He is so open for me, so willing. His groans are loud and true as I fuck him, rubbing my face in the blood on his back. I grip his hips, and stop, embedded in him. I can feel my claws extend right before I slash into his back, ripping him open. The blood flows freely, and I bathe my chest in it, bellowing as I hurl my cock into him. I wrap the belt around his neck, constricting his breath, my cock pounding him into the table, and I bite. Mulled wine. Spicy. Sweet. Tangy. I drink him down, savoring each gulp, thrusting steadily. I release his neck, hear his gasping breaths, and bite harder, feeding.

"Please, Sir," he manages in a throaty whisper.

I lift my head. "Please what, boy?"

This is the first time I have called him boy, and he whimpers at the sound of it.

"Please, Sir. Please may I come, Sir?"

I thrust into him hard, and feel his ass grab me.

"Mine. You are my boy. Mine to fuck. Mine to slash open. Mine to devour. Mine to mark. Mine to command. You may come when I sink my teeth into you again, boy. I want to hear it. Tell me you are mine, and then you may come."

I drive my cock into him, reaming him deeply, and rub my chest against his bloody back. I reach around to grab his cock, gripping it tightly and stroking it in quick bursts. I plunge my teeth into his shoulder. Gnawing him open. Snarling as I drink. My dick pumping into him. "I am yours, Sir. I offer myself freely for your use. I am so glad to be yours, Sir."

144

I explode into him, storms crashing in huge tidal waves. Drinking and coming. Releasing myself and drawing him in. His ass clenches around me in spasms as he bursts, his body bucking and shuddering. I continue to feed. When his body calms, I am sated, and I ease myself out of him slowly. I take my time licking his wounds closed, savoring the taste of him. I pull him up into my arms, smiling.

"Now let's see that cock of yours, boy."

His eyes go wide, he looks down and he starts trembling again. I lift his chin to meet his eyes, and then trace the scars on his chest lightly with my tongue. I lift my head to stare into his eyes again, and slowly unzip the jock, revealing a large black silicone cock. I pump it hard, stroking it against him, where I know he is enlarged by testosterone.

"Did you think I didn't know, boy? After all the centuries I've lived, did you think I did not learn how to read people?"

I grin into his eyes.

"You are my boy. And I am proud to claim you as mine."

I gather him to me, holding him tight, and start imagining possibilities.

THE SALT DUSK
Raith Sargent

The dark grey eyes of dusk opened, and daylight scampered away. Into the trees it ran, the sunlit beams shattering into thousands of odd-shaped splinters. In fiery rebuke of their imminent death, the fractured rays railed in raging color. Orange then a brilliant blood-red, the remnants of the day burned betwixt the shadows. But their murder was assured. Their demise foretold by a million yesterdays that were felled by the same dark hand. Ever so soon their lights dimmed to frail purples; their last breaths gasped in failing pinks. Night entered on mocking tiptoe.

From the grave of trees, a man stepped out into the departing twilight. He wore all shades of white. Cream linen pants draped over pale leather loafers. An ecru cotton, long-sleeved shirt hung open, revealing a stark white muscle shirt clinging to a strong, broad chest. His skin was the color of dark honey, his hair the shade of dark chocolate. Ochre eyes ruled handsomely over a strong jaw, a line of dark pink lips and a nose memorable in its utter mundanity. There was no ill sign of years to his face, his age a tightly spun quandary in the South American moonlight.

The man walked slowly down an old stone path, and although his gait was steady, he held tightly in his left hand a walking stick. The scarred staff was crudely carved from the wood of a monkey puzzle tree. Tiny stumps of amputated branches marred the length of the wood in a macabre collection of birthmarks and death throes. The walking stick further told its sad tale in the odd 'clop-clop-tick' dirge the footfalls played.

The dark forest at the man's retreating back lay silent and waiting.

#

Dusk tasted of salt. It was the only time of the day that the sea air traveled down the gravel road by the inn. Byrne Jacobs sucked its twang from his bottom lip and smiled.

It had been a good day, one he'd remember even if the girls did not. He was playing chaperone to his twenty-one-year-old sister and her best friend, a twenty-two-year-old ingénue from Texas. Both were beautiful and drunk, and he was there to guide their way back to their nightly beds, sans lusty strangers. They had been roaming through South America for two weeks and he had excelled at his guardian duties to the utter consternation of Tracie and Megan. The smug smile he wore on his handsome face was well-deserved; Byrne had literally been the women's worst nightmare.

The girls in sandals, shorts and bikini tops dizzily weaved their drunken steps on and off the gravel path. Byrne, in jeans and a black T-shirt, watched them from behind with a bored eye. He was twenty-seven years old, well past the 'drink me under the table' games of his wickedly raucous youth. Smart enough to be able to laze through college and attractive enough to get all the good invites, his university days had been a blur of booze and sex. Nowadays, he got off on flying his Cessna and watching the profits roll in from his small sight-seeing business off the northern California coast. It was quite a successful business, too. His thirst for adventure and his devil-may-care smile made him a favorite with many tourists and with most people in general. With his blond hair, softly tanned skin and swimmer-physique, his social calendar was still well-filled despite his wildest days being behind him. But family had always come first for him, so when his sister had gotten the crazy idea to explore the outposts of Chile, there was no way in hell he was going to let her go without him. His business was put on hold for three months and guarding his little sister and her friend became his newest purpose in life.

But right now, he longed for the northern Pacific's air. The closest he felt to home on this little island was at twilight when the breezes brought with it sweet memories of his plane and his life in the skies. So he relished the taste of dusk's salt on his lips and wished the lurking night away.

But it was of no use. The evening fell and slowly dragged the lazing trio of travelers down into the daunting Chilean night.

An eerie melody of 'clop-clop-tick' rode gently in on the wind.

#

The sweet scent of chicha swimming on a young woman's breath first marked the travelers as prey. For many months, his hunger had lain dormant inside him. It slept like a beast through winter, awaking hungry and foul-tempered.

The man and his walking stick left the stone path for the gravel road that ran by the inn.

# # # # #

In the palm of the island of Chiloe lay the Colocolo Inn. It was a bleak little house with only three rooms to rent. The light that seeped from its tiny windows was murky and yellow. It was a poor beacon home, but one Byrne and his giggling charges followed gladly. The dark rainforests of the island were frightening enough during the daylight hours, but at night the shivers they sent down the spine were biting.

He hurried the girls on with a few cheeky words, "Bubble baths straight ahead, ladies!"

His sister shot him a one-fingered salute; her friend snapped back a slurred "Fuck you."

Yes, it was definitely time to put this binge to bed …

Suddenly, in a thundering din of thrashing wing-beats, the sky fell to the earth and devoured the little inn whole.

# # # # #

One girl screamed; the other one turned to run.

After a moment of raw, seizing fear, Byrne grabbed both women by the shoulders and dragged them behind him.

In shock all three could only watch as the inn revealed itself not to be gone but only buried. Beneath a hundred pair of vulture wings, the bleak building and its yellow light now cowered. With long, sharp talons the beasts clung to the clapboard walls, spreading their wings out to their full seven-foot span. All was black feathers, the birds' blood-red heads tucked, hidden, down to their chests. The unearthly racket the vultures made was ear-splitting. Joining together their voiceless calls, the carrions trumpeted shrieking hisses to the sky.

The three travelers covered their ears and hunkered down, terrified, to the ground.

A mad scurrying of course fur and tails barreled past the ladies' bare legs, eliciting yelps and a sob from the trio that huddled even closer together. Only Byrne dared to raise eyes enough to identify the fleeing, mouse-like creatures. They were rat-sized animals, resembling

149

opossums. Black rings circled their wide, frantic eyes; their bodies were covered in short, wiry fur. Long, skinny tails curled and uncurled as they grappled for position around the foundation of the inn. A blurb and a photo in the back of some brochure flashed briefly through Byrne's mind as he remembered the animal's name: *monito del monte* or mountain monkey.

The trivial thought vanished into oblivion as three bone-jarring 'BANG!'s rifled out of the trees behind them.

Dead leaves showered down around them as Byrne grabbed the girls' arms preparing to drag them away, but a chilling laugh barked in his left ear stopped Byrne dead.

"Fool!" a deep, teasing voice spat from behind.

Pushing the girls away, issuing a fervent plea for them to flee, Byrne spun around and came face to face with the honey-skinned man in white. He had expected something horrifying; he had not expected beauty. For a stuttered heartbeat, Byrne stood waylaid by the man's sheer magnetism. It sung off his handsome figure in rolling melodies both thrumming and sweet. Surreal and addictive, the pull, however, was mostly frightening. Byrne knew he had to get his charges far away from this creature.

But the piercing steel gaze of the stranger was already locked on the running girls' backs. Not breaking his glare, the man raised his staff and swung it hard against the nearest tree.

'BANG!'

It was the same sound as before and had Byrne wincing away.

The man's face sliced open into a most horrid smile as he purred out between perfectly white shining teeth, "Come, sweetmeats, come."

To Byrne's utter horror, Tracie and Megan suddenly stopped.

"Run!" Byrne cried out in anger and fear. "Run!"

"Come," the man once again beckoned.

The girls' bare shoulders slumped, their arms falling dead at their sides. Tracie and Megan turned. They appeared half-asleep; their drunkenness was gone, replaced by a lethargy that seemed to be sucking the strength from their very core. With half-lidded eyes and emotionless faces, the girls stumbled slowly back to Byrne and the man.

"No!" Byrne screamed and started to run to his sister and her friend.

"No," in a sing-song voice, the man mocked Byrne's plea. His staff once again pounded against the tree.

'BANG!'

Byrne literally froze in his tracks, his legs suddenly rooted down to the ground. Panic flared in Byrne's eyes as he stared down at his immoveable feet. He could move all but his legs, but there was little he could do tied inexplicably to one spot. "Who the hell are you?" he twisted around and angrily spat at the man.

"I am Trauco." Coolly the answer was given, as a cruel god, on a whim, hands down a soul's damnation.

From the same place that he had drawn *monito del monte*, Byrne dragged back what he had heard of the Trauco myth …

The Trauco was said to be a grotesquely deformed goblin that lived in the holes of the trees. With a gnarled staff at his side, he would stalk young women who were foolish enough to wander into his woods. His gaze alone could entrance them, make the women fall at his feet, where he would steal their virginity and leave a child in its stead.

"But …" Byrne mumbled, trying hard to work out all the inconsistencies flying around in his terrified mind.

Trauco enjoyed the boy's confusion for a tantalizing moment or two before explaining haughtily, "Myth is a mask, dear boy. Look behind its paper eyes to find the true horror of life."

Byrne's mind refused to wrap itself around such broad concepts, when the immediate danger was so simple and so keen. In the end, there was only one thing for him to say, "I won't let you have them."

Trauco laughed and drew Byrne's attention back over the boy's shoulder. "But they give themselves to me."

As if on cue, the swaying girls reached behind their backs and released their bikinis from their breasts. Without hesitation, they then reached down to undo their shorts.

"No!" Byrne screamed, trying and failing to run toward the girls again. His cries quickly turned to pleas, "Please, no! She's my sister."

One eyebrow of the beast rose with delight, "Then I will have her first."

Rage fought with tears as Byrne battled to keep thinking straight, "Please! I'll give you anything, do anything."

Trauco snorted, and waved the meaningless words away with his hand, "I take what I want."

Byrne weighed his words for only a heartbeat before calmly offering to the beast, "Then take me."

A genuine smile of surprise rose up on Trauco's face as he conceded to the boy, "How noble."

A sad laugh gurgled up in Byrne's throat. "Not really," he confessed with a steady eye. He was terrified beyond all reason, but his cock still twitched in excitement. He had been with men before and enjoyed it. Sex was a game he played well; sex was a game Byrne could win.

Trauco nodded and slowly dragged his piercing gaze down and back up the length of Byrne's body. "And what would I do with a man?"

Byrne chuckled sourly as he challenged, "I won't play noble if you don't play dumb."

Clearly affronted by the boy's attitude, Trauco's lips curled up in a snarl. "What is stopping me from taking you all?"

"A willing fuck," Byrne boldly replied. "How long since you've had one of those?"

Interest clearly piqued, the goblin nonetheless vowed, "You resist, and I will kill you."

"You touch either of them and you'll have to," Byrne swore in return. "You let them go right now and never go after them again, and I will let you fuck me anyway you want me."

"Hardly a fair trade," Trauco snorted, though the vein in his neck beat faster.

Byrne recognized the sign of arousal and played on it with his last available move. With contempt warring with seduction he still managed to mask his voice behind a purr, "I dare you, Trauco."

"And I accept." With a flick of his wrist the girls turned away and walked slowly toward the still vulture-laden inn. As they neared, the carrions covering the door rose to the sky allowing the half-dressed women passage inside. Once the door closed behind them, the vultures returned and re-took the door and its frame. Again, the inn was encrusted in thick, black feathers. With a smug curl of his lip, Trauco turned to Byrne and vowed, "You run, you die."

"I won't run."

"Soon, you will beg to." In a move of ungodly speed, Trauco shot his arm out and wrapped his fingers securely around Byrne's neck. There was no time for a gasp as the goblin jerked the boy up on his toes. With a smile one could only call evil, Trauco hissed, "Fly for me, boy!" An upward thrust of inhuman strength flung Byrne up, ten feet off of the ground.

His arms flailing wildly, his legs all askew, Byrne tried to regain some semblance of balance as he toppled up into the night air. But as he reached the crest of his tossing, all his movements suddenly stopped. The very fibers of his skin tightened and turned to pale stone. He fell to the ground as heavily as lead, not a muscle in his body could Byrne so much as twitch. Even his eyes could not move; the ocean-blue orbs laid wide open and panicked.

Trauco stood smugly over the boy's frozen form. "Are you afraid?" he sneered at the handsome edifice of fear.

Only a gurgle from the throat of stone answered.

"I could leave you like this." Trauco looked back to the inn. "Taste of the sweetmeats in there. Gift you my son as your nephew." His eyes drew languorously back to the man on the ground.

Awkwardly sprawled, his arms and legs frozen at odd angles, Byrne resembled a magnificent bug pinned to a mad entomologist's board.

Wetting his lips, Trauco knelt down by his side. "Or ..." he slowly unzipped Byrne's jeans and pushed them and his underwear down past his hips. The boy's dick, long and delightfully full, was frozen at quarter mast. Trauco lecherously grinned, "Or I could lick of this meat." His tongue partook of the delicatessen that was Byrne's cock. Up and down, around and around, Trauco greedily lathered the shaft.

An eternity passed for the frozen man.

With cheeks rosy from his exertion, Trauco raised back up to his knees and glared down into the trapped blue eyes. "Or I could knead these balls," he palmed the rocksacs roughly, "As I prepare this hole for my seed." With his eyes burning in filthy desire, Trauco dove down to eat. The anal treasure was hard to reach, but his tongue rapturously enjoyed the journey. Once successfully there, he rimmed the boy with a gourmet's palette. Well-satisfied with the allure of the appetizer, Trauco kneeled upright again and asked of Byrne with a smirk, "And you will allow this willingly?"

The stone did not answer.

"One opportunity to prove this I give you." With a flick of his hand he released the boy from his stone casing. "A willing fuck? Show me."

In a move either bold or foolhardy, Byrne swept Trauco's legs out from under him, the goblin-man hitting the ground with an ungainly 'Oomph!' Before any lethal countermeasures could be made, Byrne threw himself on top of Trauco and shot his tongue deep within the beast's beautiful mouth. Not caring if his sanity had betrayed his mind for his cock, Byrne allowed the madness of carnal need to devour him.

Fingers of steel clamped around the back of Byrne's head, driving the boy's eager tongue farther down Trauco's throat. The goblin moaned.

Energized further by this vocal endorsement, Byrne yanked his own T-shirt over his head, relinquishing the delicious mouth for only a moment. Digging his fingers deep into the chest of Trauco, he grabbed hold of his white undershirt and ripped it free of his body. The open, long-sleeved shirt met the same violent fate.

With both men now bare-chested, Byrne slowly rubbed his hardened nipples up and down the lightly furred expanse of skin below him. He could feel the man's nubs tighten and firm as they rolled against his straining pecs. It was Byrne's turn to moan. But his assault did not lessen. Grabbing his own already displaced jeans he shoved them down to his knees and expertly shimmied them down to his ankles and then off his now bare feet.

Their tongues still tangled up together, Byrne had to push himself off to gain breath enough to gasp, "I'm going to fuck you."

Crushing the sides of Byrne's face with his hands, Trauco stared him dead in the eyes. Threats were made, accepted, re-challenged all in the silent, gladiatorial glare between the two men.

In the end, Trauco growled a breathless, "Yes."

And Byrne took him.

Linen pants were ripped off of legs already splayed wide. Shoes were kicked off with ravaging toes. Shoulders held down, nipples were bit, sucked and then bit hard again. A tongue trailed down to a navel, hot breath blew. Hands clamped down on hips. A mouth swallowed whole a cock hard and weeping. Suck, suck, suck … until balls tightened and threatened to release. Byrne drew back, yanked Trauco's thighs up in the air and slammed them down against the man's own heaving chest. The starred hole of the goblin-man opened and begged to be filled.

Byrne rammed his cock full into Trauco's body.

In a garbled gasp, Trauco cried out. Fingers dug into the earth.

Byrne pulled back, thrust deeper.

A prostate was hit. The goblin's mind disintegrated into a kaleidoscope of dizzying colors.

Thrust.

Honey-colored skin bled sweat.

Thrust.

Lungs spasmed.

Thrust.

A dark heart seized.

Thrust!

Thrust!

And as the world imploded, a goblin's cock painted a mortal's stomach white and man's cock filled an ungodly star with cream.

Each collapsed into the other's arms and dreamed.

# # # # #

Trauco awoke and shoved the man off of his chest and free of his body. Byrne only groaned as he was rolled over to his back. Trauco easily gained his feet and re-clothed himself without a glance at the spent nude body stretched out on the ground before him. Once he had regained his immaculately dressed form, Trauco took his walking stick and beat it once upon a tree.

'BANG!'

Byrne bucked once on the ground as he was ripped awake. Bleary, confused eyes widened as memory overrode the bliss of ignorance. He pulled himself up on his arms and shuffled quickly back and away.

A smile grew wildly across Trauco's face, contorting his features into something simply evil. "Every night you'll remember. And every night you'll yearn for me again."

Without awaiting a reply, Trauco pounded his staff hard upon the ground. A ball of green fire erupted from the earth and swallowed the man-beast whole. Slowly the fire burned out and the smoke died away, revealing Trauco's true self.

Gone were the clothes; in their stead sheets of bark sown together with twine covered the lengths of now-puckered skin. A dirt-colored hat with a wide, lax brim and a conical top lazed to its left, covered the creature's head. His features were grotesque, swollen and deformed. His legs were mere stumps; his arms little more than twisted flesh upon broken bone. His voice had too disappeared, replaced with grunts equally guttural and crude. The only things that remained of his previous self were his eyes. Clear and piercing, they brokered no lies as to the harm that could yet be done.

With jaws of chilled teeth and the breath of hell, the wind swept down from the monkey puzzle trees and devoured the ghastly vision whole.

As the vultures slowly departed, the mountain monkeys slipping away, Byrne Jacobs whispered to the foul-tasting air, "And you will remember me, Trauco, as the man who fucked the beast."

# # # # #

The bright white eyes of dawn opened, and the night cowered away.

REVENGE OF THE LIVING DEAD
Simon Sheppard

I struggled toward the entrance of the tomb. Gripping a guttering torch, I staggered up the long, sloping passage, desperately calling out into the flickering gloom. But when I reached the gate of the sepulchre, the metal door was shut and locked. 'Twas then that foreboding turned to fear. I pounded on the steel till my fists were bloodied, shouted till I grew hoarse. But the watchman must have scarpered back to the workers' camp, where he'd be screwing some harlot, or getting drunk on bad brandy. By Christ, I was trapped in the underground tomb of a long-dead Pharaoh, with none to rescue me until the next day! Or worse – the day after that, since it was Thursday, the day before the Muslim Sabbath.

Damn and blast! Two days confined with the relics of the long-dead past, in a stuffy tomb, which would soon, when the torches sputtered out, sink into inky blackness! Into grim, dusty silence ...

Hunger, thirst, the horrible closeness of the tomb, all were sure to prove a grueling trial. Surely, the network of small ventilation holes, which the fellahin had drilled would keep me from asphyxiation. And I remembered hearing that men could last for days without water. Nevertheless, panic gripped me by my dry throat. Would I prove worthy of the test?

I cursed myself for coming to Egypt in the first place. But what other choice had I? For I was the son of Lord John Banning, the world's most prominent, nay, exalted archaeologist. And not the favored son. My younger brother, Reggie, was the apple of Father's eye. Reggie was a renowned Egyptologist in his own right. Reggie had given Father a much-adored grandson. I, on the other hand, was a wastrel, a ne'er-do-well threatened with disinheritance. My grip on my share of the old Lord's estate had been shaky at best, and refusing to travel to Egypt to act as Father's reluctant assistant would surely have threatened my very future.

And thus came I to the Levant, the scene of Father's mightiest success, a triumph greater than the discovery of the tomb of Tutankhamun. Always a petty, resentful man, Lord John had spent several years plotting to outdo the Tutankhamun expedition. And by equal parts of ruthless cunning and utter luck, he had. He'd made the greatest archaeological find of all time: Pharaoh Kharis's tomb, a far grander site than Tut's paltry digs.

I'd arrived in Egypt, fabled Land of the Pharaohs, and found myself amidst choking dust, stifling heat, wretched peasantry. Those in Britain who idealize the mystic Orient have never had to battle off a swarm of leprous beggar-boys tearing at one's sleeves. To my father, Egypt held out the promise of even-greater wealth, even more-universal fame. But Egypt had nothing to offer me, not a bloody thing. Except Mehemet.

Mehemet was one of the laborers hired by Father, a dark-skinned young man of startlingly handsome face and form. I had noticed him when I first visited the dig. Stripped to the waist, sunlight gleaming on bronze flesh, he was hauling bucket loads of rubble from the tomb. He gazed straight at me, nay, through me with dark, knowing eyes. Insolent bugger! I thought. Yet something in his mien troubled me, and in the days that followed, our eyes often met. I soon began slipping him a piastre or two whenever I saw him. Though our fingers barely touched as I handed him the coins, the transient contact always sent a shock through my body, a strange surging through my loins.

It wasn't till Isobel's farewell party that our contact became complete. My fiancée, who had accompanied me from London, was due to depart for home the following day. A dinner in her honor was held at the English consul's house in Luxor, its open-air courtyard turned into a rough sort of banquet hall. To my surprise, Mehemet had been pressed into service as a waiter, resplendent in a gleaming white galabiyya.

The party drank toast after toast to my fiancée. But my attention was diverted by the closeness of Mehemet, his dark skin scrubbed clean of the dust of toil, his curly black hair oiled and shining. And as I grew more inebriated, my distraction grew apace.

"Are you all right, my darling?" Isobel asked, concern in her voice. In the heat of the late desert afternoon, her pale cheeks had taken on a rosy blush, adding to her loveliness. She was the very picture of the flower of English womanhood. At that moment, I couldn't have cared less.

I saw my chance. "I am feeling a mite unwell," I said. "Perhaps I should go inside and lie down for a bit."

Mehemet was clearing off the remnants of the fish course. I caught his eye as I slipped through the consulate's louvered doors. When I looked back, he was watching me. He nodded. Neither of us needed to say a word.

I made my way upstairs, to a bedroom overlooking the courtyard. I sat, smoking a cigar, and waited.

Within minutes, I heard the door click shut. I turned to look. It was Mehemet.

"Master," he said. It was the first I'd heard him speak. He hurried to me, knelt at my feet, and laid his beautiful head upon my thigh. "Master," he said again.

Tentatively, I laid a hand upon his shining curls. He nuzzled his face into my leg. My manhood, already stiffening, grew hard and began to throb. When I spread my legs, he moved his head between my thighs until his face rested upon my swollen crotch, He opened his lips and gnawed upon the erect shaft through the fabric of my trousers. My God, I thought, if we're discovered ... but I let him continue. Isobel had never done this for me, nor was she likely to. I took another puff of my cigar.

Mehemet rose to his feet and pulled his galabiyya over his head. He stood naked before me. The late afternoon light slanting through the slats of the shutters cast bright stripes over his naked, dusky flesh. His long, circumcised phallus curved upward from the dark bush of his crotch. "You can suck if you want," he said, in heavily-accented English.

I shook my head. I was a man, after all, and not about to do such a thing with another man. And I, as an Englishman, was certainly not about to do such a thing with a native. Neither, of course, would I ever allow him inside me. I'd heard that the wogs were all buggers, but viewed being buggered themselves as being beneath their masculine dignity. So it came as something a surprise when Mehemet turned his back to me, reached behind, and spread the cheeks of his fundament, exposing a tightly puckered hole. "Then you can have me back here, Master," he said, unhesitatingly. Shamelessly.

I was on my feet in a shot, trousers dropping to my ankles. He bent, half-standing, over the bed, as I stood behind him and plowed my manhood into him. A bit of spit was all the lubrication I needed; he quite obviously had been sodomized before. He opened fully for me, his insides soft and hot as the desert air.

The sound of singing – English songs – filtered through the window as I rammed into him again and again, grabbing fiercely at his shoulders, pumping my seed into his lean, brown arse.

He had the good sense not to shoot off onto the neatly-made bed. When I was done with him, he slipped his galabiyya back over his body, concealing his still-hard member, and slipped out of the room. By then, my cigar had developed quite an ash.

By the time I returned to the party, dessert had been served, and lanterns lit against the night. "Feeling better?" Isobel asked in a tone of concern.

"Yes," I replied, and meant it.

"Here, take this, my darling," she said, removing the little silver crucifix which hung around her neck and fastening it around my own. "May it protect you always in this heathen land." I smiled a secret smile at my bride-to-be.

I'm ashamed to confess that after Isobel's departure for Britain I continued my assignations with Mehemet. In a storage shed, a workman's tent, a gully in the bone-dry hills of the Valley of the Kings, anywhere we could find a few moments of privacy, we went at it. Indeed, the first time I saw him after Isobel's party, his back still bore the marks of the punishment he'd received for absenting himself from his serving duties. But they soon faded, and I'd sometimes briefly stroke his well-muscled shoulders as I mounted his arse. To me, our encounters seemed quick, brutal, signally lacking in civilized concern. But, I'm sure he enjoyed the attentions of a white man, for, like a beast, he proffered his hungry bum every chance that he got.

Until, that is, one evening, when one of my father's native foremen chanced upon us at an inopportune moment, and our indiscretions were found out.

"What the bloody hell were you two playing at?" roared my father, when I had been called before him. "I could take it out of Mehemet's hide, but he's been an excellent workman, and I'll be damned if I'll blame some benighted fuzzy-wuzzy for the depredations of my dissolute son. Well, that's an end to it, you hear me? When we return to England, you shall marry Isobel and give me grandchildren. Grandsons. And if I ever, EVER hear of such a thing again, you'll not only be disinherited, you'll be disowned! You shall no longer be any son of mine! Is that understood?"

"Yes, sir," I said, managing my most convincingly sheepish tone.

Father's eyes were still bulging, face red. "There's that foreman to be taken care of, but that should prove no problem." he said, half to himself. "But what the bloody hell am I going to do about you?"

I couldn't think of a single appropriate thing to say.

"Drop your trousers," he commanded me.

"WHAT?"

"You heard me," he sneered. "If you're going to behave like a sodding schoolboy, I shall have to treat you like one."

The stroke of Father's cane, when it came down upon my naked arse, caused an odd admixture of pain and pleasure, bringing memories of being disciplined by my handsome public school headmaster. Even back then, as a trembling schoolboy, I understood the sensations to be something beyond mere pain, something that brought forth a dark, near-unendurable delight. And now, despite myself, I found the strokes of the cane traveling straight to my soul. Only the fear of being seen erect by my Father kept my cock at bay.

And when my arse was thoroughly warmed and my trousers once again in place, I knew that I would never bugger Mehemet again, but that I would refrain out of fear of genteel poverty, not fear of the cane.

My father said no more of the matter. I never again set eyes on the foreman who'd informed on us. But Mehemet would not be placated. I tried my best to avoid him, and when he was near, never looked directly at him. But at odd moments he would appear at my side. "Please, Master," he'd whine, importuning with those liquid Levantine eyes of his. "Why won't you see me again? Why won't you fuck me? The Big Master will never know." By God, he had lost all sense of discretion, sometimes even approaching me when others were around. He would have to be dealt with.

But I realized that Father (though I assumed he had dealt with the foreman) would never solve the problem of this pestiferous Egyptian boy. Rather, the old Lord would expect me to be man enough to deal with the problem myself. And so, after one harassment too

161

many, I took the bothersome wog aside and arranged to meet him that evening by the entrance to Kharis's tomb, shortly after the workers had gone back to their hovels, but before the night watchman was due to lock the door to the subterranean tomb. I was at the end of my patience, and I full well realized that if reasoning proved ineffective, I might have to resort to something more brutal. But one more native found dead in the dusty hills of Egypt ... who would really care?

I hoped, of course, that it wouldn't come to that, but I decided to fortify myself just in case. I consumed, I'm afraid, rather too many gin-and-its, and, woozy from the heat, ducked into the tomb for a bit of shade. The workmen were finishing up their day's labors, and didn't so much as glance at me. I went ever deeper into the tomb of Kharis, into the inner sanctum. I curled up behind some packing crates piled beside the sarcophagus, intending to just shut my eyes for a moment. But I must have passed quite thoroughly out, never hearing the warning cry of the watchman as he locked the heavy metal door.

And thus was I trapped in Kharis's tomb.

To distract myself, I attempted to focus my attention upon the tomb's decor, the frescoes I'd seen day after dusty day but never closely studied before. The sloping corridor was lined by primitive paintings of scenes from everyday life: the hunting of waterfowl, fishing, the baking of bread. And beside the pictures, hieroglyphic texts that none but a few could read. At the end of the corridor, the door to the inner tomb was flanked by two statues of the jackal-god Anubis, ebony-black and gold, gilt glinting in the torchlight.

Once inside the antechamber to the Pharaonic tomb, the paintings became the usual barbaric melange of gods and goddesses: oddly shaped half-naked women with crescent moons on their heads, ocher-colored men with the heads of animals. Thoth, the baboon-headed god of wisdom, Hathor, the cow-eared goddess of something-or-other. My father's impatient lectures on Egyptian mythology vanished from my mind. Panic again arose. What was I to do, imprisoned alone for days?

I made my way back into the burial chamber itself, where the remaining torches still shone in the thin oxygen. Here, the paintings were of the dead king and his court, and of the god Min-Amun, Lord of Procreation. Pharaoh Kharis had supposedly been the manifestation of this Min-Amun, an imposing fellow always pictured wearing a headdress of two tall plumes, carrying a flail, and exhibiting a most noticeable erection. Indeed, portrayals of the mummified god showed the big, stiff thing sticking clear out of his wrappings. Most of the gods may have faded into a fuzzy never-neverland in my mind, I might have forgotten the details of Set's slaying of his brother-god Osiris, but the image of Min-Amun remained clear in memory. "And oddly enough," I recalled my father saying, "for a Pharaoh so identified with the god of procreation, Kharis never wed, and apparently had no children. He was, as far as we know, damn near the only bachelor king that Egypt ever had."

The tomb chamber was still cluttered with piles of funerary objects, though some of the most valuable finds had already been crated up and shipped off to the British Museum. But the great statue of the seated Pharaoh still stood against the far wall, and before it lay the immense sarcophagus, its massive granite top still in place, the golden coffin we knew lay within still unglimpsed, unopened. Only when most of the objects been cleared from the room could the huge lid be dragged off and the priceless golden image of the king safely be removed from its resting place.

I took some of the straw destined to crate up items for removal and made a makeshift bed in one corner of the room, near a beastly statue of a hippopotamus-headed goddess. I sat down and stared blankly at the treasures heaped before me, wishing to be anywhere but here, anyplace but this heathen country. And as I sat there, the torches, one by one, began to flicker and die.

In times of stress, I often resort to self-stimulation to calm myself. And so I unbuttoned my trousers, pulled out my member, spit into my hand, and began to caress myself, stroking and squeezing. At first, I remained limp. I tried thinking of Isobel, the shape of her breasts, her cunny, but still no response. It was not till my thoughts turned to Mehemet, to the feeling of his hot, slick hole, that my manstaff began to rise, the head reddening, slipping out past the foreskin, swelling in my hand. I pictured Mehemet's dark penis against my own, remembering his animal grunts as I'd torn into him. I cupped my balls in my other hand and pulled at them as my strokes quickened. Mehemet! I shot off, catching the flow in my hand, licking the hot, briny fluid from my palm. And felt a relaxation, a kind of peace. The room was nearly dark now, a single flame remaining. I closed my eyes.

Yes, it was a shame about Mehemet. But the situation had become quite unsuitable and, attractive though he might be, the troublesome brown boy would have to be taken care of. To that end, should worse come to worst, I'd brought along a long Arabic dagger. Fat lot of good it would do me now!

The last torch flickered out. I was alone in the awful darkness now. Instinctively, I grasped the crucifix that Isobel had given me, held it tightly enough to feel it bite into my palm. But it provided neither comfort nor peace.

And then I heard it. Felt it rather than actually heard it at first. A perturbation of the air. And then a scraping, the eerie sound of stone against stone. The grating grew louder, and a shaft of greenish light sprang up through the darkness, till my eyes could discern movement in the gloom.

I was aghast. Two men had appeared out of nowhere and, with superhuman strength, were dragging open the cover of the sarcophagus. As they did so, the ever-brightening green light took on a golden cast. Light was flooding from the sarcophagus, from the long-dead Pharaoh's bier.

And the two men! They weren't men at all! Their bodies were human, but the two had heads of beasts! Baboon-headed Thoth. And falcon-headed Horus, lifting the granite slab with his left hand, and holding in his right hand the ankh, cross-like symbol of life.

The two ghastly beings lifted the stone cover as though it were made of merest pasteboard, and leaned it against the wall. The little room was flooded with light. And then the chanting commenced. I heard it, my ears must have heard it, and yet it seemed to be echoing within my very brain. And, somehow, I could understand every word.

He has wakened, He who is in health,

And they lifted off the elaborately-carved cover of the mummy case and set it aside.

Min-Amun, Lord of Eternity, who created the Everlasting.

And they lifted off the lid of a second case, nested inside the first, also in the form of the dead Pharaoh, but even more beautiful, even more heavily gilded than the first. And now the glow from the sarcophagus was a bright gold.

His bull-horns mighty, his face beautiful,
He is the Lord of the Serpent.
His head wears the tall White Crown.

And Thoth and Horus removed the inmost case, made of purest beaten gold. It shone from within like an uncanny sun.

The gods rejoice at the sight of His beauty.
When they behold Him their hearts spring to life!

And from the coffin arose – somehow, somehow! – the long-dead Pharaoh Kharis. A golden mask was over his face. His body was wrapped in linen winding-sheets. In his right hand he held a flail, the many-tailed whip that symbolizes divine power. And from him jutted a huge, hard phallus, the shaft of Min-Amun.

He climbed, levitated really, from the great stone sarcophagus, and then approached, towering above me, glowing with golden light. I could scarce believe my eyes. I held fast to the precious crucifix around my neck, Isobel's gift, and prayed that all this would prove to be a mere phantasm.

But it was real, for Kharis's mummified left hand reached down and grabbed hold of the cross's silver chain. I gripped the crucifix as tightly as I could, until I felt its metal burning into my flesh. But the long-dead Pharaoh, with one small gesture, ripped it from my neck and grabbed it from my hand.

Praise be unto you, creator of all that is,
Lord of the Truth and Father of the Gods.

Thoth and Horus, chanting, approached me, grabbed me by my elbows and dragged me to my feet. The mummy extended a dead hand, reached beneath my jacket, and pulled my dagger from its hidden sheath. Starting at my throat, he used the razor-sharp blade to slice into my clothing, cutting open my linen shirt, cutting through my belt, down the front of my trousers. Tatters of cloth hung from my half-naked body. I stood exposed before the Pharaoh Kharis, the king who had become the god Min-Amun. I squirmed against the grip of the gods to no avail, for their ferocious grips held me tight. And to my great shame, the excitement of the moment had somehow aroused me, so that my cock was hard, as hard as Min-Amun's, if not nearly as large.

Thoth and Horus forced me to my knees, face-to-face with Min-Amun's resurrected penis. I knew what I was to do. I did not wish to do so, for it went against my very nature, but I was powerless to resist. Stripped of my will, I opened my mouth. The dead Pharaoh's phallus slid against my tongue, prying my mouth ever wider, probing the back of my throat. It tasted earthy, salty, and sweet as decay. And I gulped it down.

Oh god with countless names,
Who arises in the East

165

And sets on the Western Horizon!

Against my better will, against all judgment, I was swallowing the powerful shaft, the cock of eternity.

You who are born each morning,
And every day overthrow your foes!

What, oh what, had come over me? Greedily as a baby, I nursed at the source of life, sucked at its heft, longed to drink its steaming nectar. But it was not to be, for the musky root of god withdrew from my straining jaws. Who amongst us can name the strange spell I was under, explain why I thirsted for more?

Thoth and Horus dragged me roughly to my feet. Led to the foot of the granite sarcophagus, I was stretched over its great, hollow form, my torso over the golden casket that had, for millennia, held Kharis's mummy. Held it, that is, until now. Bent over at the waist, ripped bits of clothing still hanging from my back and ankles, I was naked and vulnerable. And yet, strange to relate, I felt something approaching peace, in readiness for whatever was to come. Using strips of linen winding-cloth, the two gods bound my wrists to large iron rings set into the sides of the sarcophagus. My ankles, too, were tied to, I suppose, similar rings in the floor.

I peered over my shoulder, at the golden mask of Kharis, the shining visage of Min-Amun. And then I looked down into the empty casket, its inner surface painted with a starry night sky. The goddess Nut, giving birth to the dawn, surmounted the infinite heavens.

And then the flail came down. Its heavy leather thongs thudded into my shoulder, stinging my flesh again and again, first one shoulder, then the other. With each stroke, the sensation intensified, began to glow. Certainly, one might regard this as "punishment," though for what transgression I knew not. But a deep part of me understood it to be something else as well: initiation. An initiation into mysteries darker than Christianity, older than time. As the flail whipped my flesh, moving down now from my shoulders to my buttocks, I stared into the emptiness of the painted sky and felt that I was flying. What should have been pain became a strange sort of pleasure, and my cock swelled and rose to its fullest extent, penetrating the empty space where dead Kharis had lain.

Baboon-headed Thoth and falcon-headed Horus had resumed their unearthly chant:

He who rescues the fearful from oppression,

Who wisely judges between the wretched and the strong,
O Lord of Understanding, from whose mouth flows power,
For love of you the River Nile arose.

The flogging ceased. I knew then what would come next, what must come next. I felt the linen-wrapped hands of Kharis upon my buttocks, kneading the flesh, separating the globes, exposing my vulnerable, virginal hole. Oh Christ! I thought. Oh no! And yet part of me wanted all this to happen, a desire which, to my shame, I still can't fully explain.

The penetration, when it came, was a sensation of sudden, searing pain, followed near-immediately by a sort of delicious fullness. With every stroke, the cock of god entered further, opening me, sanctifying me. My manhood throbbed mightily, my swaying balls were full to bursting. Over and over, with piston-like strokes, golden-faced Kharis rammed into me, shoving me against the stone of the sarcophagus, causing me to strain against my bonds.

That such a fate should befall an Englishman ... I thought, and then, unable to complete the sentence, I thought no more.

A hand appeared before my face, against the starry sky. The hand bore a golden ankh, the symbol of life. It was the hand of Horus. I kissed the amulet, as I knew I must surely be meant to do. And then I kissed the hand itself, the Hand of God. It was like kissing the Sun.

The fucking increased in ferocity, if such a thing were possible. And then the flailing resumed, striking at my outside while my insides were being torn apart. I was quite beside myself with terror and joy. I wanted it all: the revenge of the dead Pharaoh, the presence of the Living God, the nectar of heaven. I wanted, needed, Min-Amun to sow his hot seed inside me, as he had once made fertile the Valley of the Nile.

The explosion, when it came, burst forth from deep within me. The great phallus of Min-Amun let flow His seed, spurting and flooding inside me, and pushing out from my own throbbing manhood load upon load of gushing semen, great gouts which flew streaming into Nut's night sky. I called out, in words I had not known I knew, "O Ra adored in Karnak, appearing great in the House of Creation, Sovereign and Lord of the gods, all Hail!"

And then everything went black.

When I regained consciousness, Mehemet was kneeling over me, shaking me, a look of concern on his dark face.

"Master, Master, are you all right?" he asked. "When you did not appear at the appointed time, I was worried. I went to find the watchman, who gave me his keys. What has happened to you? Why are you here?"

And indeed I must have presented a baffling sight, for I was lying naked on the pile of straw in the corner of the tomb, my torn clothes in a jumble before the statue of the King.

I looked around. The tomb, lit by the light of Mehemet's torch, seemed otherwise undisturbed. The lid of the stone sarcophagus was firmly in its place. How could I explain to this ignorant brown boy what had happened, what I thought had happened, what might not have occurred at all? There were simply no words for what I felt.

I grabbed for the crucifix around my neck, Isobel's gift to me. It was gone. In its place hung the golden ankh of Horus. I suppose I must have gasped. As though impelled by an unearthly force, I lifted it from my body and slipped it over the head of the kneeling Mehemet.

Mehemet pulled off his galabiyya, draping it tenderly over my nude body, and sat upon the straw beside me, gently placing my head upon his naked lap.

I'm not altogether ashamed to admit that in those circumstances, at that time, I felt a certain tenderness toward him. I turned my head, so I could inhale the smell of his crotch, yeasty and sweet as the smell of the workers' flatbread baking in the desert morning. And then I kissed his penis, which stirred to life beneath my touch, a brown snake arising from the rushes of his jet-black hair. I took the thing into my mouth, suckling at it like an infant at its mother's breast, and fell into a deep sleep.

As Mehemet, still-naked, led me back to the camp through the chill of early dawn, I knew what I must do. I gathered my things, left a terse note for my father, and, the now-clothed brown boy at my side, headed out from the Valley of the Kings.

Using the not-inconsiderable money I had with me, we two headed north to Alexandria, where I established myself in a shabby sort of luxury. And together we lived, to outward appearance, as Master and servant. Only the gold amulet around his neck gave evidence of our true relationship. But on most nights, Mehemet stole to my bed. And on most of those nights, I would fuck him, though he never, of course, was permitted to penetrate me.

My time in Alexandria was comfortable enough. For a while. I associated with a small band of adventurers and expatriates, many of them men like myself, bachelors living with their serving-boys. Mehemet did my bidding. Life in Egypt settled into a comfortable routine.

And yet, as those of you who have tried to live in isolation from civilization know, my existence grew stale after a while. I became tired of the crowded, filthy streets, the gabble of a strange tongue, my reliance on the same small circle of friends. And my pile of cash grew ever-smaller.

Mehemet, who had once been so docile and devoted, steadily grew more insistent in his demands. The peasant cheekily let it be known that he wished, indeed took it as his right, to penetrate me. He seemed to regard my refusal as a personal affront. The boy soon granted me fewer and fewer of his sexual favors, and was sulky and distant when he did. He no longer wore the gold ankh which I'd given him, but kept it in a little box in his room. I was forced to seek solace elsewhere.

And my father, who had somehow managed to locate me, sent word that I was not only disinherited, but forthwith was no son of his.

So I did what any wise man would do in such a circumstance. One morning while Mehemet was buying vegetables at the souq, I went off to the port and booked passage on a steamship back to Britain, not neglecting to reclaim the golden ankh before I left. I bid farewell to that dusty, heathen land, my departure having left me with no regrets, none worth mentioning.

Back in London, Father's fame was in full flower. He was often asked to speak before the Explorers' Club and the like, for his explorations in Egypt had made quite a sensation. In particular, the discovery of a silver crucifix, gripped in the hand of the embalmed and buried Pharaoh, provoked widespread speculation. Some took it to be proof of the desecration of the tomb by a prior intruder, though this seemed to defy all evidence. Others took it to be a miraculous portent of the birth of Our Lord. If Isobel found the crucifix to be of familiar appearance, she never said a word. And so the cross in the mummy's hand remained unexplained, yet another of the Mysteries of Ancient Egypt.

My Father, celebrated, successful, and possessed of a swelling bank account, proved to be in an uncharacteristically forgiving mood.

By the time Isobel and I announced our upcoming nuptials, I had been welcomed back into the bosom of the family and reinstated in Father's will.

I settled into domestic bliss with my wife, who eventually gave me three children, one of them, fortunately, a boy. Isobel proved to be all that a man could hope for in a mate (although her reluctances in the bedroom did eventually compel me to make arrangements elsewhere.) Only now and again did the image of Mehemet, unbidden, arise in my mind.

All in all, my life was happy and rich. The allowance I received was generally sufficient. But when an unexpected reversal of fortune left me strapped for funds, the golden ankh provided salvation. For the amulet, whose existence I had kept secret, brought a tidy sum from a private collector. And after that, I never thought of Mehemet again, from that day down to this. His image had vanished from my memory. Though sometimes ...

Eventually, my Father died, as die we all surely must, leaving me his title and most of his estate. Only estrangement from my brother Reggie clouded my most satisfactory life. Yes, despite Reggie's mysterious, tragic death, despite the crumbling of the Empire, I've been, I suppose, quite happy. I've lived out my life as best I could.

And I never returned to Egypt again.

Now that I am an old man myself, a widower in his decline, I thought it best to set down this tale and leave it for you, my son, to read after my death. I realize my account sounds fantastical, even preposterous, and I know not what you'll make of it. I hope that you won't think any the less of me when you read how I succumbed, however briefly, to the temptations of the Levant. For I know that times have changed, perhaps too quickly, and what was unspeakable then is talked of today, albeit in hushed tones. Perhaps you'll hand this account on to your own sons, by way of a cautionary tale. Life is after all, my son, a strange affair, full of compromise and peril, and without strength of will we are left with only ... only ...

And perhaps now you'll understand why I was never able to explain to you, no matter how you wondered, however often you asked, how such a burn was made; that strange mark blazoned on the palm of your Papa's hand, that deep and abiding scar in the shape of a cross.

A VERY HANDSOME MAN
Wayne Summers

One stray cat reclining on the doorstep as if it owned the place would have been a curiosity. With a growl and wave of the hand one could have scared it off the porch and sent it scampering across the lawn to the neighbor's porch, thereby making it their problem. However, thirteen cats congregated on the porch, steps and the path in front of them is an entirely different matter.

"What do they want?" Clive asked peering through the curtains.

James, a forty-five-year-old writer who shared his spacious townhouse with Clive, glanced up from the computer screen, frowning.

"I don't know that they want anything," he replied returning his attention to his manuscript. "Why don't you go out and ask them?"

Clive's smile evaporated. He clicked his teeth and threw himself onto the Italian leather couch. The fifteen-year age difference between them was sometimes an insurmountable chasm that overwhelmed him with all its complexities. Even after being together for a decade, he sometimes got the feeling that James considered himself a little superior to him; the one with the upper hand.

"I'm serious," he continued. "Why are they out there? You have to admit it's a bit strange."

"Maybe Cook has given them something to eat, thrown them the breakfast scraps," said James, "Though I'll be pissed off if she has. The last thing I want is damn cats pissing all over the front step. Once the sun hits it, it'll reek for weeks."

Clive made a small noise of agreement but his eyes were riveted to the collection of cats.

The following morning, Clive discovered that the cats had not dispersed during the night and had in fact settled in to the point where they didn't appear to be the slightest bit perturbed when he stepped through them to get the morning mail. On the contrary, they snaked their way around him, purring and rubbing themselves against his legs as he leant down to empty the mailbox. The thought occurred to him to shoo them away, but he decided against it. If James wasn't worried about them then why should he? Nevertheless, it was disconcerting to have thirteen sets of eyes on him as he made his way back up the path. Images of Hitchcock's *The Birds* flashed in his mind's eye.

"What are you looking at?" he asked suddenly.

He lunged at one of them, meaning only to scare it, but the cat was not intimidated in the slightest. It hissed and swiped at him with four claws extended and ready for business. The attack was unexpected and set his heart racing.

"Those cats are a fucking menace," he said at the breakfast table. "You'll have to call the exterminator."

"Are you still going on about them?" asked James. "Let them be. They'll leave when they're ready. Cook has promised me she isn't feeding them, and if I know anything about cats, it's that they won't hang around if they aren't fed."

James bit down on his toast and marmalade, and thumbed through the mail.

"Bloody bills!" he muttered.

Clive shook his head and played with the strip of crispy bacon on his plate. He wasn't convinced that thirteen cats just appearing from out of nowhere was something to be ignored.

At that moment Cook stuck her chubby-cheeked face through the sliding doors that separated it from the hallway.

"Sir, you have a visitor," she announced in a rather official tone.

"Who is it?" asked James.

"I don't know, Sir. But he's very handsome."

James tore through the envelope he was holding with a butter knife and looked Cook directly in the eyes.

"Well in that case you'd better let him in," he replied dryly, before looking across the table at Clive. "Honestly, you wouldn't believe how many times I've told her what to do when she answers the door. Still hasn't quite got the hang of it after all these years."

Clive laughed. "She certainly is one in a million. Though I guess you did hire her for her cooking, not her communication skills."

There was a small knock on the dining room door before Cook slid them open.

"Mr. Lucas Santorini," Cook announced, bowing her head in a regal gesture she thought appropriate in the situation. Clive snickered as James rolled his eyes and walked around the side of the table with his hand outstretched.

"Mr. Santorini, good morning," he said. "Did we have an appointment? I don't recall having any meetings this morning."

Lucas Santorini shook James's hand and smiled a dazzlingly brilliant smile.

"I'm sorry to impose on you," he said looking across at Clive.

"Please meet my nephew, Clive," said James, turning and winking surreptitiously at his lover. The shadow of a frown played on Clive's brow. It was the same every time someone of any import passed through the front doors. The old 'my nephew is up from the country for a couple of weeks' explanation. He knew it by heart. He understood his lover's public profile meant that they had to be discreet. He really did. But understanding something didn't make it any easier to bear.

Clive extended a hand and smiled. His teeth were perfect thanks to James's generosity. That killer grin coupled with his naturally chiseled features and natural charm were a weapon James had used on more than one occasion to clinch a deal. They were a good team; each getting something from the other.

"I'm pleased to meet you, Mr. Santorini," Clive said, with a flash of blue eyes and teeth. He looked into Mr. Santorini's eyes and noticed how dark they were. There appeared to be no distinction between iris and pupil, the blackness dominating the visible eye with only white around them. His attention was distracted by one of the cats from outside rubbing up against his leg. He gently kicked it aside.

"How …?"

"Oh, I must apologize," said Lucas. "They accompany me everywhere. They're like children. So demanding. But I suppose they are a bit of company and they do protect me."

Clive's brow wrinkled.

"The cats protect you? How could a cat possibly protect you?"

"I guess that does sound rather incomprehensible, but I assure you that they have never let me down," he said with a glint in his dark eyes.

Clive noticed James regarding the man in front of him and wondered if he was thinking the same thing as he was – that despite the man's eccentricities he was every bit as handsome as Cook had described. His eyes may have been dark, but they were beguiling, and his smile was dazzling if not vaguely familiar.

The faint recollection of being in his presence at a time before this instantly became a niggling, boring irritation in his head. He racked his brains but could not for the life of him remember where they could have met. It annoyed him even more that the man was so dashingly good-looking, with his neatly trimmed moustache and goatee, the tuft of hair sticking up over his pressed white shirt and his high cheek bones and full lips. How could have forgotten meeting a man like that?

"Your nephew has inherited your good looks, James."

Clive's eyes darted from the handsome stranger to James and then to his feet. He shifted uncomfortably on the spot and then walked over to a chair. He didn't sit but rested a hand on it, a security device to help him feel less uncomfortable.

"Yes, very attractive," he said as he moved across the room to where Clive stood. He reached up and stroked Clive's cheek with the back of his hand.

"Surprisingly soft," he commented before leaning in and kissing the thirty-year-old on the lips.

"You don't mind, do you?" he asked, glancing over his shoulder at James.

James babbled something indecipherable as Lucas pressed his lips once more against Clive's. Clive felt his body tingle. As Lucas kissed him, exploring his mouth with his tongue, he felt the stranger's hand slip into the space between the buttons of his shirt. Even the touch of his made him quiver like a teenager. He let his head fall back, arching his neck and leaving it exposed. He closed his eyes as an overwhelming feeling of lust pulsed through his body. He moaned as Lucas's lips moved from his lips to his chin and then his throat. For a moment they lingered there, sucking, licking, tasting.

"Take my cock in your hand," said Clive breathily. "Touch me. Please touch me!"

There was an urgency in his voice that surprised him. He had never been unfaithful to James before and now here he was being seduced right in front of his uncle.

"That's all right, Caro," whispered Lucas as he tongued and kissed his ear. "Your uncle thinks that if I fuck you then I will forget about our little contract."

"And will you?"

Clive heard the man laugh almost undetectably in his ear.

"No."

Despite his hatred for the man, Clive could not push him away. Even scarier was the fact that he didn't want to. Rather than repel him, his arms were wrapped tightly around the man's athletic body, pulling him closer, wanting more of him. He could feel Lucas's hard cock grinding against his own through the fabric of their pants. His arsehole twitched at the thought that maybe he would feel that thick cock slide into him. Still he had no thought for his lover though for an instant he wondered what magic this man had cast upon him.

"Let's get naked," Lucas said as though it were an announcement, and suddenly all three of them were naked. "Let's get more comfortable." And they were on the carpet, arms and legs entangled, lips and tongues kissing, licking, sucking. Lucas pulled Clive's arse cheeks apart, exposing a band of puckered pink tissue surrounded by a ring of dark blonde hair.

"Lick it," he commanded James.

James leant down and flicked his lover's arsehole with the firm, wet tip of his tongue.

"Get in there. Get in there deep."

Lucas' commands were turning both of them on. Clive could tell by the way James obeyed every command. He felt James's tongue poke its way through the sphincter muscle, tasting the inside of him before withdrawing.

"Now kiss me," said Lucas. "Let me taste your lover on your tongue."

Clive looked over his shoulder as James and Lucas kissed, the stranger sucking the tip of James's tongue before taking the whole thing into his mouth.

"He tastes good."

Then both of them started licking and sucking at his arsehole, jostling for a position at the entrance to his anus. Their hot breath tickled as their tongues flickered over the puckered skin; teasing him and making it tighten and relax in equal measure. He reached around and pulled his cheeks open even further, hoping to give them easier access to his tight arsehole. He wasn't disappointed. He could now feel two tongues probing his hole, and a finger. He pushed back, offering them his arse and not caring what they did to it.

Lucas was the first to leave his arse, lying down on the carpet next to him.

"Sit on my cock," he said, his eyes sparkling. "Sit with your back to me, so you can see your friend."

Clive did as he'd been asked and lowered himself gently onto the man's thick cock. He grimaced as the head pushed through his tight sphincter, but closed his eyes to enjoy the rest of it slipping deeper into his bowels.

"How does that feel?" the stranger asked.

"Feels so good," he replied, opening his eyes and seeing that James was looking directly at him. But there was no anger or jealousy in his eyes, only love. He saw James smile at him and he smiled back.

"Now lean back on me," Lucas said. "Lie down on my chest."

At first Clive wasn't sure what the stranger meant. He felt the man's arm wrap itself around his waist and pull him gently back. He rested on the man's torso, his hairy chest tickling the fair skin of his back. He liked the way it felt and moved ever so slightly to enjoy the soft, scratchy feeling once again.

"Fuck him," he heard Lucas say. "Stick your cock in your boy."

Clive's eyes widened. He was too tight to have another cock inside him. He opened his mouth to protest, but as if the stranger could read his thoughts, his hand came up and cupped his mouth.

"Do it," said Lucas.

James knelt between Lucas and Clive's legs. He spat a great glob of saliva onto his hand and massaged the slimy spit over his erect seven-incher. He spat again and smeared the results over the top of Clive's arsehole before gently pushing the head of his cock inside.

Clive grimaced. His eyes were closed tight. James's cock was an average size was coupled with the enormous organ Lucas had him impaled upon it was almost torture. He could feel James at his arsehole valiantly trying to get his cock inside, but the strange thing was as he thought about two cocks being inside him his arse muscles relented slightly, enough for James to push his fleshy mushroom head inside. The rest was easier to take, especially since James had the courtesy to let him get used to the two cocks.

When Lucas started thrusting, ever so gently, his taut hole throbbed with a radiating heat.

"Oh yeah," Clive moaned. "Fuck me."

He opened his eyes a crack and smiled as James was smiling at him. Their lips came together, and as they kissed he could feel the two cocks moving ever so slightly inside him, sliding over each other inside him. The thought had his whole body tingling. Waves of heat washed over him, from inside out. Soon he was finding it difficult to breathe. Lucas had brought his fingers up to tease his nipples while James sucked and kissed the sensitive skin of his neck.

For a moment James took his lips off his neck and leaned over his shoulder. He could tell by the way James had lifted his head that they were kissing. The thought of them with their mouths locked together while their two cocks thrust ever closer to imminent climax inside him started his own cock leaking pre-cum.

Lucas was the first to start thrusting hard. While his lips were still on James's his hips started bucking, pushing his fat tool deeper into him. James seemed to keep the same rhythm he had kept from the beginning, but the heavy breaths in his ear told him that he was nevertheless close to blowing his load.

"Breed my hole," he said. "Both of you. Blow your seed into me."

Clive moaned as he pulled James deeper into him. His lover's back was taut and sweaty. He loved the way his body felt on top of him, so muscular, so heavy, so masculine. And again his thoughts turned to the two cocks inside him, about to blast their loads inside him. He spread his legs wider and grabbed James's buttocks with his hands.

"I'm going to come!" he shouted.

His cock swelled and then exploded between his lover's body and himself; his grunts and gasps setting the other two off.

"Take my load, lad," cried Lucas, thrusting powerfully up into Clive, lifting both him and James high up off the floor.

"Me, too, baby," said James, leaning back, his face screwed up and his hips pressing harder against Clive's body.

For a moment there was a frenzy of activity as both men emptied their balls into Clive. And then nothing. Clive let his head roll to one side as James lay panting on top of him, the sweat from his brow dripping onto his cheek.

The three men lay in a state of communal bliss for a full five minutes. No one talked. But then something changed in the room. There was a slight shimmer and the atmosphere seemed stuffy and warm. James looked down and shrieked. He went to get up but his cock was still inside Clive. He fell backwards pulling himself free and sending spears of pain through Clive's abdomen. There was another wave when he realized that he still had the stranger's cock inside him. He reached down between his legs and pulled Lucas's still semi-hard cock out of his arsehole and leapt off the man.

"What the hell did you just do to me?" Clive snapped.

"See for yourself," said the stranger nodding towards the space between Clive's legs. Clive looked down as a dribble of cum escaped his arse. From the side of his eye he saw the man get to his feet.

"Now in answer to your question, Clive; the one you were thinking about before our little, um, interlude. Allow me to refresh your memory," said Lucas, the smile dissolving from his face as he turned to face James. "Think back to your university years, to the dark days of despair when you wrote and wrote and could not find anyone to read your stories. Think back to that stranger who answered your anguished prayers."

Clive looked from Lucas to James and noticed how the blood had drained from his lover's face. But there were other changes in him as well, the slight sheen of perspiration that had appeared on his forehead, the slight tremor in the hand that he raised to wipe his brow and the deep swallow.

"Yes, it's coming back to you now, isn't it? That early morning moment of torment when you teetered on the edge of suicide ..."

"What's he talking about?" asked Clive, his brow heavy as he moved to comfort James.

"Yes," smiled James nervously, ignoring him, "but I didn't think that you were serious. You couldn't have been, I mean, you can't be serious."

Lucas approached James, his brow heavy and his full lips pressed tightly together, until their faces were only inches apart.

"Well, I was and am very serious," Lucas snarled. "And in case you've forgotten, I have a contract that you signed in your own blood. Furthermore, I explained at the time what signing that contract would mean. You have your luxury townhouse, your career and your wealth. You have everything you wanted, and now I have come to collect what I want as stipulated in our deal."

Clive rushed at the stranger with fists raised, but a stinging pain in his leg stopped him dead. He looked down to see the black cat getting ready to claw him a second time. Then, just as he lifted his leg to kick it away, another cat leapt onto the table and another onto the chair next to him; all three hissing as they were joined by others.

Lucas smiled. "That, my friend, is how they protect me," he explained. "Now it is very valiant of you to want to protect your, er, uncle, but he knows full-well that I speak the truth, and we did in fact have a deal together."

James made use of the stranger's attention being taken and dashed towards the sliding doors yet he was too slow. With one wave of his hand, Lucas had the doors fixed shut.

"Now James, you can make this easy on yourself or difficult. I suggest the former since you also have a nephew to consider. Or should I say lover. Let's drop the pretense."

"What is it he wants?" Clive asked, his tone accusatory.

James hung his head.

"It's the age-old deal," Lucas explained. "What does one usually sell when they have nothing else to offer? When they have a burning desire, but no means to attain their heart's desire?"

"My soul," James replied with a sigh that encapsulated every ounce of defeat he was experiencing. "He has come for my soul."

James spun around and tried the doors a second time. He dug his fingers into the groove between them, clawing and scratching at them until they bled; until his face was so red that Clive thought he would burst a blood vessel.

"I have warned you!" growled Lucas.

Suddenly the room was full of energy. With a wave of Lucas's hand, Clive was sent crashing into the wall and James was flung across the room, landing face-down on the polished surface of the dining table. There was a great snapping sound as two of the table legs broke off, sending the end of the table thudding to the floor with a crash that sent Clive's heart racing. As he climbed to his feet, rubbing the back of his head, he noticed that while the table was at a slant James stayed where he had fallen. He hadn't slid an inch. His eyes darted from James to the stranger. He watched, helpless, as Lucas pulled two large nails from his jacket pocket and threw them into the air. In the blink of an eye they were embedded in James' hands, holding him securely where he lay.

Clive tried to get up when he heard James's agonized cries, but an invisible force had him pinned against the wall. The cats, stealthy and fearless, had also begun to congregate around him, hissing at his slightest movement. Tears misted his eyes as he saw blood pouring from the wounds in James' hands; the streams of red bleeding into the fabric of James's shirt. Agony was etched on a face that was rarely expressive, the gritted teeth and the screwed-up nose an advertisement to the pain he was enduring.

Lucas summoned Clive with a gesture. At first, Clive stayed where he was and debated whether he would do what the stranger wanted him to. It was his misfortune, however, to pause for a moment too long and the decision was made for him. A great force lifted him to his feet and propelled him across the polished floorboards of the dining room. Despite what was happening to him, his eyes never left his lover. As he passed the broken dining table, he saw the mighty iron nails that had pinned him to the thick wood of the table; the blood around his wounds almost black.

"Are you all right in there?" called Cook, after hearing the dining table crashing to the floor.

In a flash, Lucas had his eyes on the dining room doors, his eyes shadowed by a frown. It took him no more than a couple of seconds to assess the complications a loose-lipped cook could cause for him before he melted the skin of her lips together, and the skin of her nostrils for good measure. Her wails as her dermis began to bubble and blister became muffled as the flesh cooled and dried, leaving an impenetrable barrier of scar tissue.

"What are you doing?" Clive demanded. "Leave her alone!"

There was an almighty crash as Cook hit the floor, her hands clawing at the skin that fused her lips together. Lucas pulled her energy in through the minute gap between and around the doors. It was smoky grey and shadowy, and wafted across the room until Lucas caught the tip of it between his lips. He sucked, his chest heaving as Cook's spirit disappeared down his throat. For a moment his dark eyes flashed golden then he wiped his mouth as he would if he'd just finished a delicious meal.

"Now go and hold your lover's arse cheeks apart for me," Lucas said.

Clive looked the stranger in the eye. "No!" he snapped.

"Never mind," Lucas replied. "It makes no difference to me whether you do as I say or not. I will be done regardless, and you will suffer for your disobedience."

At that moment, a sharp jolt of pain pierced Clive's skull. For a second or two everything went black. He stumbled about, knocking into a chair. But as the pain abated, his vision returned, at first blurred but then as clear as it ever was. Lucas' perfect smile being the first thing he saw.

"Now, are you ready to give me what I have come for?" Lucas asked James.

James grunted unintelligibly.

"Speak up, man," said Lucas.

Clive glared at the stranger. This interloper was enjoying every minute he spent torturing his beloved. He seethed in silence, hoping that Lucas would slip up and give him the opportunity to crack him over the head with one of the chairs.

"It will never happen," Lucas said shooting Clive a stern look. "I know your thoughts before you do." He returned his attention to James. "Now, James, our deal. What's to happen?"

"You get nothing!" James spat.

Lucas tut-tutted, shaking his head slowly as James's legs were spread wide open and nails hammered into the soles of his feet. James bellowed with pain, his sobs like knife wounds to Clive's heart.

"You're enjoying this, aren't you?" Clive snarled. "You sick fucker!"

Lucas laughed theatrically. "I am merely taking what is mine from a man who refuses to deliver on a promise. Besides, I am no man. Please don't insult me by saying that I am. Is it so difficult, after all you have seen, to deduce who I am?"

Clive was not going to say it. He was not going to say the name Lucas wanted him to say, though Lucas's smile made it clear that words were not necessary. Lucas knew that the penny had dropped for Clive.

"I grow tired," Lucas announced. "I'd put a small amount of time aside to get what I came for, and already I am late for another appointment. You people are all the same, eager to sell your soul when you are desperate for things that a bit of hard work and time would get for you anyway, but when it comes time to pay the piper, you reveal yourselves to be the self-centered, simple-minded creatures you always have been. Now pull your boyfriend's arse cheeks open. Let me see the pink lips of his arsehole."

Clive felt sick. An acidic taste hit the back of his throat. He forced it back.

"W-w-w-what?" he stammered.

Lucas sucked his teeth. "I am asking you a third time to pull your boyfriend's arse cheeks apart, so I have a means to extract his soul."

"Can't you get it another way?"

Lucas grinned. "Of course I can, boy. But this way is so much more humiliating for him. And for you. Now show me his arsehole!"

Clive shook his head and took a step back from the table.

"Very well then," said Lucas. "Obviously you are incapable of learning from past mistakes. Your services are no longer needed."

Clive heard a mighty scraping sound to one side. He gasped as the bricks of the fireplace began separating, opening outwards into the room. Then a great force sucked him into the brickwork, which quickly closed around him. Clive blinked the settling mortar dust out of his eyes. At least he was still alive, but when he went to move, he found he couldn't. He couldn't even move his face. He cast his eyes downwards and saw his tongue spitting out fragments of dust and bricks through lips that were several bricks down. To the side he could just catch a glimpse of a couple of fingers sticking out of the mortar. He wriggled them, and they moved, but they felt separate to him.

"I'm rather proud of that one," Lucas grinned. "Not the least reason being that you may still see what I am about to do to your beloved James."

Lucas whistled, and with a flick of the wrist, two cats scampered across the rug towards him. Clive watched in horror as both creatures began to morph into something larger, taller and infinitely more frightening. Both felines had become bipedal, their skin stretching till it was so thin that Clive could see their innards amongst the fur that stuck out in isolated clumps dotted all over their bodies. The female's sex was swollen and red while the male cat-creature's thin, red cock wobbled erect as the demon moved towards James. They were now almost as tall as the six-foot Mr. Santorini and seemed unsteady on two feet, although that was possibly due to the lack of elasticity in their skin.

"Open that arse!" he ordered them.

The cat-demons took up position on either side of the table, each raising one paw into the air before bringing it down with such a force that each claw was buried to the pink padding of their paws in the tender flesh of James' arse.

James roared; his bloodied body writhed and twisted in agony.

"Open it!" Lucas demanded.

The cat-demons jerked each cheek apart, sending another wave of white-hot pain ricocheting through James's body.

"Very nice," Lucas smiled looking at the pink, puckered flesh. "A bit hairy for my liking."

He leaned in. Clive's eyes widened. He was feeling nauseous, despite not knowing where in the brickwork his stomach was.

"What are you doing? You sick fuck!" he yelled. "Leave him alone! You leave him the fuck alone!"

Lucas looked up. "Put a brick in it!" he said and suddenly there was an explosion of pain in Clive's mouth as it was filled with the taste of blood and baked clay. The pain was fierce. His lips had split and he'd swallowed a couple of teeth. A torrent of vomit rushed into the small space left in his mouth, but he could not swallow it back. He began to choke as he watched Lucas position his head directly in front of James's open anus.

"Are you ready, James?" Lucas asked. "Are you ready for me to take what you so easily could have given? You could have saved yourself this pain, but you people never know when the party is over."

Lucas exhaled a long and icy breath then paused before sucking in again. At first nothing happened, and then slowly he began to draw a blurry, shadowy energy from deep inside James's body. It came out in wisps at first, as if it were as reluctant to be taken as James had been to give it, but in no time at all it was streaming out, thick and soupy.

Clive felt his eyes brim with tears, and his hands were too far away, locked forever in the bricks and mortar of the fireplace, to wipe them away. He saw through his tears James's face, looking at him, imploring him. He saw Lucas Santorini sucking hard at the hairy hole of his lover, Hoovering up his soul; drawing it in until the veins in his neck were taut and his olive skin began to almost glow red. Small tears began to appear in the flesh surrounding James's anus. Blood trickled down over James's balls and down the table, collecting in a small pool on the floor beneath. Then Clive saw James's eyes close, as though he had fallen asleep. But of course, he was not sleeping at all.

Lucas wiped his mouth, picking a pubic hair from his lip and flicking it into the air. He collapsed backwards onto one of the dining room chairs and sat there gasping for breath.

"That was tough," he puffed. "A real challenge. Your boyfriend really didn't want me to have it, did he?"

It was a rhetorical question since Lucas didn't care about the reply, and Clive was unable to give it.

"Well I should be off now. Capobell and Ursula, thank you for your service. You may return to form now."

The two cat-demons began to yowl. Their skin suddenly looked too big for them and was hanging off in great sheets. Underneath they were getting smaller and smaller until they had returned to their terrestrial size and form. They took a moment to lick themselves as their skin closed in around them, and then both scurried out of the room behind Lucas and the other cats.

"I'm really sorry about the mess," he called back over his shoulder, "but I can assure you that you won't be the one who has to clean it up."

Clive heard the front door slam.

"At least the bastard never got his claws into my soul," he thought to himself triumphantly as his eyes glazed over, and the room disappeared into a thick fog.

He shivered. His whole body felt limp. Through heavy eyelids he saw the first wisps of his spirit waft across the dining room and out the door. And somewhere near the front gate, Mr. Santorini stood, eyes closed and once more sucking in another soul.

ON THE DARKEST NIGHT
R. J. Bradshaw

"I think we should spend the night at your place next month," I say, looking over my shoulder at him with a sly grin. I'm mixing a rye and ginger from my mini-fridge, for myself only; Callahan doesn't drink, or eat. No need for hosting when he's around, something I like about our little visits.

Callahan smiles, a wide smile that exposes his long sharp teeth. He sits on my bed at the other side of the room, his bat-like wings folded behind him, his whip-shaped tail resting on the sheets. "The cathedral?" he questions, his voice too deep for a human to mimic. "We have not done that before. I suppose I could climb down and get you."

Glass in hand, I turn around to face him. I stand motionless, allowing Callahan to get a good look at my naked body. I don't think I'm exceptionally attractive. I'm in my twenties, thin, but certainly not muscular. Yet Callahan can't take his eyes off me, something else I like. My body's as foreign and alluring to him as his is to me. I watch the progression of his gaze moving slowly down my pale skin, from my lightly-haired chest to my flat stomach, and eventually to my flaccid cock. His gaze lingers there for a few seconds before meeting my eyes.

He, too, is naked. He doesn't wear clothes, ever. Clothes wouldn't fit him, which isn't something that I'm complaining about. I've never tired of seeing his gray hairless skin, his lean solid body, his above average dick. And maybe this makes me slightly freaky, but I'm attracted to the other stuff as well: the tail, the wings, the horns. I even like his teeth, although I have to go without certain pleasures.

"That could be fun," I state enthusiastically, picturing myself tossed over Callahan's shoulder, being carried up the side of a building. I suddenly imagine flying with him, though I know his wings only allow him to glide.

He pats a clawed hand upon the sheets to the left of where he sits, enticing me to join him. For someone who doesn't eat, he looks hungry. "You will admire my view of the city," he comments. "It is very ... enchanting."

I might think he's joking if not for the seriousness of his expression. Besides his small horns and pointed teeth, Callahan's facial features are remarkably human. His jaw is strongly defined and his cheekbones high. His wide nose is slightly off-center, and his eyes are dark gray, the same shade as his skin. He could get me to do nearly anything when he traps me in his gaze, especially when he looks at me like this.

Leaving my rye and ginger on the dresser, I make my way over to the bed, resting a bare leg against his cool skin as I lay down.

"Better?" I ask.

Callahan inhales my musk, something I can't do with him since he doesn't have a smell. He lies down on his side to avoid damaging his wings, tracing a taloned finger gently across my stomach and chest, peering at me with stony eyes.

"Indeed," he says, pushing his lips against my neck. I'm always surprised by the lightness of his kisses, pointed teeth hidden behind his lips. His touch is always cool, but he is not hard as one might expect. His body is solid with muscle, but his gray skin is soft, comforting.

Slinging my left arm over him, I slide my hand across his folded wings and strong polished back. With my free hand, I direct his face to mine, my lips touching his. Callahan's lips remain closed as I kiss them, nibble them, first his upper lip, then his lower. He is afraid he will hurt me should he reciprocate the actions. As my nibbles turn to biting, a growl of pleasure rumbles in his throat.

The gray hand that had traced my stomach and chest now pulls me tightly against him, our cocks pressed together, hardening. My mouth moves across Callahan's ear and neck and downwards to his right nipple, my teeth still biting, my tongue toying with his dark flesh. Down his body, my mouth travels, from his stomach to his stiff cock as my own erection glides down past his knees, past his ankles and taloned feet. Callahan tangles a clawed hand into the curly blond locks atop my head while I lick his hairless balls. They are tasteless, Callahan doesn't sweat. My tongue moves up his thick shaft, and I pull back his foreskin before taking the tip of his cock in my mouth. A low moan escapes him, my hand and lips swallowing his penis, his cockhead dragging across the roof of my mouth. With one hand, I pump his shaft as I slip his penis in and out of my mouth, wet with my saliva. I fondle his smooth balls with the other.

"Please stop," he whispers, almost purring. "I am nearing ejaculation, and I want to make love to you."

I release his cock from my lips, lifting my blue eyes to meet his gray ones.

"You mean you want to fuck me before you come."

Callahan huffs, disapproving of my language, but still he flashes his teeth in a smile.

"Yes," he admits. "I would like nothing more."

"Okay," I tease, "but your ass is mine next month on top of the cathedral."

"I will enjoy that," he replies.

Knowing that Callahan can't lie on his wings, I rest my head on a pillow, spreading my legs, allowing him to be on top. I'm on my back; I want to watch him as he fucks me.

Callahan positions himself above me, bent legs beneath mine, back straightened. His claws grip the sheets by my midsection, the sound of fabric tearing. He unfolds his massive bat-like wings, which expand outwards, nearly reaching the walls on both sides of him. His tail is whipping behind him, left and right. This is Callahan in all his glory.

Grabbing lubricant eagerly from my night stand, I pour it into my palms, rubbing some onto his hard cock, some onto my asshole. After playing with his erection for several seconds, I direct it to my hole, inviting him in. Slowly, gently, he enters me, his thick cock stretching me, my breath catching.

"Is that okay?" he asks, genuinely concerned that he might hurt me.

I groan.

"Keep going."

Callahan pushes into me until his tip reaches my prostate, forcing a loud cry of pleasure to burst from me. Grinning, he pulls out slightly before pushing in again. He repeats this motion, finding his rhythm, slow at first, but gaining speed. The muscles of his upper body constrict and relax as he thrusts into me, his wings beginning to flap, air being jostled, stirring up random papers around the room.

"Fuck me," I yell, as if he isn't already. The bed is scraping on the floor, my hands are clutching the sides of the mattress. Panting uncontrollably, I look up to see Callahan leaning back, biting his lower lip in sheer ecstasy, black blood dripping onto his heaving chest. His stony eyes are closed, his tail is lashing the air. It might be the hottest fucking thing I've ever seen.

"I am going to ejaculate," he tells me, every muscle of his sculpted body tightening, his wings expanding to their full width, remaining rigid. His liquid spills inside me, cool like his skin. Yet still, he continues to thrust, his arms quaking. It feels so good, I never want him to stop. "It is getting very ... sensitive," he says, "but I want you to ejaculate also."

"I know," I reply, my breath heavy. "I've been meaning to try something new that might alleviate that problem."

"What is that?" he questions, pulling out of me, his wings folding in.

"Well ..." I begin, smiling up at him, "you did something a couple of months ago when we were having a disagreement ..."

He's confused.

"What did I do?"

"When I tried to shove you away from me, you turned your feet into rock, so I couldn't budge you."

"Yes ..." he responds, urging me to continue.

"I guess I was wondering if you could do that with your dick," I suggest.

Callahan lets out a booming laugh, a rare incident.

"It does not work that way," he tells me. "The transformation must start in my feet."

"That's okay," I say. "Make everything rock up to your waist then."

He cocks his head slightly, deliberating.

"I want you to do it while your dick is still pointing up," I hasten. "Maybe you should sit on the floor, so you don't break the bed."

"Okay," he says, giving in with more deep laughter. "It could be rather titillating."

Leaving me on the bed, Callahan sits on the floor. He puts one hand on the carpet behind him to keep himself propped up, his other holding his erection in place. He crosses his legs, and I scramble to the side of the mattress to watch him. I get the impression that he's already transforming his lower body to stone, but it's barely noticeable. The color of his skin doesn't change, but his dark veins start to vanish, and his legs become unusually still.

"It is done," he states.

"Really?" I ask, climbing down onto the floor in front of him. Somewhat skeptically, I touch one of his knees. It's hard, colder than usual, and I know that he's telling the truth. I reach over and stroke his stone cock, smooth and totally rigid, a perfect dildo.

"Can you feel that?" I ask.

"Not at all," he responds, his anticipation clearly building, wanting me to use him.

My asshole still well-lubricated, I rise to my knees and put one on each side of his immovable legs, lowering my ass onto his rock-hard dick. I gasp as I slide the stone shaft inside me. The sensation is strange but intensely satisfying.

When I start to ride it, Callahan wraps a clawed hand around my erection, careful not to scratch me.

"You are incredibly sexy," he growls as I fuck his hand, his dark gray eyes twinkling with lust. His stone cock is so cold it almost burns, pleasurable pain. I grip his horns as I tighten my hole around it. Sweat is beading on my skin. If his tail wasn't rock, I would tell him to whip me with it like he has so many times before, never hard enough to make me bleed, just hard enough to get me off. I imagine it now, so near to coming ...

My body convulses, semen shooting onto Callahan's chest, mixing with his now dried blood. My muscles constrict, my vision blurs for a moment. I slide my hands behind Callahan's head, forcing him to me, kissing him.

"We really have to do that more often," I pant, sliding my asshole from his stone hard-on. By the time, I sit back down on his lap, his skin is soft again.

"Gladly," he responds with a sharp smirk, but he seems distracted.

"What's wrong?" I ask, pulse still racing.

"I am feeling the pull," he answers sadly. "I have to leave you soon."

Callahan is only granted life on the darkest night, the night of the new moon. At the end of this night, there's some kind of magnetic force that draws him back to his perch on the cathedral wall, a pull that he can't withstand for long.

I glance at the time.

"Fuck," I mutter.

"My sentiments exactly," he sighs as we stand together, Callahan towering at least a foot above me. We amble towards the balcony door. "Remember, I'm going to your place next month," I tell him.

"I will remember," he replies, kissing my forehead. "I will be waiting."

I can't think of anything else to say. I have mixed feelings when he leaves, Callahan sees me nearly every minute of his living state, but I see him for only a small portion of mine, leaving me with alone my fantasies, waiting for the new moon. So I simply watch him as he opens the door, stepping out into the waning night. His seductive eyes scan my face and naked body once more before his wings extend and he leaps from my balcony. The bedroom is quiet. Walking over to the dresser, I down the rest of my drink.

AT-WILL EMPLOYMENT
Mark Apoapsis

Luke looked pale in his dark suit and kept scratching under his stiff collar. All our lives, I had rarely seen him dressed in anything but a bright-colored tank top and short pants, full of life as he effortlessly ran to intercept my Frisbee. He usually had a tan a couple of shades darker than his blond hair. I stepped up to stand beside him. His shoulder, when I squeezed it in silent sympathy, was a little scrawnier than I'd expected, it had been solidly muscled the last time we'd embraced.

I had many happy memories of our grandmother, and the best ones all involved Luke. Finally, I murmured, "First time we see each other in two years, and it has to be in front of a coffin."

Luke jumped and gave me a strange, fearful look.

"I've missed you, dude," I whispered. "What have you been up to?"

"Sorry. I don't get out much, with my job."

He didn't seem comfortable talking at the funeral, and I had to get back to my brother and sister. I did get his cell phone number.

#

A few weeks later, I called and managed to talk him into meeting at a coffee shop. My cousin still looked pale, even in a white turtleneck, and uncharacteristically subdued. Maybe he was just tired. He kept yawning despite the coffee, which was odd because he'd always been a morning person.

"You know what we should do?" I said. "We should go camping. It'll be like the old days, only just the two of us."

"Except that we both have jobs now. Our summertimes are gone, man."

"That's what vacations are for. It'll be great. If we had fun then, just imagine what we could do without adult supervision."

That got a smile out of him. "I wish I could. My boss won't let me take any time off."

"So quit. I'm sure Grandma would have approved of your spending your inheritance on getting free of a job that makes you unhappy. You can look for a better one afterward, or go back to school. I'd be glad to lend you my share, if it'll help."

"No, I like the job. He's a nice guy. Plus, I get free rent in a big beautiful old house."

I knew my cousin well enough to tell he was feeling deeply conflicted for some reason. Following a hunch, I asked, "This old guy you're working for. Living with." Luke blushed slightly, so I forged ahead. "Has he ... made advances toward you?"

Luke hung his head. There was no mistaking the shame on his face.

"Damn him! Did you tell him you weren't interested?"

Luke looked like he was about to correct me, but stopped himself and remained silent.

"Look, dude, you can tell me, of all people. If you've gotten involved with this guy, and it's consensual – well, I'd be surprised, but there's nothing to be ashamed of. Just because I happen not to like old guys myself doesn't mean I'm going to freak out." Luke was a good-looking man, tall and blond and blue-eyed. I'd go for him myself in a minute, if he weren't my cousin. And so absolutely straight.

"He doesn't seem old, now that I've been with him so long," Luke mumbled.

"Dude!" I crowed, hardly believing. "Why didn't you ever tell me? Does Aunt ..."

"You don't understand. I'm not ... It's not like that." He sobbed, scratching under his turtleneck. "The way he ..."

"What? Is he forcing himself on you? Beating you?"

"It f-feels ... It's so ..." he began, then buried his face in his hands.

Maybe it was a good thing that he was my cousin, and straight, or I'd never have felt free to do what I so casually did next. I leaned close to him across the table, hooked a finger in his turtleneck, and bared his neck. I half expected bruises. What I found was peculiar: six pink scabs.

"Bug bites," he said.

# # # # #

I discreetly followed Luke home in my car and watched him enter a nice old house that was easily worth seven figures these days. As far as I could tell peering around the gate at the end of the long driveway, he let himself in; I was half expecting either a butler or the old man.

Saturday afternoon, I dropped by unannounced. Luke answered the door in his undershirt and boxers, rubbing his eyes. His blond hair was tousled.

"Sorry, man, did I wake you?" It was three in the afternoon.

"No, I was working out," my cousin lied.

I invited myself in, and we sat on the couch. As my eyes adjusted, I discerned four scabs on his shoulder, two inside one arm, six inside the other, eight down one leg. The six on his neck were almost gone, but there were two new ones.

I grabbed his forearm. "Where'd you get these?"

"Bug bites. Mowing the lawn."

They didn't look like bug bites to me. Bug bites usually leave bumps; I'd heard somewhere that the bump was a reaction to the anti-coagulant that bugs inject. These looked more like the tooth marks left after a neighbor's dog had bitten me once, only neater. Whatever had bitten Luke, it hadn't injected him with anything he was allergic to.

But I said, "Try wearing a long-sleeve shirt."

"Too hot. I always wear a tank top."

I yanked up his undershirt. One pair of matching bite marks on his belly, neatly straddling the almost invisible line of hair I knew ran down his torso.

"Except when I take it off," he amended lamely.

He struggled half-heartedly, weeping, as I examined him further. "Do you always mow the lawn in the nude?" I shouted, letting his waistband snap back.

"The boss ordered me not to t-talk," he whimpered.

This was pathetic. What happened to the strong-willed cousin I'd known all my life, the confident man he'd become? Was Luke being tortured? Why hadn't he walked out? Gone to the police?

"Get dressed! I want to have a talk with this boss of yours."

"He's sleeping."

"I don't care!"

When Luke led me to the basement, and I saw the coffin, my first thought was that it was all an elaborate prank. But fun-loving as

193

he'd once been, my cousin never could keep a straight face, so there was no way he'd be able to keep me going so long. Anyway, I knew exactly how much a nice coffin like this would cost, having recently been in the market.

"Um, your boss is what, exactly? Just so we're clear."

"H-he's ... I-I can't even say it," Luke stammered.

# # # # #

It was late afternoon by the time I had located a saw, a large file, a solid wooden table leg, and a heavy silver paperweight. As Luke hung back, I lifted the coffin lid, fully expecting to see a dark-haired older man in a black cape. There was a man inside, but he looked younger than we were: twenty at most. He was dressed in what many normal men sleep in: flannel pajama bottoms. Sandy-haired, he looked fit and healthy, and his pale, rosy skin was utterly unscarred and unblemished.

His chest was slightly cool to the touch, and unmoving. I felt a single heartbeat after a few seconds, then nothing. I placed the makeshift stake – the table leg, filed down to a point – against the defenseless young man's bare chest. With a trembling hand, I raised the heavy paperweight.

That was as far as I got. I just couldn't bring myself to smack it down on the table leg and drive the point into his flesh. Maybe if he'd looked waxen and corpselike – but he looked like a normal, healthy guy whose life I was about to end. I reminded myself that the healthy, ruddy glow was no doubt the very life he'd sucked out of my cousin, and raised the paperweight again. But, I still couldn't gather the nerve to bring it down.

Finally, I turned to Luke, who was watching silently with tears streaming down his face, and said, "Dude, I can't do this. I've never killed anyone before."

He looked at me pathetically and didn't answer.

"Fuck!" I said, hurling down the stake and paperweight in frustration. I paced the length of the basement twice, then whirled on my cousin. "Will you help me carry him outside? The sun'll kill him, right?" Somehow my instincts didn't rebel at the thought of carrying an unconscious man into the sunshine, the way they did against driving a stake through his heart.

After a long hesitation, Luke said, "All right. I'll take his feet."

I leaned down and lifted the limp arms far enough to snake my hands past his armpits and interlace my fingers in front of his sternum. Together we hoisted him out of the coffin and carried him up the stairs.

As we carried him across the living room, I noticed that despite the drawn curtains, his bare skin had already reddened noticeably. Not exactly sunburn yet, but if I saw that color on a buddy lying beside me on a beach, I would nag him to put on a shirt. Reluctantly, if the buddy looked half this good.

Our path to the front door took us through a beam of sunlight shining through a crack in the curtains. As it played across his exposed skin, he awoke with a panicked gasp and took in the situation.

"No, please," he said in a groggy voice.

I kept walking. He began to struggle in my arms, weak as a kitten. He turned his soft brown gaze on me, pleading silently, and it took all the willpower I had not to release him. Then he turned it on my cousin, who was looking miserably over his shoulder.

"Luke, please! You wouldn't really do this to me, would you?"

Luke looked torn for a moment, then he released his grip on the bare feet. His young boss scrabbled to a standing position, but I still had my arms locked firmly around his torso. He jabbed me in the abdomen with his elbow, but so weakly I barely felt it.

"I'm going to carry him out if I have to do it myself across my shoulders." I spun him around and grabbed his wrists, slamming his back against a wall. Pinning his wrists over his head as he struggled feebly, I caught my breath and tried to decide between dragging him over to the front door and trying to get it open one-handed, or hurling him through the glass of a window – another idea I flinched at. Maybe it would be enough to just open the curtains. Or maybe that would just fry him slowly before my eyes, and the full sunlight outside would be more merciful. He looked so helpless like this, with his bare chest heaving and the wispy nests of hair in his armpits exposed.

Then Luke grabbed me from behind, locking his arm around my throat. He'd always liked chokeholds and was pretty good at them. In the past, when we were just fooling around, I'd always submitted immediately when he got me in one. Now it was for real, there'd be no crying "uncle" to my cousin this time. I tried to pull his arm away. Weakened as Luke was these days, I almost broke his grip, but the next thing I knew, all three of us were hitting the ground, and his boss had managed to pin one of my arms under his weight and entangle the other in his own limbs. My cousin maintained the pressure on the sides of my throat, and dark spots began to swim across my vision.

# # # # #

I awoke to find my cousin tying me to a chair in the dining room. "I couldn't let you do it," Luke said, weeping.

"I just wanted to free you, dude," I said softly.

"I know. I'm sorry. I didn't want to get you mixed up in this, but you wouldn't let it go."

"What happens now? Is he going to kill me?"

"Do you really think I'd be tying you up if I thought he would do that?"

"Why are you tying me up at all?"

"Well ... he asked me to."

"Really."

"It's hard to say no to him."

"So what do you think he'll do with me?"

"I – I've got to go throw some covers over him. Try to relax, man. I'm sure it'll be okay."

# # # # #

Luke came back to offer me a drink and keep me company, but he left at sunset, and when he came back half an hour later, he wasn't alone. His youthful master was fully dressed now. Still no cape, just a well-worn pair of jeans and a casual shirt. I noticed the jeans were bellbottoms, and gathered that he didn't exactly go out and shop for every season's latest fashions. His handsome face no longer had a trace of sunburn.

"You won't hurt him, will you?" Luke asked him. Getting no response, he said boldly, "If you hurt him, I swear I'll ..."

His master gave him a mild look that stopped him in mid-sentence.

"Unbutton his shirt."

"Yes, sir."

After my cousin had carried out his command, he brushed him aside and leaned close to me, spreading my shirt wide and inhaling deeply and appreciatively.

"Your brother?"

"Cousin," Luke said.

"I like him," he said, toying with my dark chest hair. Luke's chest was smooth, something I'd taunted him about ever since mine had grown in. "He smells a lot like you. And he's got great shoulders." He squeezed them gently, then pushed my shirt out of the way to expose one. "Oh, yeah! Just what I want to sink my teeth into."

It wasn't anything like I'd expected. I thought it would hurt, like the time that dog had bitten me, but the intense sensation was more like exquisite pleasure than pain, as his teeth pierced my skin, slid through my flesh, and teased apart the fibers of my shoulder muscles. By the time he was finished, I actually felt pleasantly relaxed, and disinclined to move, something like the way I feel after lying on a beach, or after sex. It was as though he'd sucked the strength out of my muscles, and stress and fear along with it. The bite was already closing.

Then he turned to Luke and casually began pulling his shirt over his head.

"Please," Luke protested. "Not in front of my cousin."

In answer, his master merely adjusted my chair, so I'd have a better view. He did this by casually lifting it clear off the ground and setting it gently back down as easily as if it were empty.

Still tied up, I watched helplessly as he unbuckled my cousin's belt and pulled his pants down, then his boxers. He lifted Luke's unresisting form in his strong arms and bent over him, exploring every part of his body with his mouth. To my amazement, Luke seemed to reluctantly enjoy it. He seemed to be trying not to react, but small moans of pleasure were drawn unwillingly from his quivering form, and he was even starting to get a hard-on.

When he was finished with him, he stretched Luke out on the floor. For a moment I worried that he'd killed him.

"He's out cold," he said a gloating affection that sounded more like a fraternity brother after a party, or a lover after a hot night of sex, than like a boss. He demonstrated by lifting Luke's arm and letting it drop limply onto my cousin's bare chest. Then, grinning at me wickedly, he lifted Luke's limp cock with his fingers and let that drop. Then he rose and loomed over me.

"Are you going to kill me now?" I asked meekly.

"Of course not." With his finger, he traced the trail of wispy black hairs that run from my navel downward, as I squirmed helplessly. "I can think of better things to do with you."

This time he didn't limit himself to my shoulder. He untied me first and laid me on the floor not far from my unconscious cousin. I tried to resist, but he grabbed my wrists in a gentle but unbreakable grip and put his mouth wherever he wanted to. After sampling three areas of my chest, he stretched my arms over my head and bit into the muscle on the side of my armpit.

By the time he removed my shoes and socks, rolled up my pants leg, and bit into my calf, I wasn't even trying to resist anymore. Why should I, if a hot guy wanted to rip my clothes off?

Eventually, I found myself stripped to my boxers – with an embarrassing erection making an obvious tent in the fabric – cradled in his inhumanly strong arms as he stood there looking down at me almost tenderly. I waited for him to select the next part of my exposed body to invade with his teeth.

Instead, he said, "It's just like food for me, you know."

"I sort figured out that out," I said weakly.

"No, I don't just mean that I need it to live, or to keep me strong. I mean I enjoy the subtle blend of flavors. Luke hasn't been afraid of me for a long time, so that first taste of you was a nice change of pace. But you know how you taste now? I know that taste of helpless submission very well from your cousin, but you've got a strong under-taste of desire that he's got barely a hint of. And he always tastes of shame, tonight more than ever because I humiliated him in front of you. Shame is one of my favorite flavors, but I like variety. You're not ashamed at all. It's refreshing. You've got this delicious taste of humiliation, but I can tell the difference."

"You should let him go now that you have me."

"I don't know about that. You really bring out the flavor in him. I'm pretty sure he brings out certain flavors in you, too. I'll have to experiment." He began nuzzling my throat.

# # # # #

I woke up in bed, naked, sprawled on my back. My cousin's body had been draped on top of me and the covers tucked neatly around us. I could feel his cock, as limp as the rest of his body, squashed against my belly. I felt more relaxed and content than I'd ever felt in my life, but I also felt embarrassed at finding myself in this compromising position. I didn't remember how we got into bed, and assumed we'd been placed here while we were both unconscious.

"Dude?" I whispered. "You awake?"

"I am now," he murmured without raising his forehead from my shoulder.

"You're kind of heavy. Can you roll off me?"

"Dude," he said languidly, "if I could move, do you think I'd lie here with my nose practically in your armpit?"

"Sorry," I said, and with an effort managed to shift my arm. Luke turned his head slightly and settled into a position with his unshaven cheek brushing mine and his lips an inch from my neck. With a contented sigh, he settled back to sleep.

I may or may not have dozed off like that, but then I heard the door open. Our master loomed over us and brushed the hair back from my forehead. "I really shouldn't take any more tonight, but I just can't resist such a complex blend." He nuzzled my neck and whispered, "Contentment. Affection. Protectiveness. Ah. Now I think I detect a hint of shame."

Rising, he stripped the covers off of us, exposing our naked embrace. He lifted my cousin up by his shoulders, slipped a hand under his chest, and slid his whole body down along mine until his cheek rested on my thigh, so close to my crotch that I could feel his warm breath stir my pubic hair with each snore.

"Yes. Definitely shame. An irresistible combination!"

# # # # #

That sated him for days, and he went easier on us both after that. Within a few weeks, I was back to full strength, and to my delight, so was Luke. Apparently, two of us were enough to satisfy his needs without leaving us feeling drained. It also helped that he generously fed us a hearty and healthful diet.

He didn't make us share a bed after what he did to punish us, and entertain himself, that first night. We each had our own room upstairs. Luke liked to hang out in my room, and we'd often stay up late talking well into the morning. But if he fell asleep in my bed, I'd always either wake him up or, if we'd been drinking, carry him over my shoulders to his own room and put him to bed.

We were even allowed to get up early and spend the latter part of the afternoon enjoying the sun, tossing a football around, shirtless in the huge back yard. I felt more full of life than ever before, despite getting it sucked out of me regularly, and more free than I had before

I'd been enslaved. Once, on a whim, we even had a water balloon fight stark naked. The back yard was completely private, and it was broad daylight, so no one would ever know.

After the sun got low, we would usually play video games, sometimes for hours if our master decided to sleep in. We could easily afford the latest entertainment system with what he paid us on top of our free rent. I gathered that he owned the house free and clear. He bragged that he had stock holdings dating back to when the Dow was still under 500, although these days he seemed to enjoy placing trades online, and liked to refer to himself as a "day trader."

One evening, he came up behind us, side by side on the couch intent on gunning down virtual zombies, and playfully grabbed us, pressing his head down between our shoulders and breathing deeply.

"Do you know how many decades it's been since I've tasted such joy and camaraderie? Hold still."

Pulling my collar down to expose my shoulder, he took a small taste of me, then repeated the process with Luke. He'd just woken up and was still clad only in his pajama bottoms. He was getting more comfortable being casual around me now. Until recently, the last time I'd seen him shirtless was the day he'd been struggling helplessly in my grip. I enjoyed the casual familiarity, but I fantasized about going further. Someday, I hoped to explore that torso with my own mouth, run my tongue over that perfect skin, even tug down those pajamas with my teeth and do a little sucking of my own. I'd fantasized about it last thing every morning for the past week, right after kicking my cousin out of my room for the day.

"I'll get dressed for breakfast while you two decide who's on the menu," he said when he was done with Luke.

"Your turn," Luke told me.

"No way, dude, it's your turn."

We never took turns these days. It was just an excuse to wrestle for it.

"Either you're getting strong again, or I'm getting weaker," I grunted into his armpit.

"I was strong enough yesterday when I carried you upstairs after he had a little too much," he reminded me.

Nevertheless, I beat him this time, and when our master returned, freshly showered and dressed, Luke was stripped to the waist and I had his arms firmly pinned at his sides.

I could feel every shudder of pleasure that wracked my cousin's body. Luke had managed to get my shirt completely unbuttoned, so my chest was plastered against his back, transmitting every quiver like an electric shock.

When he finally pulled back from Luke, leaving him sagging in my arms, he said, "I can't resist. You both just smell too good today to pass up."

When he occasionally decides to break the informal rules like that, it's not as if there's any way we can stop him. But lying there afterward, in an tangled shirtless heap, skin-to-skin on top of my cousin, I decided it wasn't too high a price.

MY NIGHT DEMON
Jay Starre

It was well past two o'clock in the morning and I still wasn't ready to call it a night. Seated before my computer, I randomly cruised the internet, checking out porn sites while nursing a hard-on.

Image after image of hot men, nasty hard cocks and lush, spread asses popped up on my screen one after the other. It was mesmerizing and chaotic all at once. I was actually too tired to jerk off even though my cock drooled unsatisfied in my fist.

Following links in a dream-like jumble of sexual visions, I stumbled on a site of bizarre gay erotic art. Paintings of wild monster-like men in fantastic sexual positions bombarded my half-awake consciousness. Both vivid and surreal at the same time, they seemed to jump right off the screen at me. For a brief instant, I was terribly frightened and wanted nothing more than to get out of that strange Website.

But my fingers would not move on the keyboard. Colors pulsed in odd waves. The leering, crouching, fucking savages on the screen appeared totally, fantastically real.

I found myself stumbling toward my bed across the room. With a mixture of relief and disappointment, I realized I'd somehow escaped the mesmerizing computer screen and its bizarre images.

My cock was still stiff and throbbing. I tumbled into sleep while gently rocking into my fist.

Falling into the warm darkness of sleep, my cock was the last link with reality, stiff and dripping. The humid heat of a summer night's sleep opened up like the opposite end of a yawning black tunnel even as it closed over my consciousness.

Appearing out of a dark mist that was cloyingly warm and thick, I saw the dream lover ahead of me. Naked, he crouched on all fours with his back to me. I stared in absorbed fascination at his hefty, hairy ass growing larger as I effortlessly floated nearer. The fleshy cheeks were lewdly parted – and just below that deep crevice a pair of fat balls dangled close to his body.

I tore my eyes from that large ass and those full balls. I saw black bat-like wings protruding from the night demon's shoulders. The semi-folded wings jutted out from the sides of the black vest that covered his back. I noted with an odd clarity that both wings and vest appeared to be made from the same dark leather. That opal-dark hide glistened with a moist sheen.

He grasped a whip in one hand, also dark and leathery. All that leather seemed to be a part of him. Wings, vest, and whip were an extension of his flesh, foreboding in a moist, dark and sexual manner.

I woke up.

Bathed in a sheen of moist sweat, I stared out the open window across from my bed. It was morning! It hadn't seemed like more than a moment had passed. That vivid nightmare still clung with a throbbing tenacity to the edges of my consciousness. I stirred and rose to get ready for work. Monday. My boring job in a boring office building beckoned like stale bread and sour milk.

I faced the mirror and realized I didn't want to shave. My clean-cut looks were always so important to me, but that morning, I thought fuck it. The dark stubble on my face looked somehow right.

At work someone commented on how much they liked my new beard. I thought that was odd until I happened to look up in a washroom mirror and was stunned to see the stubble of the morning was more than that. I had a beard, short, yes, but thick and dark. My blue eyes seemed brighter, my teeth whiter, my nose more craggy and masculine.

A vivid image abruptly reared before me in the mirror. Darkness. Then, hairy butt-cheeks and a divided ass crack. Leather wings rising above a kneeling, vested figure. I stumbled from the washroom, shaking from head to toe. It was only a dream. Graphic and detailed, yes, but far from realistic. There were no sex demons in real life.

The remainder of the day, I worked in a fog. I felt eyes on me, co-workers glancing at me and smiling strangely. Men who hadn't given me the time of day were cruising me! I fled work in a near panic at the end of the day.

I ate supper and avoided the computer and that demon-porn site, sure it had somehow spurred that awful dream. I tried to stay awake as long as possible, but I had to work the next day. I was tired and so very sleepy.

I was also electrified by a strange sexual ambivalence.

Without consciously deciding, I stripped naked. Not sure how I got there, I now lay on my bed in the darkness. The open window blew in summer air. The fresh aroma of nearby fields mingled with the stench of a muddy irrigation ditch beyond that.

I was asleep before I realized it. The fog of darkness was complete, but I was aware. I was dreaming and I knew it.

My demon was there.

Again, crouched on all fours with his back to me. My eyes returned to the obscene crack of his ass, where the last time I'd dared to look before waking.

A tangle of blindingly bright platinum-blond hair sprouted to curl around his dangling ball-sack. Those balls were so full and fat, I imagined gallons of jizz in them just waiting to spurt out. I was unable to look away from those plump nads, hypnotised by their juicy fullness as they hung down below that open, furry ass-crack.

He turned his head toward me.

Burning heat and an icy chill battled all along my naked spine. An urgency all at once possessed me as I dared gaze into his face. It seemed like an oddly heavy face, the square jaw covered in a silky luster of that same platinum blond hair, which also sprouted on his scalp in a shockingly bright spike. The utter contrast of those dark wings and black leather vest against platinum hair on his head, face, down there in his deep ass-crack, and over his ballsack, struck me like a slap to the face.

He smiled.

That smile gapes like a huge hole as his mouth opens and physically sucks me forward. I am suddenly on my back and he is kneeling above my prone body. His big gloved hands, also of opal-dark leather, are on my shoulders and a drooling cock is thrust toward my face.

It was morning. I breathed in and out deeply, the heat of the previous day still lingering like my nightmare. I rose to go to the bathroom, and once there, I turned to face the full-length mirror.

I was shocked. My dark beard was thick and full. I'd sprouted a fine coat of dark hair across my chest, something I'd always wished for but hadn't been naturally graced with. Not only that, my body was no longer the lean machine of years of gym toning. I was bigger, larger than ever before. My stomach was rounded, somehow more sexually alluring that way. My thighs were massive. Fat, which I'd dreaded with near-phobia, now coated and enhanced the muscles I'd worked so hard for.

My cock was rock-hard, but I didn't touch it. I was afraid. Very afraid. What was happening to me?

Work was a blur. Eyes followed me, and I imagined every male I encountered lusted for my newer, fuller body. I felt heavy as I walked, powerful, dark and foreboding. The thought that the demon of the night had insinuated himself into my soul sent shivers of fear coursing through my bloodstream.

My job was routine, mindless. I performed effortlessly. I didn't think. I was too afraid to do that.

Night came, and I hadn't dared yet go home. I wandered the city streets to the edge of town, where my apartment building fronted the fields and woods. Tonight, they looked richer, more alive. It seemed like the grass was growing right before my eyes. The smells were so acute, mud, flowers, forest mulch, animal manure, they hit me like a punch to the gut.

I climbed the five flights of stairs to my apartment with my new, powerful thighs propelling me upwards like tree trunks come to life. I felt afraid, very afraid, but bizarrely exhilarated, too. I ate supper mechanically, not tasting anything as I prepared for bed with a fearful purpose. I had decided.

I wouldn't run. I would face my demon.

I lay down on my back, naked, running my hands through the silken curls on my chest. I licked my lips, sighing, breathing deeply as I let my thoughts go. I surrendered to the night.

I felt wind whipping across my body, and the flap of wings in my ears.

Darkness enveloped me like a warm blanket, then dissolved. I literally cried out with joy as he appeared again. It was exactly as I'd left it, the dream, the nightmare. The demon crouched with his back to me, then he turned his head.

Urgency fluttered in my pounding heart. The same panic-excitement from the last time I'd gazed into his face possessed me all over again. I gawked, hypnotized by the heavy face, the square jaw covered in a silky luster of platinum beard, the scalp topped by that bright spike of the purest white hair

Again, the demon smiled.

That smile gapes like a huge howl as his mouth opens and physically sucks me forward. I am suddenly on my back and he is kneeling above my prone body. His big gloved hands, also of opal-dark leather, are on my shoulders and a drooling cock is thrust toward my face.

I steadied, awake but asleep. My hands, without even the slightest tremble, went up of their own accord. I groped his open ass and those big round balls with a sudden greediness that was more than lust. The heavy sack was as fat as it looked. With ferocious greed, I rolled and massaged it. He hissed at me in a deep, purring voice …

"Love my ballsack, love it before it fills you with its thick milk. Love it before it spurts into your guts through your gaping mouth. Love that full sack before its juices flood in a torrent into your yawning asshole."

I sensed more than saw the aura of cold fire that surrounded us, with only stygian darkness beyond that. The glare of unfeeling flames burned in eerie oranges, purples and magentas. The black leather of his body and attire glowed with garish reflections of that pulsating flame. My demon was on fire, but it was a cold flame. It didn't burn me outwardly, rather it kindled a searing heat within so powerful it felt as if it was bursting through the very cells of my body.

That heat took on life, transforming into a pulsing ache of utterly desperate need.

He feeds me his cock as he kneels over my chest. His thickly-muscled thighs press against my sides and trap me in hairy, hot flesh. Turgid cock thrusts into my open mouth past my slurping lips. That cock throbs with scorching stiffness. I suck it in with a moaning mewl, my eagerness to have that fat shaft in my throat totally consuming. I want it so bad I cry out, my voice muffled by his meat. The knob slides over my tongue, tasting of sticky goo, thick and tangy. I swallow and suck, more of the gunk oozing from that fat head. I swallow hungrily as his cock pulses out its slow trickle of juice.

My hands fondled his balls. I felt both the big nuts in their sack. Round and huge, solid and full. I massaged them greedily and rolled them in my hands as I sucked more love-juice from his leaking shank in my mouth. He writhed above me, slowly. Pumping his shaft between my lips in a steady thrust, his blond-furred thighs suddenly yielded to fall open over me, wide apart.

"Yes," he sighs in that hissing whisper. "Yes, suck me into your being. Take my essence for your own. Feed on me. I am yours and you are mine."

His voice transmitted a wave of delicious shivers that radiated throughout my body. My cock ached, lying hard on my belly in its own pool of leaking nut fluid. My entire body was as hard as my cock, thrusting up into the warm thighs that trapped me. I became aware of an equally hard stone bed beneath us. Our love bed was rock, cold and hot at the same time, solid and unyielding, slippery with a sheen of moisture that was somehow exactly like human – or demon – sweat.

One of my demon's hands moved to encase mine in an irresistible grip. He pulled that hand up into his own asscrack, sliding it slowly over the warm crevice, through the silky curls of platinum fur. Farther up, the demon settled our fingers on the puckered slot pulsing between those massive nether cheeks. I gasped around the cock in my mouth as I felt the convulsing pit welcoming me.

I strummed the lips of a quaking volcano of asshole. The hole swelled and protruded, wet with slick lubricant. I rubbed my fingers all around the slippery entrance and quivering lips as he encouraged me with the pressure from his gloved hand. I stroked the hot rim lovingly, feeling it clamp and gape as it accepted my intimate caress. I knew without any doubt, that hole wanted my fingers on it. It was alive, and calling to me. I shivered as I petted the wet slot, rubbing all over it from top to bottom and into the slick center. It squeezed tight against my fingers, then pouted outwards with hungry heat.

More juice flowed steadily into my throat as I massaged his fat balls with one hand and rubbed the demon's swollen anus with the other. His gloved hand on mine began to push at my fingers. I understood their urgent need, and pressed into the center of his butt pit. It gaped open and three of my fingers slithered into a gooey maw of torrid fuck tunnel.

"Oh yessss…" he hisses again.

Around the cock in my mouth, I looked up and back. His eyes burned ice-blue as they glared down at me. For a frightening moment, I felt as if I was staring into my own eyes, equally blue and bright and icy, but the face below was bearded blond, while I was dark, raven-haired. We weren't the same! We couldn't be the same!

The demon's mouth opened, and a fat tongue lolled out between wet lips as he panted and squirmed against me. Those eyes and that mouth evoked pure hunger, compelling, and absolutely irresistible.

I stared into demon eyes as my fingers explored inside demon hole, massaging throbbing fuck-walls and searching out the walnut of prostate. I discovered that hard pleasure-nut and rubbed it as I frigged in a deep, leisurely in-and-out glide with my fingers. My demon grunted above me as he squirmed his big ass around my hands. The hole all at once yielded to me and a fourth finger was up his ass. I was amazed and awed.

My hand searched around in his bowels, stretching the unresisting butt-lips and kneading the rubbery prostate. I sensed he was an open pit for my pleasure, and I sucked his cock deep into my throat. I thrust four fingers far up into his squishy, wet asshole. I twisted them in his guts, then yanked them out, feeling his anal walls follow them possessively. I paused at the hot, oozing entrance, then shoved deep again. I began to pump his ass with my fingers, slamming in and yanking out.

His cock pumped more nut-milk into my throat. His balls roiled in my palm, even fuller than at first. His asshole pulsed around my fingers as it swallowed them and expelled them alternately. I couldn't get enough of that hole and shoved even deeper. His sweet anus yielded, taking my fingers with hungry need.

I gasped, then snorted air through my nostrils as I swallowed more of his gooey spooge. The fire around us that seemed cool was now blistering. We were rising. The demon's wings distended and flapped in a wild cadence as his cock invaded my throat and my fingers sank into his asshole.

The sky was inky black. I could feel hot wind against my naked back and butt and thighs. I hung suspended from his clamping legs, dangling a thousand feet from the ground as he effortlessly cradled me in his powerful limbs. We raced through the endless night as he crooned to me his love and his desire.

"Feel my ass, love it like it is all there is. Feel it deep with your hand. Feel my cock buried in your throat as I fill you with man-seed. Feel my full balls feeding you their joy."

I pushed into his ass with my fingers, two or three or four. The sucking anal walls enveloped and then released like a suctioning pump. It was lava-hot in there, as hot as the giant column of cock in my throat.

His balls nestled in my palm, continually feeding me their spunk. I fingered his warm asshole greedily and sucked his juicy cock with slurping lust. That suctioning anal pit captured my hand while his steely cock impaled my throat. I was connected to him in a heated lust of fingers and mouth.

I flew along, fingering his suctioning asshole with increasing passion. I rammed deep, his hole pulling me in, his sphincter clamping around my fingers. I yanked out, his anal walls following and blooming outwards as I abandoned him. I plunged back in, his asshole pulling me into his insides, into his guts, into his very soul. I fucked him with my fingers, his powerful, hairy limbs cradling me and his stiff cock filling me while his hot hole gaped open for me. I couldn't get enough of that hole. I could never get enough of it.

We were on the ground again, on that solid rock of earth with fire around us and with no more breeze blowing around my naked ass. My hand slipped from my winged lover's pulsing asshole. My ass-wet fingers moved up to cup his massive fleshy butt-cheek. That solid flesh was utterly different from the yielding maw I'd just been probing. Then, that empty pit descended as his butt dropped down to suddenly engulf my drooling cock.

I reared up in a violent exultation as my body twisted impossibly so that my cock was in his ass while my mouth remained full of his cock. I fucked deep into that gooey butt-hole. It throbbed tightly now, wrapping soft lips around my meat to yank out the seed locked up in my own balls. I came in a raging torrent up the winged demon's clamping fuck-hole.

I sucked greedily on his cock while I spurted far up his welcoming asshole. My demon laughed then, a throaty, frightening – and exciting caw.

He was rising off of me, his cock sliding from my mouth while my cock slipped from his clinging butt tunnel. I found myself staring up at that asscrack again. The hefty, hairy nuts with their platinum blond fur dangled above me, and that deep asscrack yawned open above it. The shock of blond fur sprouting from the base of that crack parted for the distended pit of his asshole, now slick with my cum drooling from it.

My winged demon turned and lifted me. Cradled in his arms we were soaring in the air once again.

210

Magenta-orange fire burned all around us as air blew along my open ass-crack. His cock nestled up in there, a shaft of steel, throbbing and pulsing along my butt valley in insistent need. It had not emptied yet. I felt its need as it slid all along my crack in a writhing rhythm. His enormous balls rubbed sensually against my flesh. His bat-cock took aim at the quivering center of my asshole. I shivered and moaned as that wet knob pressed and rubbed against my hole. I clamped my thighs around his waist and thrust up into his stiff shank. It slithered down into my aching asshole like a giant snake of scorching desire.

He fucked me in the air while I screamed and screamed and my demon laughed and laughed.

I awoke in a pool of my own cum. My asshole throbbed. I rubbed the sticky cum along my belly and fingered my warm asshole.

This time I couldn't face the dawn, or my boring job. Not now. Maybe never.

I fell back asleep with my finger sliding up my butt and a crazed smile on my face.

I went looking for him. My winged night demon.

Myself.

WHO RIDES SO LATE THROUGH NIGHT AND WIND?
David Holly

Professor Terhuff's history exam had been a bitch, but I had aced it. After a celebratory supper of three spearmint milkshakes at Burgerland, I studied Germanic poetry for an hour, followed by another hour of differential geometry. To assuage my lingering hunger, I devoured a five-pound bag of chocolate mints while I studied. My head heavy with "*Wer reitet so spät durch Nacht und Wind?*" and the intrinsic properties of curves and surfaces, I brushed my teeth with peppermint toothpaste and climbed into bed. My roommate's empty bed spoke volumes. Another one had dropped out, overwhelmed by twisted nightmares, haunted excursions, and nocturnal emissions.

I slept blissfully until a tiny silver bell awakened me. The bell's tinkle drowned out the other sounds of the winter night, though the sound came to my ears alone. Above the wail of the wind, a human voice chanted, "Come, demon, for to thee my mouth is promised. Come, demon, for to thee my mouth is promised."

The fire of desire consumed me. My lust sharpened to a fiery point. I rose naked from my bed, passed through the wall, and flew over the campus. The gibbous moon threw long shadows, but I cast none. Sitka Spruce shivered in the December cold as I flew between their frosted boughs, over Faustus Hall and past the bat-infested Clock Tower. Who rides so late through the night and wind? Hoffmann Dormitory stood like a trembling cock near the edge of the campus. I passed through its ivy walls and into a dorm room not unlike my own.

Travis was sitting on his bed with the tiny silver bell in his hand. His roommate was fast asleep in his own bed. I caused a deeper sleep to come over the roommate. The next day, Travis's roommate would be troubled by the haunts of erotic dreams that eluded memory but left him perplexed.

213

"Come, demon, for to thee my mouth is promised," Travis chanted softly. He was wearing green briefs, which bulged with his erection. He fingered his dick as he chanted and rang his silver bell.

"I am here," I whispered to his soul. I made my demonic form visible, naked, protuberant, and fabulous. My thick uncut cock swam before Travis' eyes. "Keep your promise, now," I demanded. "Suck me off. Suck me until I feed you my unholy cum."

I wasn't surprised to see that I knew Travis by day. He was a fellow student in my biology class, but though I easily recognized him, he could not know me in my true shape. At the hour of midnight, I was the rapier of masculine force and the glowing object of homosexual desire. No male who summoned me could then resist me.

Travis asked, "What are you?" Without waiting for my answer, he touched his lips to the hood of my cock.

"I am an incubus of unrepressed homosexuality," I said. "I brandish the gigantic dick. I shoot the shape-shifting semen into your body. When you have taken my cum, your secret desires will stand exposed to the whole world. Now fulfill your promise. Suck in your damnation."

Oblivious to the implications in my words, Travis fastened his mouth upon my cockhead. I was already leaking a thin stream of cum, enough to ensnare him forever. He shuddered as my pre-cum dripped onto his tongue, shuddered, gasped, and sucked more ferociously. "You are mine now," I said. "I claim your cocksucker's soul for the Seven Lords of the Underworld."

I love cocksuckers. They never complain about the size of my dick, not like the butt-boys do. The butt-boys always gripe, "It's too thick. It'll split me." That's what they always say just before they open their asses and take my whole package. Oh, yes, I love them, too. The opening sphincter. The hot asshole. The grainy chute. The vulnerable prostate. The deep channel. The yards of intestine waiting for my thick cum. No matter what they say, they love the penetration, the motion, and the gift of cum. Butt-boys are eager harvests, and I love shooting my shaping cum into their chutes. And after the turning, their asses swell and grow until their contours spelled Butt Slut.

However, my classmate Travis was a born cocksucker. He kissed down the side of my shaft, licking around it. His mouth reached my dark pubic hairs. I laughed ghoulishly – though he could not hear the astral merriment – as he extracted a crisp hair from his tongue.

Freed from the hirsute distraction, he licked my shaft up to the head, licked around the foreskin, pushed my hood back and flicked the tip of his tongue under it, and tightened his lips on the end. Rapturous sensations claimed me.

I trembled on the periphery of the hellish rapture while long minutes spun their webs. My cock leaked thin streams of pre-cum into Travis's mouth.

"My lips are tingling," he said, wondering.

"They will tingle," I whispered preternaturally. "They are coming alive to their infernal duties, and your mouth will reflect your desire so long as you live."

He took my whole cock then, so it rode down his tongue. The moist chute that was his throat encased my cock, drawing it toward an entangling orgasm. Tremors of staggering pleasure vibrated through my loins. My demonic fires pumped into my balls, and my Luciferian cock prepared to cast my seed into this college boy's sucking mouth.

My pelvis contracted as cum arose from my seminal vesicles, and the volcano of pleasure erupted. The first taste of my cum made Travis my personal possession, one more notch in my pistol, one more link in my chain, one more bead on my necklace of human conquests. He could not have resisted me then, even if he had been so inclined. I could have made him commit sexual acts known to the foulest fiends only.

My orgasmic explosions increased, growing to a world-shattering eruption of pleasure. The demonic muscles at the base of my penis relaxed, constricted, relaxed and constricted, time after time, so that my stinging jizm splattered against the back of Travis's throat. Bursts of rapture shook me, minute after minute, and each burst came with an enjoyable ejaculation of stygian spunk.

The next morning, I grabbed the seat beside Travis in the science amphitheatre. "How are you doing, Travis?" I asked.

Travis gave me a blank look. His lips were puffier than they had been. His secret desire was starting to show, but he had not yet accepted the change. I laughed when I pictured what he would eventually become.

"I'm Weylyn," I said.

"Oh, yeah, fine," he said, turning his attention to Dr. Ghulper's lecture on hagfishes, lampreys, sharks, rays, coelacanths, and lungfishes. Travis didn't know me from the Nine Lords of Hell, but after sucking my dick his lips had gone purplish. He had cocksucker written all over his mouth.

"Pretty lips," I said. "I bet you can give a hell of a blowjob."

A sophomore at a large public university, I had known my true nature for several years. The truth came out during my junior year at high school. I was living with my mother in the apartments above her psychic reader and fortune-telling shop, when I received a letter from a local attorney. I went to the lawyer's office after school, and he told me he could arrange a meeting with my father, whom I had never met and about whom I knew nothing. My mother would never say a word about him. When I agreed, the lawyer escorted me to a coffee shop down the street, made a brief introduction, and departed.

The man whom the lawyer had introduced as my father returned from the counter with two lattes with eight squirts of peppermint each. My eyes crossed with bliss when I took a sip. My father hissed, "Your reaction proves you're the Spawn of Hell."

Spawn of Hell? "Holy shit."

A peal of demonic laughter issued from his throat. Nonplussed, I looked around to see if the manager was coming to toss us out. However, no one seemed to notice. They saw only a father and a son pleasantly sipping coffee on a Saturday afternoon.

He can't be my father. He doesn't look like me. Hardly had the thought crossed my mind before I realized how many features we shared. He was rapier thin, with hair of jet, ruby lips, and demonic eyes. Despite his slender build, his muscles were satanically defined, his buttocks billowed, and his cock made a devilish print in his Dockers slacks. I had always had the same problem. My cock was so big that its dimensions were obvious right through my clothing. In high school gym classes, my fellow students had teased about the size of my cock. My mother once admitted that the doctor refused to circumcise me. "This fellow is going to have a whopper. No way would I trim it," he had said.

I took a second sip from my cardboard cup. The sharp peppermint taste suited me. I let the flavor roll around my mouth before I swallowed. Spawn of Hell. "What the fuck?" I said. "Who are you, really?"

"Oh, I am your father," he said with a wicked leer.

"So where have you been all my life?"

"You were your mother's responsibility. She summoned me. I've fucked more than three hundred thousand women. I can't help it that she got knocked up."

If I hadn't been his son, I would have stomped out then. As it was, I knocked back another slurp of my coffee and favored him with a smirk. "If you're a dammed hobgoblin and Mom is Old Poker's slut, what does that make me?"

"An incubus. Imp of Hell. Child of a demon and a human woman who summoned the forces of darkness to her bed – numerous times, I might append."

A diabolic pride suffused me, but I didn't want to be gulled.

"Prove that I'm an incubus."

"You have passion for mint in any form, but candy in particular."

"So?" Any fool could have blabbed about my craving for mint.

"You're stacked, sexy, hung like a horse, and you can't jack off." How the fuck did he know that I could not masturbate – no matter how hard or how often I tried?

My expression must have spoken volumes for he went on. "Nor have you fucked – you are incapable in human form. That is why you've never dated. Soon you will awaken to your pandemonic nature. We ride late, but once we ride, we go nightly. A sound or a scent through the astral plane – the tinkle of a bell, a whiff of feverish incense, an incantation for puckish cock, the smoke from black candles, a trumpet call for penetration, or a diabolist's whispered plea – shall pull you from your bed. You will rise into the air, you shall pass through walls, you shall fly upon the wind, and you shall cast your demonic seed into the bodies of the women who summon you. That is ..." my father hesitated. "Unless ..." He stopped again.

"Unless what?" I shivered as the imp of the perverse climbed my spine.

"Unless you are the last of our line."

That did not sound good.

"What do you mean?"

"Each demonic lineage has a certain term to work upon the Earth. Each line has an ending place, and your ancestors have been going to and fro for eons."

"What happens to the last of the lineage?"

"Each demon casts one child, a son, into one of the summoning women. In my case – and yours – it was your mother. However, if you are the last of our line, you will bear no children because you will cast your seed into no woman born."

"You mean …?"

"Yes, it is possible, even probable, that you will be a gay incubus."

A nameless thrill shot through me – not a thrill of dismay.

"Is that bad?"

"Not in the least. A gay incubus receives a special reward after he passes from the Earth. Do not ask, for I do not know its nature. That reward will not be mine to claim. I have spent my time upon this world satisfying the lusts of concupiscent bitches."

"The way you put it … it sounds dreadful."

After father recovered from another din of ghastly mirth, he added, "I know two gay incubuses. Both claim that the pleasure of man to man is greater than that of man to woman. They say that men love cocks better than woman do, and so men give stupendous blowjobs. According to my friends, coming in a man's ass is better than getting off in any woman's twat."

"When will I know what I am?" As if I didn't already feel my gayness in my bones.

"Soon. You have nearly reached the age of your first summons."

As it turned out, a year slipped by before a man called for me. I awoke lickerish from the smoke of black candles, passed through solid concrete and stucco, and rode cloud scud to the home of Mr. Newburn, one of my neighbors. Home alone while Mrs. Newburn was attending a travel agents' convention, Mr. Newburn had evoked an incubus. When I slipped through the wall, he was standing naked in a chalk circle with black candles illuminating his flesh.

I was under compulsion to fuck him, but if I didn't turn into a supernatural being nightly, I would have fucked his ass any day of the week. Mr. Newburn was just thirty. A personal trainer, he practically lived at the gym. His muscles were toned and his butt provocative. I crossed into the chalk circle, manifested my demonic form behind him, and bent him forward.

"Oh, God, what are you?" he gasped. I would learn that my summoners frequently called upon Providence. They went to the trouble of summoning a gay incubus but discredited the evidence of their senses when I arrived.

Although it was my first time, I knew exactly what to do. My cock released a load of slippery fluid as I pushed its head against his asshole. I lubricated him with my hellborn juices and pushed inside. Mr. Newburn gasped as I dilated his anus, but I didn't hesitate. I pushed harder so that he toppled forward, me still mounting him. I pushed my cock in until my pubic hair tickled his buttocks. I began humping him in earnest then, and he yelped with joy (and some terror) while I did him. I stroked thirty times in his ass; abruptly, he yelped, "Oh, you're hitting the spot. Oh, fuck, you're giving me an anal orgasm. Here I come. Here I come."

A sensation such as I had never felt claimed me. My body was aflame with tingles. My cock was engulfed in his hot, contracting ass, which sent raptures through my dick head. The tingles grew into a long vibration of delicious sensation. Then the muscles at the base of my penis contracted, and I felt the burst of jizm that poured into Mr. Newburn's ass. The mind-boggling orgasm went on for several minutes while I pumped out gigantic squirts of my cum.

I butt-fucked Mr. Newburn in three positions, stuffing him with a gallon of my demonic cum before he released me. That cum would produce a telling effect on his posterior, one he'd be hard pressed to explain to Mrs. Newburn. I returned to my bed sexually relieved for the first time in my life.

A week later, I was walking down the street and saw Mr. Newburn doing butt-toning exercises in his yard. His buttocks were bulging. His gym shorts so defined his rear that they shrieked sodomite.

"Trying to reduce your rump, Mr. Newburn?" I asked roguishly, conscious that exercising a sprite butt would make it curvier. I'd given him a new silhouette for life.

"One body part got bigger than it was supposed to, Weylyn," he said, never suspecting that I was the incubus who'd exposed his love of anal penetration. "I'm going to adjust my gym routine."

"I can't imagine why," I replied. "You've got some stupendous booty. I'll bet an ass like yours pulls in guys with perpetual hard-ons."

I earned As on my final examinations. Supernatural intellect came with my supernatural cock. As I checked my grades online, I ate a half gallon of chocolate chip mint ice cream with peppermint syrup for kicks. By the time I finished eating, I was feeling randy as hell. I brushed my teeth with spearmint toothpaste and climbed naked into my bed, eager to receive the night's summons.

Eddy, the football quarterback, used his key to invade the team locker room after hours. Draped naked over a bench, he blew a trumpet, rang a cowbell, and offered his ass to demons. Eddy gasped when I touched him. "It worked," he yelped.

"A trumpet and a cowbell," I remonstrated, my demonic voice whispering supernaturally between the lockers redolent of sweaty boys. "You're lucky the racket didn't fetch a coach."

"Are you real?"

Holding him in position with one hand on his back, I shifted into visibility. He shrieked when he saw my cock. "It's too big. You'll kill me with that."

Laughing fiendishly, I pressed my cock head between his butt cheeks and squirted my lubricating fluids into his asshole.

"You're making me wet," he cried. The touch of my juices dilated his sphincter. I opened him wide and slid in the head of my cock. Eddy emitted a shuddering gasp. "I don't have any choice, do I? I gotta go through with it."

"The commitment is absolute," I agreed. "Once you summon me, you must receive my cum into your ass or your throat."

"Fuck my ass," Eddy said. "That's what I want."

I pushed my dick deeper into his hole. Eddy's asshole received me like an old friend, so I rammed my cock up his grainy chute. His sphincter began contracting around my dick, and Eddy moaned. "Ah, fuck," he said. "I just got off. I must be a total pansy. Stick a dick in my ass, and I come before you hump me."

"I'm making you an anal whore, Eddy," I promised. "You'll orgasm every time you take a dick." I didn't mention what else he was going to get. He would find out soon enough when his pants didn't fit his ass.

Pulling my hips back, I started humping Eddy. My evil cock violated his anal tube. Eddy's ass was so hot and so tight that my movements produced torrents of painfully good pleasure. I groaned as I fucked him. "Oh, Son of Gomorrah, you have a killer ass," I moaned. My voice echoed from the Other World.

Eddy put his hand in his mouth as I fucked him.

"Uh, I'm gonna go again," he managed, biting his fingers in his delicious distress.

Throbbing ecstasy stunned my cock, and I thrust harder. I grabbed Eddy's hair, short but long enough to get a grip, and pulled his head back as I fucked him. With my other hand, I grabbed his chin. Eddy promptly bit down on my hand.

"I'm going shoot my cum up your ass," I hissed, the pain in my demonic hand irrelevant. "It's unholy seed, Eddy. I'm making you my fairy. You're coming out of the closet, Mr. Quarterback. After tonight, the team will know that you're a gay boy. After tonight, the world will know that you love taking big cocks up your ass."

"Yes, that's what I want," Eddy howled. "Free me." He bit ferociously, but no teeth marks would show on my hand. His ass, on the other hand, would be a revelation.

"I'll carry your sulfurous seed until we meet in Perdition," Eddy shouted. "Pour your pernicious spirit into my sacred soul."

"You'll be the hottest butt-slut in Gehenna. The Derrière Devils will gangbang your ass in the Chthonic Regions."

My orgasm was a thunderstorm of lightning, thunder, and pouring rain. Pour I did. I unloaded my stygian seed into Eddy's hellishly-fine poop tube.

"Oh, uh," Eddy grunted, biting my hand as I fucked him, came into him, and made him come.

I fucked his ass until a cock in the college barns crowed in the morning sun. I flew through the gymnasium, coursed through the tops of the wintery trees, and sailed back to my bed.

During the Yuletide break, Eddy's ass grew to a damnable size. He secured a pair of the largest size football pants and took them to a tailor. Nothing in stock came close to fitting Eddy's stupendous rump. To his shock, his teammates applauded him when he announced that he was gay, and even the football coaches, with imperceptible hesitation, shook his hand.

Ten years later, I had graduated law school, passed the bar exams, and sued a famous brand of snack foods on behalf of an obese client until the company pissed money. I purchased a penthouse with a rooftop garden complete with tropical foliage and swimming pool. One evening just past the dinner hour, my father knocked on my door. My servant Seabridge, a swishy West Indian, rang up as I lounged under a coconut palm beside my pool.

"Says he's my father, does he? Rather Byronic-looking gentleman? Escort him up, Seabridge."

To my astonishment, my father looked forty. He ran his eyes over my well-packed swim briefs and gave forth with the demonic laugh I remembered.

"You have aged," I said. "I'm surprised. I seem to have stopped aging at twenty."

"As did I," my father said, as Seabridge served him green Chartreuse. "I looked twenty for five hundred years, and thirty for another four hundred. But time is catching up with me. Before I reach my fifteen-hundredth birthday, I will take my place in the Pit."

"So how long have you got?"

"Five hundred years." He shrugged off the mortal chill.

"That sucks."

"Not at all, my boy. The Pit is our destiny. Our line has walked this world since Dagon was a minnow. Our time is passing. But not yet."

"What happens to us in the Pit?" I really wanted to know.

"I haven't been there, Weylyn," he replied. "I was born into an Earthly body, just like you were. I can't remember anything that happened before August 13, 1019. Except what my father told me. He was born during the Roman Republic."

"How long have I got?" That was the vital question. What did I care when the old man was going to blazes. It was all about me.

My father issued his demonic laugh again. Seabridge returned in a pink thong bikini. He minced toward the pool and cautiously lowered his charcoal body into the shallow end.

"Has your servant ever summoned you?"

"You can see that he has not," I said. Seabridge's lips and buttocks retained their natural shapes. "How long will I continue on this Earth?"

He shrugged. "Gay demons last for a long time. Three thousand years. Five thousand. Who knows? It's we straight demons who cross the Styx after ten-to-fifteen centuries."

"Tell me about our family," I urged.

"That's why I'm here, Weylyn." The night deepened while he told stories of my male ancestors from time out of memory to the beginning of writing and of the notorious women who'd summoned them. I was trying to absorb the strange stories, when he interrupted my musings: "I'm glad that you are supporting your mother."

"I'm paying for her new age psychic center: card readers, book shop, trinkets, occult classes, and the rest of the works. She's in heaven."

"Ugh," my father shivered. "Not a word we use."

"Sorry." I indicated my striped swim briefs and the pool where Seabridge was floating serenely upon his back. "Would you like to take a swim?"

"No. I'll sip a nightcap of this fine Chartreuse, but then I must prepare for my summons."

He did not get a chance to prepare. We received calls at virtually the same instant. Wafts of incense tickled my nostrils accompanied by the thumping of a small drum.

"What is yours, Weylyn?" my father asked.

"Three young fellows hoping for a sex orgy with a demon. I haven't done a group for a couple of years. It's fun, but draining. How about yours?"

"It's your mother – again." He made a wry face as he added, "I envy you. Frequently, I wish I had been the homosexual incubus."

I snickered at the thought. The woman must hound him incessantly. "Be careful," I teased. "I don't want any little brothers."

He laughed as he rode into the air. "Have no fear, Weylyn. Our race is granted only one impregnation."

And I am granted none, I thought with glee. I levitated, leaving Seabridge floating obliviously. Father and I slid through the glass greenhouse panels three stories above my garden and parted in the night. I sped across the city and down toward the manicured lawns of the college campus. Leaves were falling, and the air was crisp with autumn. I swooped along a lawn decorated with windfall black walnuts and through the walls of the college gymnasium. In this building, I had turned out the quarterback Eddy, but this time my mission waited two stories underground where the Olympic sized swimming pool dominated a floor.

"The swim team – no surprise there," I hissed. Athletes are gayer than the average male, and swimmers, wrestlers, and bicyclists topped the list. Perhaps the chimera of Lycra enthralled the homosexual soul. Whatever the case, the odor of gayness scented the gymnasium. Straight men watched sports on television, guzzled beer, devoured fattening snacks, and grew bags of guts that overflowed the couch.

The ceiling above the indoor pool crouched in stygian darkness, but the underwater lights made the blue-tiled pool glow luridly. Pots of summoning oil simmered, and the drum lay near them. Three college boys were swimming a lane, each following the bare body before him, naked and marvelous. Only then did I realize that I had already graced one of the three with my favors. His bulging buttocks and puffy lips told the tale. Robbie had summoned me twice, taking my cock in his mouth and in his ass. He had cocksucker and bunbury boy echoing from every pore.

"The devil's here," Robbie shouted when I stood naked and erect beside the pool. "What did I tell you guys?"

"Holy fuck," Riley said.

Bray was struck dumb by the sight of my demonic dork. I could see his thoughts as clearly as I saw his rising dick: He's going to stick that monster up my asshole. He's going to fill me with cum, cum that will give me huge curvy buttocks that will sway like a girl's rump when I walk. Oh, fuck, yeah! Game on, Mr. Incubus!

I took Bray first, bending him over the edge of the swimming pool and filling him to the hilt. He shrieked with joy as I banged him. "I love a boy who gives it up so enthusiastically when I fuck him," I hissed into his mind. "When you burst into Hell, you'll receive a demonic gang bang, which you're going to love, and then the Lord of the Underworld is going to install you as a fucktoy in the Wall of Asses."

"What's a demonic gangbang like?" Bray gasped, his asshole contracting around my shaft.

"You'll be strapped down on a butt-fuck board while a thousand demons line up to take their turn coming into your ass. There will be demons of every description, from the breathtakingly beautiful light bearers to flapping, flopping, squishing, squirming monstrosities, and all of them will love fucking your damned ass."

The description of this future bliss made Bray come like a bitch. He howled as his human cum flew out of his dick. His asshole contracted and expanded, milking off my demonic dick. My orgasm began normally, then it swelled to an overwhelming crescendo. My crotch was an orchestra playing low notes at a high level. My cockhead sang *Carmen* in Bray's ass, while my balls wailed Robert Johnson's "Hellhound on My Trail."

I fucked Riley's ass next, and he was eternally grateful. I made grandiose promises about the presents he would receive in Hell. Of course, I was lying like a goddamn fiend. I had no more idea about the nature of the Realm of the Damned than did these mortal boys. I had only my old man's word for what would happen in the netherworld, and he hadn't been there either.

"You're next," I told Robbie.

"I'm already huge," Robbie exclaimed, pointing toward his rear.

"I have to fuck your ass before I am dismissed. You joined in the summoning ritual, so you must receive my cum again."

"Will I get even sexier? More gay than I am already?"

"The more devil's cum you receive, the more powerful the effect."

Robbie threw himself on his back and raised his legs. "Take me this way," he demanded. "I'll make myself your submissive anal slut forever." Like he had a choice.

I fucked Robbie until I unloaded a quart of cum into his ass. I fucked each one twice more, giving them my all. The three swimmers were sprawled naked alongside the swimming pool, their assholes tightly holding my cum inside, and deeply dreaming of their future conquests as I rose through the floors of the gymnasium and soared across the campus. I returned to my penthouse apartment atop the skyscraper and assumed my former position, complete with green stripped swim briefs, beside the swimming pool. Seabridge gradually came to himself.

"Pardon, Monsieur Weylyn," he apologized. "I must have fallen into slumber while floating."

"Quite all right, Seabridge," I assured the servant.

"Will there be anything else, Monsieur?'

I tipped the last of the green Chartreuse into a glass. "Nothing further. Pleasant dreams, Seabridge."

"Pleasant dreams, Monsieur," said he.

What seems a dream to the innocent is a shattering orgasm to those who share unholy bloodlines. I adjusted my drained balls in my swim briefs, sipped the aromatic liquor, and looked forward to five thousand years of summons.

ABOUT THE AUTHORS

MARK APOAPSIS's ("At-will Employment") previous work includes several erotic SF stories in *Muscle Worshippers*, *Men on the Edge*, and *Taken by Force*; a plain old erotic stories in *Ride Me Cowboy* and *Service with a Smile*; and an early story in issue 13 of the online magazine *Velvet Mafia*. He also has five unsexed stories in *Chilling Tales of Terror* and the *Supernatural*, a collection of gay and lesbian horror flash-fiction – although only three of those include an actual act of unsexing.

MICHAEL BRACKEN's ("The Loophole") short fiction has been published or is forthcoming in *Best Gay Romance 2010*, *Boys Getting Ahead*, *Country Boys*, *Flesh & Blood: Guilty as Sin*, *Freshmen*, *Hot Blood: Strange Bedfellows*, *The Mammoth Book of Best New Erotica 4*, *Men*, *Teammates*, *Ultimate Gay Erotica 2006*, and in many other anthologies and periodicals.

R. J. BRADSHAW ("On the Darkest Night") lives in Saskatoon, Saskatchewan, where he founded a romantic greeting card company to showcase his poetry. His short fiction has previously been published in *QueeredFiction's Queer Wolf* and *Queer Dimensions* anthologies.

H.L. CHAMPA ("The Eighth") has appeared in numerous anthologies including *Tasting Him*, *Like Magnets We Attract* and *College Boys*. If you prefer your erotica in electronic form, shorts stories can be found at *Clean Sheets* and *Ravenous Romance*. Find her online at heidichampa.blogspot.com.

R. W. CLINGER's ("Nocturnal Nolan") work with STARbooks Press includes stories in *Pretty Boys & Roughnecks*, *Teammates*, *Boys Getting Ahead*, *Video Boys* and the novels, *The Pool Boy* and *Soft on the Eyes*.

DAVID HOLLY ("Who Rides So Late through Night and Wind?") is neither an incubus nor a demon, so readers can only summon him with the mundane tool known as e-mail. His stories have appeared in the STARbooks Press anthologies *Cruising for Bad Boys* and *Unwrapped: Erotic Holiday Tales*. Readers will find a complete bibliography and his e-mail address at http://www.gaywriter.org.

MARK JAMES ("Running with the Pack") is a writer of gay erotica with several published short stories, and two published novels, *The Iron Hand* and *Escape from Purgatory*. He resides in Dallas, where summers are hot, the land's flat, and the cold winters lend themselves to long days spent indoors writing. He is currently working on *Razor's Edge*, the sequel to *The Iron Hand*.

KYLE LUKOFF ("Lunacy") is a young writer and bookseller living in Brooklyn, New York. He has published a wide variety of erotica from many different perspectives and orientations.

JEFF MANN's ("Whitby") books include two collections of poetry, *Bones Washed with Wine* and *On the Tongue*; a book of personal essays, *Edge: Travels of an Appalachian Leather Bear*; a novella, *Devoured*, included in *Masters of Midnight: Erotic Tales of the Vampire*; a collection of poetry and memoir, *Loving Mountains, Loving Men*; and a volume of short fiction, *A History of Barbed Wire*, winner of a Lambda Literary Award. He teaches creative writing at Virginia Tech in Blacksburg, Virginia.

WAYNE MANSFIELD ("The Vampire Heart" and "A Very Handsome Man") was born and raised in rural Western Australia. He left home at seventeen to study teaching in that state's capital city, Perth. He now lives in Mount Lawley and works as an English language teacher and counselor. As well as several stories for STARbooks Press and Torquere Press, he is the author of the best selling hardcore erotica story "Highway Patrol" and of "Tracing The Devil," which is shaping up to be just as popular. Find out more and check out his blog containing a full history of publishing credits at http://www.myspace.com/darknessgathers.

There's a reason guys growl for **G. R. RICHARDS**'s ("The Wishing Wall") erotica. You would never know it by the love of public television documentaries and great food in high-end restaurants, but G.R. Richards pens some of the world's steamiest guy-on-guy stories. Be on the lookout for Richards' two hot Christmas stories, "Ivy League" and "Vintage Toys for Lucky Boys," from Dreamspinner Press, and "A Descent into the Mailroom," a gritty BDSM office menage tale coming to eXcessica Publishing in June 2010. Richards is also a contributor to the upcoming anthology *Skater Boys* (Cleis Press). http://www.grrichards.webs.com/

ROB ROSEN, ("The Gatekeeper") author of the novels *Sparkle: The Queerest Book You'll Ever Love* and *Divas Las Vegas*, has been published, to date, in more than sixty anthologies, most notably the STARbooks Press collections: *Ride Me Cowboy, Service with a Smile, Unmasked II, Cruising for Bad Boys, SexTime, Pretty Boys and Roughnecks, Teammates, Boys Getting Ahead, Unwrapped,* and *Video Boys.* His erotic fiction can frequently be found in the pages of *MEN* and *Freshmen* magazines. Please visit him at his Website, www.therobrosen.com, or email him at robrosen@therobrosen.com.

RAITH SARGENT ("The Salt Dusk") is a thirty-seven-year-old, full-time writer with a Masters in Art History, a minor in Literature and a nasty habit of surviving his mind.

SIMON SHEPPARD ("Revenge of the Living Dead") is the author of the award-winning *Hotter than Hell and Other Stories; In Deep: Erotic Stories; Kinkorama: Dispatches from the Front Lines of Perversion; Sex Parties 101* and the forthcoming *Sodomy!* He's also the editor of the Lambda-Award-winning *Homosex: Sixty Years of Gay Erotica* and *Leathermen,* and his work has been published in over 300 anthologies. He writes the weekly column "Notes of a Cranky Old Fag" for CarnalNation.com, and hangs out at www.simonsheppard.com.

Published in dozens of gay erotic anthologies, **JAY STARRE** ("My Night Demon") pumps and grinds out fiction from his home in Vancouver, Canada. He has written regularly for such hot magazines as *Torso, Mandate* and *Men.* His work can be found in titles like *Love in a Lock-Up, Don't Ask, Don't Tie Me Up, Unmasked, Ride Me Cowboy,* and *SexTime.* His steamy gay novels *Erotic Tales of the Knights Templar* and *Lusty Adventures of the Knossos Prince* are published by STARbooks Press.

XAN WEST ("Willing") is the pseudonym of a NYC BDSM/sex educator and writer. "Willing" was previously published in *Leathermen.* Xan's story "First Time Since," won honorable mention for the 2008 National Leather Association's John Preston Short Fiction Award. Xan's erotica can be found in *Best SM Erotica Volumes 2 & 3, Hurts So Good, Love at First Sting, Men on the Edge, Backdraft, Frenzy, Best Gay Erotica 2009, DADDIES, Pleasure Bound, SexTime, Cruising for Bad Boys,* and *Biker Boys.* Xan also wrote the introduction to *Wired Hard 4.* Xan wants to hear from you, and can be reached at Xan_West@yahoo.com.

LOGAN ZACHARY ("Werebear") lives in Minneapolis, MN, where he is an avid reader, writer, and book collector. His stories can be found in *Hard Hats, Taken by Force, Boys Caught in the Act, Ride*

Christopher Pierce

Me Cowboy, Service with a Smile, Surfer Boys, Ultimate Gay Erotica 2009, Time Travel Sex, Best Gay Erotica 2009, Biker Boys, Unmasked II, Unwrapped, College Boys, Boys Getting Ahead, Skater Boys, Video Boys, and *Queer Dimension.* He can be reached at LoganZachary2002@yahoo.com.

ABOUT THE EDITOR

Christopher Pierce is the author of *Kidnapped by a Sex Maniac: The Erotic Fiction of Christopher Pierce*, as well as the novel *Rogue: Slave* and its sequel *Rogue: Hunted* (all STARbooks Press). He co-edited the *Fetish Chest Trilogy* of anthologies (Alyson Publications) with Rachel Kramer Bussel.

For STARbooks Press, he has edited the collections *Men on the Edge: Dangerous Erotica*, *Taken by Force: Erotic Stories of Abduction and Captivity* and *SexTime: Erotic Stories of Time Travel*. His short fiction has been published in more than thirty anthologies, including *Rough Trade* (Bold Strokes Books), *Surfer Boys*, *Leathermen* (both Cleis Press) and *Ultimate Gay Erotica 2005, 2006, 2007* and *2008* (Alyson.)

Visit him on-line at christopherpierceerotica.com.

g in the park. He was wearing these really tight jeans, so tight y
aring any underwear. "Excuse me," I said, having a hard time lo
inded by that bulge in his crotch, "but don't I know you?" "May
nd of t
with Ray
loser?
id. "Lik
e body
ly, he
up to t
staking
, I coul
od rac
ng with
we go
ll see
d?" he
ivacy.
hard. I
, traci
d it, ha
with m
bing, I
e sound of unzipping filled the small space. I don't know who's
but before I knew it, I had his rod in my hand, and mine was in
to do?" he asked, his tone challenging. I knew exactly, and san